"A fun, Rick Riordanesque escapade." —*Booklist*

The Star Thief

Lindsey Becker

ISBN 978-0-316-34853-9

9 780316 348539

5 07 99

EAN

PRAISE FOR

The Star Thief

"[An] adventure of the galactic variety.... Infused
with references to constellations and Greek mythological
creatures, and stocked with ships that sail through the sky
and civilizations succumbing to power and greed over and
over again, the **invigorating** plot ultimately leaves Honorine
with only one choice to make. **A fun, Rick Riordanesque
escapade.**" —*Booklist*

"**The pace is fast, the characters believable, and the
setting original.**... The breakneck pace will not give readers
time to ponder.... And they probably won't mind a bit. Readers
enjoying **a mix of fantasy, adventure, and a clever heroine**
will fall for this one." —*Kirkus Reviews*

"**Readers will find it easy to connect emotionally
with Honorine** as she tries to navigate a world with no
clear answers, while fantasy lovers will appreciate the
mythological underpinnings of this imaginative new world.
A fine addition to large fantasy collections."
—*School Library Journal*

"Featuring both cannonballs and magic, the story will
appeal to fantasy and adventure readers alike.... But **the
book is perfect for any young reader.**"
—*School Library Connection*

"The zippy pace... **moves from one epic battle,
chase, or discovery to another.**... [Honorine is] a
smart, daring girl." —*The Bulletin*

The Star Thief

Lindsey Becker

LITTLE, BROWN AND COMPANY
New York Boston

Text copyright © 2017 by Lindsey Becker
Illustrations copyright © 2017 by Antonio Caparo

Cover design by Marcie Lawrence. Title lettering by Antonio Caparo. Cover art © 2017 by Antonio Caparo. Cover copyright © 2017 by Hachette Book Group, Inc.

Little, Brown and Company
Hachette Book Group
1290 Avenue of the Americas, New York, NY 10104
Visit us at LBYR.com

Originally published in hardcover and ebook by Little, Brown and Company in April 2017
First Trade Paperback Edition: April 2018

Little, Brown and Company is a division of Hachette Book Group, Inc. The Little, Brown name and logo are trademarks of Hachette Book Group, Inc.

The publisher is not responsible for websites (or their content) that are not owned by the publisher.

The Library of Congress has cataloged the hardcover edition as follows:
Names: Becker, Lindsey, author.
Title: The star thief / Lindsey Becker.
Description: First Edition. | New York : Little, Brown and Company, 2017. | Summary: "Young parlor maid Honorine and her friend Francis find themselves in the middle of an epic feud between a crew of scientific sailors and the magical constellations come to life"— Provided by publisher.
Identifiers: LCCN 2016023401| ISBN 9780316348560 (hardcover) | ISBN 9780316348553 (ebook) | ISBN 9780316348584 (library edition ebook)
Subjects: | CYAC: Fantasy. | Inventors—Fiction. | Constellations—Fiction. | Mythology, Classical—Fiction. | Sailors—Fiction.
Classification: LCC PZ7.1.B43475 St 2017 | DDC [Fic]—dc23
LC record available at https://lccn.loc.gov/2016023401

ISBNs: 978-0-316-34853-9 (pbk.), 978-0-316-34855-3 (ebook)

Printed in the United States of America

LSC-C

10 9 8 7 6 5 4 3 2 1

For Katie and Sunshine

The GASLIGHT

CHAPTER
· 1 ·

The Omen Stones

Honorine realized it was going to be a difficult night when she stepped into the east parlor to do a bit of light dusting and found it on fire.

"Sharps and mercers!" she said as a spray of hot embers erupted from the fireplace. There were plenty of other rooms in the enormous Vidalia Estate that might have burst into flames—like the empty bedrooms upstairs kept for guests who never arrived, or the pantry with its thousands of pieces of silver, which had to be polished even though no one used them—and she might not have minded one bit. Instead, the room that had caught fire was the east parlor, Honorine's favorite room in the house. It was full of strange and delightful artifacts, books and bones, skulls and carved tusks, insects pinned inside shadowboxes, and glass cases of dead birds stuffed with oiled cotton, all acquired by Lord Vidalia on his extensive travels.

She quickly set down her dusting rags and lantern and went to work putting out the flames.

"Don't worry, sir," Honorine muttered as she stamped the smoldering rug with the worn heel of her boot. "I'll save your treasures!"

Lord Vidalia, as always, did not reply. He simply watched from the painting over the mantel, where he sat ever silently with his beautiful, elegant wife and their infant son, Francis, on the deck of a ship, surrounded by dark water and thousands of stars. It had been painted in 1879, according to the signature scrawled in the lower corner of the canvas, and was the only existing portrait of all three Vidalias together in the same frame, because shortly after it was finished, Lord Vidalia vanished.

Honorine hurried to get to every errant spark, stumbling around the furniture, the display cases, and the mounted specimens of animals packed into the huge and terribly cluttered room. She tripped over a red fox as she stomped about on the rug, then grabbed the nearest vase of fresh cut roses, snuffed a burning ember in the mane of a regal Barbary lion, and ran straight under the belly of a giraffe to toss the contents of the vase—water, roses, and all—into the snarling fireplace. The flames expired at once, hissing out a tremendous ball of sooty smoke. Honorine winced as it washed over the oil painting above the mantel. She grabbed a broom and waved it about to clear the air.

"Who was supposed to be tending this fire, anyway?" she asked, but the specimens declined to reply. Fires burned throughout the night, even in the empty rooms of the manor house, because Lady Vidalia kept strange hours and was deathly afraid of the dark. But fires were always to be attended, no matter how tedious a chore it might be. This was the inspiration for Honorine's lantern, a device of her own design and making. With more electric light, there would be less need for open flames burning all over the house and many fewer hours spent waiting around in otherwise empty rooms. Her latest prototype included a voltaic pile battery powering a squat lightbulb, which sat inside the glass chimney of an old kerosene lamp. With the fire now out, Honorine picked up her little lantern to inspect the damage.

To her relief, the painting was unharmed. The Vidalia family looked exactly as they always did. Lord Vidalia, noble and dignified, with thick streaks of gray in his hair. Lady Vidalia, luminously beautiful, with her burnished bronze skin and her black hair a magnificent crown of waves and ringlets set with shimmering green gemstones. The baby, Francis, sitting on his father's knee, was a bundle of white lace with a round little face and huge brown eyes.

Nothing above the fireplace seemed to be burned beyond repair, but there was something else that troubled her.

The mantel was empty.

"And what happened to Lord Vidalia's things?" Honorine said with a scowl. His hat and gloves and sword usually rested under the family portrait. She peeked quickly into the cavernous fireplace, worried that the heap of charcoal and ash might be the gloves and hat, but there was no sign of the sword, and that shouldn't have burned to dust even if it had been tossed into the flames. The rest of the room seemed undisturbed, until she came to the little alcove containing

Lord Vidalia's old writing desk, surrounded by framed charts of the sea and the stars. Someone had riffled through the desk, leaving doors ajar and drawers hastily shut with corners of parchment sticking out like sharp little tongues. Honorine found the missing items from the mantel on the floor beside the desk, along with a handful of odd black feathers and several small books dropped in a careless pile.

Honorine placed the sword and the gloves gently back on top of the mantel, and then, after a quick peek around to see that the room was still empty, she placed the hat over her dark red hair. Picking up her broom to sweep the hearth, she imagined that instead of standing in the parlor, she was at the railing of Lord Vidalia's ship, looking down at the golden sand of an uninhabited beach, ready to jump into the surf and charge ashore...when the broom straws brushed over something odd lying in the ashes.

It was another small book.

With one of her dusting rags, Honorine brushed the wet soot from the cover. It was similar to the books on the floor near the writing desk, bound in soft leather, roughly the size and weight of a deck of playing cards. The cover bore the image of a pointed crown with star-shaped jewels set at the tips. It seemed familiar, but it didn't belong in the parlor collection. She had cleaned and tended every item in this room dozens of times, and she was certain she had never seen this book before. Honorine gingerly opened to the first page.

Vidalia Field Almanac
of the
Celestial Constellations
Both Known and Extinct

This was mostly nonsense to Honorine, except for one word. *Constellations.* Being a sailor, Lord Vidalia had plenty of maps and charts of the sky all over the manor house. Following the patterns of stars was a very reliable way to navigate on the vast open sea, where there were no roads or landmarks to follow. Francis had been much more interested in the subject than Honorine, but she still knew many of the constellations by name. She and Francis had spent plenty of evenings and early mornings locating the patterns in the stars as Francis attempted to learn oceanic navigation from a bench in his mother's rose garden.

Honorine was more interested in the myths of the creatures and heroes themselves—the scorpion, the archer, the crow—and the legends about how they got their names and places in the sky. But Lord Vidalia had few books on such subjects in his libraries. His work was much more practical in nature, and Francis was only interested in the subject as it related to sailing.

Honorine ran her thumb along the pages, which stuck a bit because of the water and singed edges. When she eventually managed to pry them apart, she stared at the open book in amazement.

Gorgeous illustrations of fantastic beasts galloped and clawed and soared through an enchanted sky. Beautiful spotted bulls and golden lions, shining silver serpents and coal-black eagles, satyrs, centaurs, unicorns, and dragons—all painted with grotesque, snarling expressions in shimmering, iridescent ink. She pulled her fingers back from the page, almost afraid to touch them.

"Honorine!" snapped a stern voice from behind her. "What are you doing?"

Honorine quickly tucked the book in her apron pocket and flushed pink as she turned around to face Agnes, the head parlor maid.

"Dusting," she replied, tipping her head back to see Agnes's face under the brim of Lord Vidalia's voluminous hat. "As you requested. There was a small problem with the fireplace, but I saw to it promptly. We might want to get someone to sweep that chimney. I believe the flue may be stuck."

Agnes shook her head almost imperceptibly as she stood with her arms tensely at her sides and her mouth tightened into an impressively sour pucker.

"Take that off!" she demanded, looking over her shoulder before snatching the hat off Honorine's head and replacing it on the mantel.

"It's only a hat," Honorine said. Agnes wiped her hands hastily on her apron as if the hat had left a residue on her fingers.

"And Eve thought it was only an apple," Agnes replied, narrowing her eyes in warning. "These are not playthings. If you have time for nonsense and foolishness, then I haven't given you enough work."

Then she noticed the fine burns on the rug and the last thin coil of black smoke still twisting over the edge of the mantel. "Oh! Hono*rine*!" She clutched her heart as she examined a peppering of faint singed spots across the top of a cherrywood cabinet. "Scorch marks on the furniture! Burns on the rug! Was this lion on *fire*?"

"Only briefly," Honorine replied. "He's fine now."

"And did *that* have anything to do with...all this?" Agnes pointed accusingly at Honorine's lantern.

"No!" Honorine insisted. "It was the fireplace, I promise."

"And just look at the state of your uniform!"

Honorine looked down at her smart gray woolen dress and her white apron trimmed in lace, once crisp and bright, now splattered and smeared with black ash and flakes of soot.

"Oh, bother and bobtails!" she said as she batted at the dirt on the hem of her apron. She rather liked her uniform. The dress matched her gray eyes, and she even had a bit of gray velvet ribbon to tie back her hair. It was nothing as fancy as Lady Vidalia's gowns, but it was far better than the damp, sticky clothes one had to wear to work down in the kitchens or the laundry.

Agnes took a very deep breath and exhaled slowly, bringing one brittle hand to her tired eyes.

"Do you know what will happen to you if you lose your position here, Honorine?"

"Yes, Agnes." Honorine sighed. "It would be straight to the mills for me."

She had heard it from Agnes many times before, and from the other help, though they mostly stayed far clear of her. No other manor house would take her in, once she had worked for the Vidalias. Their house was known to be cursed or haunted or at the very least bad luck, and the other fine families in town were deathly afraid that servants from the Vidalia Manor would bring the ghosts in with them.

"That's right," Agnes added. "Where you would work twelve hours a day in the weaving rooms."

"Crawling on the hot floor under the looms to gather up the cotton lint to be spun into cheap yarn," Honorine continued.

"That's right," Agnes said again with a firm stomp of her boot heel on the wooden floor. "That's where I worked when I was your age. Not waltzing about a grand manor house in a fine dress. You are only working upstairs at the request of Lady Vidalia herself. So I have done my job dutifully, even though it has been far too much work for me to keep you presentable up here, where you might be seen by guests."

"Yes, Agnes," Honorine said. "And thank you." However, in all her years at the Vidalia Estate, Honorine had never seen anyone come to visit except for servants and other persons hired by Lady Vidalia, mostly doctors and mystics and fortune-tellers. They were shown up to the chambers in the west wing, where Lady Vidalia lived mostly in seclusion, surrounded by protective amulets and talismans.

After Lord Vidalia's disappearance, Lady Vidalia began collecting all manner of trinkets to counteract the curses and jinxes she thought must be hanging over the house. She had bundles of herbs hung over the doors and mystical runes carved into the stone turrets in the high brick fence around her property. She even had protective rocks she called omen stones strung up and draped like garlands in every window and doorway in the house, in the stables, over the gates in the fences, and across the glass roof of the old, nearly abandoned greenhouse out on the grounds. The stones resembled thick, broken yellow-green glass, strung on tangled silk lines, giving the effect of spiderwebs heavy with insect carcasses.

"I still think it was a mistake," Agnes continued to lecture as she moved about the room. "But it's too late now to change it. The downstairs help wouldn't have you anyway, even if they do need the extra hands."

She pulled back the heavy drapes and opened a window to air out the stench of smoke and burned silk.

Honorine gasped.

The omen stones were glowing.

Agnes's face drained to pale gray. She snatched the curtains closed.

"How are they doing that?" Honorine asked, watching the faint light shine out around the edges of the velvet drapes. "Where is that light coming from? Have they ever done this before?"

But Agnes, for once, said nothing at all, not even to scold. Her silence chilled Honorine right down to the bone.

Suddenly, a great, deep boom like a distant explosion rattled the windows and made the old house tremble.

"Agnes?" Honorine asked in the thinnest of whispers. "What are omen stones...omens...*of*?"

Honorine's words settled like falling ash, and the whole house went still and silent. She could hear only her own breathing.

After another moment of quiet, Agnes snapped back to attention.

"Go up to your room, find something clean and acceptable to wear, and take your filthy uniform down to Jane so it can be cleaned before tomorrow," she spouted.

"But what was that?" Honorine asked. "What's happening with the stones?"

"The next time I see you, I expect you to be presentable," Agnes continued, her scolding skills returned to full form. "Do not make me tell you a second time!"

Honorine stayed half a moment longer in protest, then nodded and started across the room. Agnes went out the modest door tucked away at the back of the parlor, into the servants' hallway, which allowed maids and footmen to have minimal interaction with guests and the upstairs residents. Such hallways traveled like arteries up and down the interior of the house, though they were rarely used in the mostly empty manor.

Honorine gathered her lantern and dusting rags, a little bit upset with Agnes. She must have known what would make the omen stones glow as if they were electrified. Well, Agnes could issue all the orders and chores she wished. Rocks magically turning into light-bulbs was not the kind of thing Honorine could simply ignore. It was the kind of thing she planned to investigate immediately.

Then the noise began.

A great knocking started overhead, as if someone were stomping about in huge, heavy boots down at the farthest end of the upstairs hall. The sound grew louder, and closer, until the chandelier in the parlor began to shudder with each step. Then the knocking simply stopped, vanishing like a snuffed-out flame. Honorine felt her heart hammering in her chest as she waited and listened. All was still, until she raised her boot to take a step toward the parlor door.

A second sound echoed through the house. This was lighter and faster, like the feet of a galloping animal racing down the hallway overhead, then down the stairs, then onto the polished marble floor of the foyer. Hard nails rattled on the smooth stone as the unknown creature raced straight toward the parlor.

Honorine extinguished the lantern light and shrank down to the floor, crouching behind the stout front paws of the Barbary lion. Out in the foyer, she could see stones beginning to glow in the huge arched window over the front entryway. Across the hall, the dark sitting room was also peppered with tiny spots of faint yellow-green light. The footfalls on the marble floor slowed to a walk. The stones began to burn brilliant yellow. Then the footfalls stopped.

The creature in the foyer howled. Or at least, a howl was the closest Honorine could come to describing the wild, ghostly call. It echoed down the cavernous hallways, rattled the windows, and cut through Honorine like a shot of ice-cold water.

When the howl faded away, the house was silent. Honorine looked up to see the stones fading back from pure golden yellow to a deeper yellow-green. As fast as she dared and as silently as she could manage, Honorine hurried to the doorway and cautiously peered into the dark foyer. The marble floor was bare and shining, as always. But leading up the carpeted stairs was a trail of paw prints, singed into the silk fibers of the rug, still smoldering hot orange around the edges.

Her eyes traveled up the grand staircase to the first landing and its huge leaded glass windows, also covered with a web of glowing stones. One window, though, was wide open.

Honorine slipped out of the parlor and snuck silently up the steps, carefully stepping around the burning paw prints in the rug. Each one was enormous, larger than her hand with all her fingers stretched out to their very widest. They led directly to the open window and then stopped abruptly, as if the creature that made them had leaped out, taking a rather bold two-story plummet onto a solid stone patio below.

Cool evening air blew in the open window, pushing something off the windowsill and onto the carpet at Honorine's feet.

It was a feather. A black feather, with an iridescent sheen of purple and green that swirled across the surface like oil spreading across dark water. Honorine plucked it from the ground, remembering the black feathers near Lord Vidalia's writing desk. But as she tried to make sense of the paw prints, the howling, the open window, and now the feather, it began to dissolve into violet embers, like the edge of paper curling as it caught fire. There was no heat, just a brief, faint glow as the feather crumbled into fine ash.

The stones in the window went dark. The smoldering paw prints extinguished across the rug. And Honorine was left with nothing but soot-stained fingertips.

Chapter · 2 ·

The Nocturnal Girl

I told you to go right up to your room and change your
filthy clothes."

Honorine's bones jumped inside her skin. She looked
up from her sooty hands to see Agnes standing at the
top of the next flight of steps, wearing her fiercest scowl.

"There was some...one in the house," Honorine
said with a squeak, pointing to the open window, and
then down the stairs at the singed paw prints. Agnes
bustled over to the landing, pulled the window shut,
and drew the curtains tightly closed.

"You didn't see anything," Agnes said, as if it were both a question and a statement. "And you will not speak about this to anyone."

"Did Lady Vidalia—"

"Any. One," Agnes repeated, and pointed up the branching staircase. "To your room now."

With her brow furrowed in silent protest, Honorine turned and marched up the stairs, the soot still on her hands and the book in her apron pocket.

The rest of the staff lived on the lower floors of the east wing of the house, in rooms near the kitchens. Honorine stayed in a nook up in the attic on the west end of the building, in the oldest part of the house, where rough, ancient stones and enormous wooden timbers were still visible in the walls and ceiling of many of the rooms. There she had a quiet little space with a snug bed, a tiny fireplace, and a large dormer window that looked out over the gardens and the northern sky, all tucked up under the very oldest rafters, where the roofline was uneven and impossibly steep. Her window was, of course, adorned with yellow stones, hung in a string across the very top of the glass. They were, to Honorine's disappointment, dark and exceptionally ordinary at the moment.

She set her lantern down, untied her apron, and emptied her pockets onto the bed. Along with the small leather-bound book, today she had gathered a pocket watch, a music box, and a carved wooden kaleidoscope, all broken, to add to her collection of projects gathered on the stout wooden mantel over her fireplace. She often tinkered with them in the late hours of the night, sometimes fixing them, sometimes taking them apart and building something new. But tonight she took no interest in her malfunctioning treasures.

Instead, she picked up the little leather-bound book, still dusted with drying soot.

It was beautiful. The cover was tooled with the image of a crown made of stars, and mythical beasts shimmered on the inside pages. A great phoenix with silver and gold feathers and reptilian eyes stared out from the heart of a raging fire. On the next page soared a copper-colored stallion with tremendous black speckled wings that reached to each end of the paper.

"'Pegasus,'" Honorine read from the text penned in tiny script along the edge of the inked drawing. "'The winged horse. Visible in the autumn sky. Do not be fooled by his beauty, for he is bloodthirsty and vicious.'" She looked up. "Vicious?" He certainly looked hot-blooded, but far more vicious was the centaur on the next page, and the dragon covered in claws and spines a page later. The creatures were made all the more frightening by the curious iridescent ink that gave an illusion of movement as light hit the page.

Other pages held detailed drawings of engine components and bizarre machines, which she found fascinating, if impossible to decipher. There were also hasty journal entries listing what must have been important dates and events on some kind of expedition.

April the Eighteenth, 1879—Hit edge of hurricane in Azores. May the Fourth, 1879—Second engine test a complete success. One entry was signed *B. Vidalia*.

"Lord Vidalia wrote this!" Honorine whispered. A little spark of electricity pricked her fingertips as she flipped through the pages. This wasn't just an almanac of his work; it was his actual journal, written in his own hand as he had traveled.

A few other brief journal entries were scrawled among the illustrations. In August, there was bad weather. In early September, a baby was born to Lord Vidalia's fellow explorer, Nautilus Olyphant, and his wife, Anne. Then, several pages seemed to have been torn out, leaving little ragged edges tucked among the binding.

Several times, she encountered the word *Mordant* printed among the drawings. The very last page was filled with an image of a slender man posed very elegantly and artificially, holding out a glowing golden pear as if he were offering it to the reader. He had wild hair and vibrant blue eyes, and there was a great deal of text written beside him, but much of it was blotted out with spilled red ink. Or perhaps, she realized with a slither of disgust, blood. Between the smears and splashes, she managed to read a few lines of text.

…myth of the Stolen Fire…known most commonly as the Mapmaker…Viciously guards his identity. Known to kill…I have concluded that it is far too dangerous to continue pursuing this particular Mordant, and accordingly, I have destroyed all of my research on the topic.—B. Vidalia, January the Ninth, 1880.

"'Eighteen…eighty'?" Honorine read aloud. She repeated the date to herself a few times before she hit on why it stood out. Lord Vidalia had vanished in early 1879, just after the portrait of the Vidalia family was painted and hung in the east parlor. He had not returned to the house again, yet somehow this book had found its way back into his study, and then wound up in the fireplace.

Honorine closed the book and held it tightly in her hand, as if the creatures within might sneak out from between the pages. She wondered what to do with it. This was a book about dangerous things, and someone had tried to destroy it.

She kept turning this puzzle over in her skull as she changed out of her soiled gray dress and into a pair of patched overalls that Agnes found appalling. But it was well after dinnertime now, when the rest of the house prepared for bed, and Honorine began her favorite part of the day—a few quiet hours of tinkering with her little gadgets and contraptions. If Honorine was quick, Agnes would never see her taking her sooty clothes down to the wash.

Before she could reach the door, she was distracted by the sound of something tapping on her window. She looked up excitedly, expecting for a moment to see the stones glowing again, but instead she saw something small and shimmery hovering outside the glass near the windowsill.

It looked like a large bee, made of copper and brass, with little stone eyes and crystalline wings. When she opened the window, it flew straight in and landed on the bib of her overalls.

She had seen a bee like this several weeks ago on the carpet in the east parlor. She had nearly swept it away, thinking it was just a dead insect. Then she noticed the strange coloring and heard a soft ticking, like clockwork gears moving somewhere inside it, and realized that it was a tiny machine. It appeared to be broken, and she took it back to her room, intending to examine it more closely after completing her daily chores. But that first bee had vanished from her mantel by the time she'd returned.

Perhaps this was the same one, and it had somehow fallen through a gap in the floorboards or flown unsteadily out through the chimney. This time, it wasn't getting away. She wrapped the bee in a handkerchief and tucked it in her pocket along with Lord Vidalia's book. She was running out of time to get to the laundry, and Agnes would still expect her to be in presentable clothes the next morning.

The clock at the end of the hall began to chime ten as Honorine picked her way down the servants' stairs to the lowest level of the house. The kitchens were busy with the end-of-day tasks, some servants still cleaning up from dinner, some scrubbing the cooking areas, others preparing for the next morning, setting out bread dough to rise and bringing in wood to stoke the ovens before the first light of dawn. Honorine gingerly carried her bundle of dirty clothes toward the washing machines in a separate alcove off the main kitchens.

"Good evening," she said to one of the cooks, and was met with a glare.

"And good-bye, then," she muttered under her breath as she made her way into the laundry. There she was confronted at once by Jane, a scullery maid who had never been particularly fond of Honorine, for reasons that seemed very obvious to Jane and were a complete mystery to Honorine.

"What are you doing down here?" Jane snapped. Her eyes narrowed when she saw the dirty clothes. "I'm almost done for the day, and you've gone and ruined your fancy little outfit?"

Honorine felt a flicker of anger in her cheeks. "It was either get my apron a little dirty or let the house burn down. I can wash them myself if it's too much trouble."

"Ha!" Jane said. "And have you ruin your uniform? Who would get blamed for that?"

Honorine leaned around the angry maid to look at the washing machines. They resembled half barrels on legs, with a gear and crank on one side to stir the water in the tub, and a second crank that ran the set of rollers used to wring out the wet clothes after they were washed. Beside Jane's tub was a second tub, where another laundry maid, Mattie, laboriously turned the crank to keep the hot water agitating, huffing and sweating and turning a brilliant, patchy red as she worked.

"You know, I—well, it would be possible to fix a motor to that," Honorine said, pointing to the crank handle. "To turn the agitator, so you don't have to do it all by hand." She could see not only how it would work, but also exactly how to build it. One little motor with a belt turning the crank and the paddle, another keeping the wringer moving.

"Oh," Jane said. "So the machine would wash all the clothes for me?"

"Yes!" Honorine said. "It should be much less work that way."

"And then what would I do all day, if a machine could do my work for me? You mean to put me out of a job?"

"Oh, no, not at all!" Honorine said. "You misunderstood."

"I heard you perfectly!" Jane said. She was no longer annoyed. She was angry. "We're already running on a skeleton crew down here. And there's nowhere to go if we lose our positions. You'll have us all out in the streets or the workhouses!"

Honorine fumed and felt the blush in her cheeks blazing to a full rage, but she choked it down.

"Fine," she said. "It was a terrible idea. Forget I ever spoke."

She spun on her black booted heel, walking as calmly and confidently as she could until she was out of the room. Then she ran up the steps, through the servants' dining room, and into the empty hall, getting her anger out through a good foot-stomping on the solid wooden floors.

She marched all the way back up to her room, her mind filled with Jane's scowling face and Agnes dismissing her as if she deserved no explanation about the stones or the paw prints or the noises.

Something suspicious was going on, but Honorine was angry, and only one thing ever really helped to clear her mind when she was upset. So she closed the door to her room and got to work on a prototype washing machine motor. Once the idea ignited in her mind, it grew like a fire, filling up all the space for practical things or responsibilities. Even if Jane didn't want it, now she had to try to build that motor.

She dismantled a few other half-finished projects to construct her new invention, letting the worries and grievances fade away as she focused on choosing suitable parts and fitting them together, until she had a roughly assembled motor in her hands. By the time she had finished, it was so late that night had slipped into very early morning. With everyone else asleep, Honorine put her brand-new motor into a pillowcase and carried it and her lantern down to the kitchens.

The soft sulfur-yellow light of her lantern shone on the wet stone floor and the scrubbed pots hanging from the ceiling near the stoves. Thick shadows swung across the brick walls, the sacks of grain, the bins of salt and sugar and cornstarch lined up in the open pantry. Honorine threaded her way past all of it to the alcove in the corner and pulled her washing machine motor from the pillowcase.

It was attached in no time, and with a few twists of the gears, the belt began to turn and the motor began to run. Honorine climbed up onto the sorting table, pulling her knees to her chest, and watched with delight as the agitator spun in the water, turning the soap into delicate, glistening foam. Jane couldn't possibly be mad after she had a chance to use this splendid new machine.

Honorine rested her chin on her knees, enjoying her quiet moment of victory. Her eyes wandered over the rest of the dark kitchen, searching for the next project. She looked at the ovens and wondered if she couldn't build some type of a more effective thermometer or a machine to knead the bread. For surely, once the rest of the staff saw that she could make everyone's work easier, they would not all look at her with such suspicion whenever she entered the kitchens.

It was times like this that she missed Francis.

He would have been excited to see the washing machine, turning on its own power, and her lantern, flickering away on the table. Francis had been her closest companion when they were the only children in the house, and they had spent a good part of each day together, eating their meals or spending afternoons in the garden, and later taking lessons together from Francis's governesses. As they grew, they had both developed a fascination with inventing and building machines. But then, last year, Francis had been sent away to school for the first time. Lady Vidalia had decided it was time for him to begin meeting and socializing with other children of his same station.

After the first semester, he had come home for holiday break with tales of classes and dormitories and dozens of other boys studying mathematics, history, biology, science. Honorine longed to visit such a place. But though Lady Vidalia might have been willing to pay a governess a little extra to give some lessons to the young maid, she wasn't going to pay to send Honorine to a proper school.

So Francis went back to school, and Honorine went back to work, spending her time that used to be for lessons with Francis building clockwork games they could play together when he returned for the summer holiday. She had made one with ducks that moved on a glass pond with magnets, and another with little windup elephants that flipped marbles through the air with springs in their trunks.

But when the school year ended, instead of Francis, a letter arrived, excitedly describing his intention to stay over the summer and continue his studies. And at the end of the summer, another letter came stating that he was looking forward to a new year of classes.

Honorine often wondered what he was doing at school while she was dusting bookshelves or watering potted ferns, or sitting in the kitchen in the dark hours of the morning, observing her prototype washing machine motor, which was making a surprising amount of bubbles. Too many to be contained in the tub, she realized, and climbed down from the table to switch it off before they spilled out onto the floor. But before she could reach the machine, she was distracted by a faint flashing light at the far end of the kitchen. Not another lantern, and not a shaft of moonlight, but a spattering of green among the jars of extracts and pots of herbs gathered along the windowsills.

The omen stones. Again.

Honorine spun around. In every window, the omen stones glowed, flickering and waning like the cold twinkle of tiny stars.

She quickly switched off her lantern and the washing machine motor and snuck up the flagstone steps into the dark central hallway above the kitchens. Far down at the other end, something was moving in the foyer, much more lightly than before, tapping carefully across the marble floor. Honorine rushed down the hallway as quickly as she dared, to the edge of the archway leading to the foyer and the east parlor.

Yellow lantern light spilled out of the parlor, along with the sound of muffled, unfamiliar voices. Whatever was making the omen stones glow was in the house at that very moment. And this was her chance to see what it was.

Pirates in the Parlor

S he came in here," said the growling, unfamiliar voice of someone who did not belong in the house.

"Are you certain?" replied the cold voice of someone else who did not belong in the parlor in the middle of the night.

"There's feathers all over the floor."

"Lots of things got feathers."

The intruders moved farther into the parlor, their voices growing too faint to hear.

Honorine slunk across the foyer until she was tucked behind a tall potted lemon tree standing just outside the parlor. From around the carved terra-cotta pot, she could see a pair of men standing on the singed rug, just in front of the hearth.

"Feathers like these, Bloom?" said the growling one, holding up an iridescent black feather exactly like the one that had crumbled to ash in Honorine's hand.

He was a huge bulldog of a man, with a boxer's face and knotty shoulders bulging under his snug blue coat. His face was burned and bleached, with the red skin and white hair of a fair man who'd spent too much time in the sun. The bridge of his nose was smashed nearly flat, leaving a little lumpy nub with round, flaring nostrils over his iron jaw. On his shoulder rested the long barrel of a rifle made from what appeared to be copper, painted wood, and glass.

"You're right, Salton," said the one with the cold voice. "That's definitely her."

He was a pinch shorter and much leaner, with mismatched eyes and hair in wild tangles. His face was deeply tanned, and his teeth glinted with gold when he spoke. He wore the same style of long blue coat, tall cuffs on his high black boots, and jewelry fashioned from bones. He held a lantern like nothing Honorine had ever seen before, a sort of glass-and-iron orb atop a short copper baton, which he could point in any direction to aim the illumination. He also appeared to be carrying two guns and a variety of knives.

They were sailors, Honorine realized, though this did not provide any further information as to what they were doing in Lady Vidalia's house in the dark of the morning, nosing about in the fireplace.

Then a third figure entered the room through the servants' entrance. She was dressed like the others, in breeches and tall boots, with a billowing shirt and a knee-length blue coat, though hers was adorned with a few extra bits of brass and braiding. She was rather tall—nearly the height of the Salton fellow—with a serious face, and a tremendous amount of thick black hair swept up into a sturdy but messy knot on the top of her head. She wore spectacles with thin yellow lenses and silk gloves over her hands, which she used to examine the room, occasionally running a finger along a surface and inspecting the tip of the glove.

"Professor du Ciel," Salton said with a nod to the woman.

"Gentlemen," she replied without looking at either of them. "Have you found anything useful?"

"Astraea was here," Bloom explained. He held up a clutch of feathers, which were already curling into embers and ash.

"But you've touched them, so now there's nothing left to study," said the professor with a sigh of annoyance.

"There are prints on the carpet," Salton added, waving a meaty finger toward the foyer, where Honorine crouched behind the lemon tree. "Wolf, I suspect."

"Yes, too small to be the lion," Professor du Ciel observed.

Wolf? And LION? Honorine thought, looking quickly over her shoulder. The foyer was, for the moment, dark and still.

"And what about the book?" Professor du Ciel continued.

Honorine felt a cold prickle around her collar. They must be talking about the one she had pulled from the ashes and was now resting in her pocket beside the odd mechanical bee.

"Not here," Salton replied.

"Not in this room, anyway," Bloom added.

"Then we keep looking," said Professor du Ciel. "The Mapmaker wouldn't come all this way to find a book and then leave without it."

Honorine's cold prickle turned to a flush of goose bumps at the mention of the Mapmaker. He was someone, or something, that even brave Lord Vidalia considered too dangerous to discuss in his own private journal.

The three of them turned away from the fireplace, heading toward the foyer. Honorine huddled into a ball and pressed herself against the wall.

"What if he already has it?" Bloom asked.

"They wouldn't still be on the ground if they already had it," du Ciel replied.

Just when she was sure they were going to discover her, Honorine looked up to see a girl standing on the staircase landing. She was no older than Honorine and dressed in a short silvery tunic and leggings that seemed to be woven from wide silver ribbons. She had dark skin and a wild mane of glossy black hair falling past her knees, all illuminated by a faint outline of soft violet light.

The girl held up a finger to her lips, gesturing for Honorine to stay silent, then pointed very slowly to the sitting room across the foyer from the east parlor. Honorine turned to see something huge, white, and glowing with blue light moving silently among the silk-upholstered couches and tall potted ferns.

"There's one of 'em!" Salton said, raising his rifle as he and Bloom ran for the sitting room, no longer bothering with quiet footsteps.

"Put down your weapon!" Professor du Ciel commanded, marching after them. They didn't appear to heed her instruction.

As their boots clattered across the marble and the trio headed into the sitting room, Honorine heard a sharp, faint voice call to her.

"Hurry!" it insisted, as if right in her ear, though when she looked up, the girl was making her way silently down the stairs, gesturing for Honorine to come toward her.

Between the thieves with guns and the little girl in the silver tunic, Honorine opted to follow the girl. She padded across the foyer as fast as she dared as the sailors stomped through the sitting room.

"Outside," the girl whispered, pointing to an open door leading onto the patio overlooking the gardens. "Go. Fast. Before they find you."

She heard the crack of gunfire, then an angry bark: "I gave you an order." This was followed by, "You're not in command of this expedition." And then further muffled arguing.

"Run," said the girl flatly. Honorine ran.

Her feet pounded down the carpeted hallway, slapping so hard when she reached a bit of wood floor that her heels stung. As she skipped over the threshold of the terrace doors and into the night, the girl slipped out after her, pulling the door shut very quietly.

"Who are you?" Honorine asked, panting and looking back over her shoulder at the dark house. Strange lights flashed through the windows. "Who are *they*? And what are they doing in Lady Vidalia's house?"

"I am Astraea," said the girl. Her eyes sparkled very dark green. There was something both familiar and uncomfortable about her stare, as if she were seeing more when she looked at Honorine than Honorine saw when she looked back. "And *they* are dangerous henchmen, though not as dangerous as the man they work for. There are many more of them, and you must come now, before they find you."

"Wait," Honorine panted, suddenly aware she was standing out in the yard, in the dark, with a complete stranger, who, though she looked harmless enough, was no more supposed to be in the Vidalia house in the middle of the night than Salton or Bloom or Professor du Ciel. "How do I know you're not dangerous, too?"

"Oh, I'm very dangerous," Astraea said. "But only to them."

Honorine looked back to see Salton and Bloom lurching toward the terrace doors.

"Aren't you supposed to say something comforting, like 'there's nothing to be afraid of'?"

"I could, but that would be a lie," Astraea replied.

Salton burst through the doors, his rifle cocked and aimed.

"Get to the greenhouse," Astraea said, though Honorine wasn't certain she had said anything aloud. Then Astraea sprinted to the terrace railing, hopped onto the stone banister with one graceful step, and leaped off. Something rose up behind her, as if she had caught part of the night and was pulling it around her.

"Wings!" Honorine gasped. What she had mistaken for long, glossy black hair was actually a pair of wings. The feathers shimmered violet and green in the pale starlight.

Salton took a terrible shot, which exploded in a ball of hot, sulfurous green smoke. While the men were choking and wiping their watering eyes, Honorine tumbled over the railing and dropped onto the lower level of the terrace a few feet below. Her heart pounded, and she could feel her pulse racing through her ears. She would have expected to be terrified, having just been chased from her house by men with rifles. But there was something more than fear racing through her veins. There was excitement, like a shock of ice water. After all, she had just seen a girl with *wings*.

She ran down the cascading veranda steps and onto the damp green lawn, where she was quickly surrounded by mist and shadows. In the darkness, the yard looked much bigger than it did from inside the house. Lantern casings filled with yet more omen stones, instead of oil and wicks, hung on tall poles along the garden paths, swaying lightly in a rustling breeze. The stones glowed here, too, casting diffused yellowish-green light over mounds of manicured shrubbery, making them appear to swell and ebb like the bellies of great, slumbering beasts.

From the safety of the garden path, Honorine dared to look back up at the house. Astraea had vanished. Salton and Bloom were running along the terrace toward the garden steps. Professor du Ciel was nowhere to be seen.

Honorine turned away from them and snuck down the path toward the tall, sturdy brick garden wall and the tiny greenhouse tucked up under a lilac hedge, hidden from view of the main house. There was a soft flash of light from within the greenhouse itself as she approached, and a gust of wind rattled the glass in its lead frames.

"Radicchio?" she called out meekly, as loudly as she dared, though she knew that whoever was inside was not the gardener. Honorine took a deep breath. "Radicchio! There's someone in the greenhouse!"

A hound howled on the other side of the garden wall, and yellow lights blazed to life in the big black barn. The stable hands were awake. They would come to investigate the noise, she hoped. Honorine stepped toward the greenhouse door and gripped the curved handle.

Pulling it open, she immediately reeled back from the powerful smell. The greenhouse was hot and damp and crowded. The leaded glass windows were fettered with ropy vines of ivy creeping and climbing across nearly every surface. Back in the corner stood a long-dead palm tree. It was moldy and withered and infested with some breed of stinging ants, but the palm had been the last gift from Lord Vidalia before he vanished, so Lady Vidalia refused to allow it to be removed.

"It's disgusting in here," Honorine muttered as beetles scattered across the floor.

"Why, it is only nature," a voice replied.

Honorine froze, her hands pinned to her sides, as a black-clad figure moved from the shadows and into the wavering yellow-green light of the omen stones hanging across the glass ceiling. A silhouetted hand brushed over an enormous white flower blooming from a knotted vine.

"Nothing beautiful in all the world exists without something a bit vile to balance the ledger," the figure said.

Honorine trembled as she stared up at him. He was a tall, slim man with a faded yet still handsome face. His hair was gray and wild, his eyes a brilliant shade of blue. He wore a long, dark duster jacket, and his clothes underneath were rather old-fashioned, with a little ruffle on the cuffs of his shirt and a cravat tied neatly under his high collar. On his shoulder sat a ragged black crow, and beside him stood a white wolf, so tall that it stood at eye level with Honorine, its coat shimmering with blue illumination that reminded her of the reflection of sunlight off water.

"So, this is her?" the man asked. Astraea stepped forward from even farther back in the darkness, her arms crossed tightly over her chest.

"This is her," she said with authority.

The man leaned down to bring his face closer to Honorine, until he was looking directly into her eyes.

"Lovely to meet you, Miss…"

"Honorine," she replied.

"Honorine," he repeated with a bob of his head. Then he stuck out a hand stained with ink and blood. "They call me the Mapmaker."

CHAPTER
· 4 ·

The Mapmaker

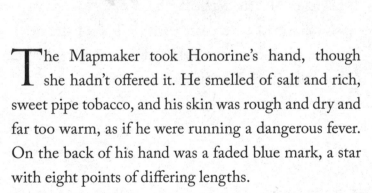

The Mapmaker took Honorine's hand, though she hadn't offered it. He smelled of salt and rich, sweet pipe tobacco, and his skin was rough and dry and far too warm, as if he were running a dangerous fever. On the back of his hand was a faded blue mark, a star with eight points of differing lengths.

"It's a...pleasure...to make...your acquaintance," Honorine mumbled as the Mapmaker grasped her little hand. His eyes seemed to brighten to a lighter shade, lifting from deep navy to a kind of sapphire.

Honorine had never seen eyes shift in color like that. The intensity of his stare made her even more uncomfortable. She looked away, down to his hand, and saw that the blue star seemed to glow, sending an unsettling sensation through her fingers. Her hand felt as if it were going numb to the point of being painful, until she pulled it sharply away. The mark disappeared under his cuff.

"Remarkable," he whispered. "You see, Astraea? I knew there was something else here. Nautilus wouldn't come all this way just for a book."

Astraea's black wings bristled. Honorine flinched at the mention of a book. The Mapmaker's unnerving stare remained on her.

"Honorine, you seem frightened," he said, and his eyes went very soft, lifting from sapphire to a near sky blue. "It isn't us you need to fear. We've come to help."

"We really must hurry this along," Astraea said with another irritated rustle of her feathers. "They know we're here. We shouldn't be away from the ship much longer."

"I know," the Mapmaker said curtly. "But some things must be done properly, without a hurry. This girl doesn't even know who we are, and with all she's seen tonight, I don't blame her for being frightened out of her skull."

The Mapmaker finally looked away from her, and the moment his gaze broke from Honorine's, she realized she was not afraid of him. Excited and a bit anxious, but the pure terror she had felt at the first sight of the Mapmaker had washed away, replaced by a hungry kind of curiosity.

"Honorine," the Mapmaker said again, "my apologies for omitting the proper introductions. I believe you have already met Astraea." He gestured to the winged girl. "Our other winged friend here is Corvus." He nodded to the crow. "And then, of course, Lux." He rested his hand on the wolf's shoulder.

"Pleased to meet you," said the wolf.

"He talks?" Honorine asked. She leaned toward him in amazement.

"Yes, and he bites," the Mapmaker said.

Honorine recoiled and tucked her hands behind her back.

The wolf narrowed his eyes at the Mapmaker. "I would never dream of biting *you*," Lux said, looking back at Honorine with yellow eyes that were not at all reassuring.

"You're the Mordant," Honorine said. "Lord Vidalia wrote about you in his journal."

"Yes, we are. You're a rather bright girl," the Mapmaker said. "And that journal, I suspect, is the very one Nautilus has come all this way to pretend to find."

"Who is Nautilus?" Honorine asked.

"We've been away from the ship for far too long now," Astraea warned. The Mapmaker nodded and waved a hand at her.

"The intruders you saw in the house work for Nautilus. As part of his... acquisitions department, let's say. The one called Salton is the head gunner on a steamship known as the *Gaslight*, which is right now lurking in the sea just a few miles offshore. His companion, Bloom, is also known as the Black Rat of Normandy and the Scourge of the North Atlantic. In his day, he was a beast of a pirate, more feared than Blackbeard or William Kyd. Between the pair of them, they have raided a hundred ports, slaughtered a thousand men, and taken ten times as much in plunder, leaving a wake of chaos and destruction. They have never failed to obtain a treasure they were tasked to find. They have never given up on a bounty, never let a man go free when they had the chance to claim his life. And now they are searching—with their guns and shackles and knives—for you."

"Me?" Honorine squeaked, though she wasn't sure the word had made it out of her throat. The fear that had left her just a moment ago flooded back. All the light and sound in the world seemed to rush away, and her eyes blurred until the only thing she could see was the faint blue flicker of the Mapmaker's eyes.

"You can't say things like that to her," someone said. It sounded like the wolf. "She's just a child, after all."

She felt a tingling in her hands, as if she were touching a mild electric current. Her vision snapped back to focus, and she found herself leaning into Lux, her hands and arms buried in his thick, slightly prickly fur.

"Careful there," Lux said. "You nearly fainted."

Honorine stood back up, leaving one hand on Lux's shoulder. Somehow the feel of the wolf's fur both calmed her and began to build in her a sense of strength and confidence.

"Thank you," she said to Lux. "I feel much better."

"That's courage," the Mapmaker said, followed with a smile and a pat of Lux's flank. "It's what he's good for. And what are you good for, Honorine?"

The courage only lasted until she pulled her hand away from Lux's coat. Then the dark and the cold and her smallness in the world seemed to become suddenly very important. Trying to ignore her thudding heart, she said, "I don't know."

"Well, they do," the Mapmaker said, pointing up toward the house while looking intensely at Honorine.

"What would they want with me? They were looking for a book." The crow on the Mapmaker's shoulder hopped up onto the potting bench and pecked at the glass.

"Yes, yes, I'm going as fast as I can, Corvus," the Mapmaker said testily. "Our apologies, Miss Honorine. A smart, young thing like yourself is very right to be suspicious. However, we are in a bit of a tight spot at the moment, so I must be embarrassingly blunt, I'm afraid. I don't know *exactly* why, but those men are hunting us. But I believe that before the night is through, they will be hunting you as well. And you won't be much of a challenge for them. I would like to propose that, instead of being captured by the likes of Salton and Bloom, you consider joining up with us instead."

Honorine blinked and furrowed her brow.

"You want me to come with you?" she asked.

"It's either us or them," Astraea said, nodding toward the house, and the men armed with rifles and knives wandering the gardens.

"What if I don't like either of those choices?" Honorine asked, looking from Astraea to Lux to the Mapmaker. "You broke into Lady Vidalia's house and tried to burn Lord Vidalia's journal. What else did you take? Are you thieves?"

The Mapmaker brightened at this.

"I always thought I'd make a rather dashing thief," he said. "But no. We're not here to take anything that doesn't belong to us already."

"That book wasn't yours," Honorine said. "It belonged to Lord Vidalia, and I think *you* tried to destroy it." She motioned to Astraea. "I saw your feathers near the fireplace."

Astraea turned toward Honorine, her eyes blazing, and looked as if she was about to say something a little more than harsh, but the Mapmaker stopped her with a wave of his hand.

"And what about the information inside?" he asked Honorine. "If Lord Vidalia wrote something down that could harm us, have we no right to protect ourselves?

We can't let that information fall into the hands of someone who would use it against us, can we?"

"But there wasn't anything dangerous in it...." Honorine said at the same moment she realized that might not be entirely true. "Was there?"

"Could I have a look at it?" the Mapmaker asked. "It's in your pocket right this moment, isn't it?"

Honorine hesitated. Lord Vidalia did not trust this Mapmaker. But then, his journal had been written many years ago. Perhaps he had been mistaken or he hadn't had all the information. The Mapmaker had not threatened her or harmed her in any way. He had, in fact, offered to help.

She pulled out the little journal and placed it in his hand.

"Thank you," he said, his eyes a calming shade of ocean blue as he flipped through the book. "Log notes, some rather nice illustrations, diagrams of machinery... but not the information that Nautilus is really looking for."

"Who?" Honorine asked. "You keep saying that name. Who is he?"

"The captain of the *Gaslight*, Nautilus Olyphant," answered Astraea. "The worst of the lot."

"We've been observing him," Lux said. "Keeping track of where he travels, trying to find a way to stop him from coming after us. We first found it curious that he would come here. But then word reached us that Nautilus was looking for a rather important piece of work created by Lord Vidalia, a lost journal, and that he was traveling across the whole of the North Atlantic to find it."

"Well, I didn't believe it," the Mapmaker said. "Not entirely. I was certain there must be something else here, something even more important, for Nautilus to go to all the trouble."

The Mapmaker looked down at Honorine.

"Now I understand," he said. "I would have come to find you much, much sooner, had I known you were here all along."

Lux moved suddenly, knocking past Honorine to get to the windows. "You'll have to explain it to her on the ship," he said. "We're out of time. He's here."

Behind him, the moon hung low and full and yellow, brushing the tops of the trees, and beside it, Honorine saw a second large, round shape resting in the sky as if the moon were casting a shadow. A flicker of golden firelight illuminated the underside of a huge blue dirigible growing closer and larger every second.

"What is that?" Honorine asked.

"Nautilus's airship," the Mapmaker huffed. "This is it, Honorine. We have to get back to our ship. It is the only place where Nautilus cannot catch us. There will be time to ask all the questions you'd like once we get outside his reach."

Honorine felt the dread building in the greenhouse as Astraea, Lux, Corvus, and the Mapmaker stared up at the looming airship, waiting for her to give them the signal to flee to safety.

"What about the others?" she asked. "Lady Vidalia is still in the house! And Agnes and the other maids! I can't just leave them behind!"

"Nautilus is looking for us, not them. If we go away, he will follow," the Mapmaker explained.

A deep, powerful explosion rang out in the dark morning sky, rattling the glass in the greenhouse windows until several panes cracked.

"What was *that*?" Honorine asked.

"That would be cannons," Lux said.

"Are you ready, Honorine?" the Mapmaker asked before the echo of the cannon fire had completely faded.

This was it. The adventure Honorine had always dreamed of, right in front of her. The kind that Lord

Vidalia had undertaken, traveling away from the manor house and the garden walls to bring home all those treasures and artifacts. The kind of adventure that had taken him away forever, she realized, perhaps had even been his demise. There would be excitement and mystery and discovery. And cannons.

"All right," she said finally.

"You'll come?" Lux asked, his ears pricking up brightly.

"Yes, I'll go with you."

She expected him to be pleased, but the Mapmaker's first reaction, just for a moment, was one of melancholy. He nodded, then put a hand on Honorine's shoulder.

"Welcome back," he said, giving her a pat. "Now, we have to get to the *Carina* before Nautilus works out that we're still here, wandering around unprotected."

The Mapmaker moved to the tangled dark at the back of the greenhouse, brushing aside a shriveled rope of vines covered in yellowing leaves, and slid open a panel of glass leading to a narrow gap in the brick garden wall. Astraea and Corvus went through after him, leaving Lux and Honorine alone under the glowing omen stones and dead palm fronds.

"You first," Lux said with a nod toward the little brick doorway. "I'll be right behind you. I promise."

Honorine took a breath and one last look back at the Vidalia house, then ducked through the wall, leaving behind the manicured gardens and the elegant estate—and entering the dark, wild woods.

CHAPTER
· 5 ·

At the Edge of the Forest

The Vidalia Estate was surrounded by a hundred acres of wild woodland, mossy ravines, and dark, silent groves of old oak trees. Honorine and Francis had often wandered in the woods, but she hadn't been out past the garden wall once in the year since he'd left home for school, and she'd never done so at night.

There was not much to see, except what was illuminated by the Mordant, who each gave off a faint aura of ethereal light. Lux was a bluish white, Astraea was a faint violet, and the Mapmaker was a color she had never seen before. It was something like ocean green, but with a phosphorescent tint. They gathered on the far side of the wall, taking a moment to observe the forest before they headed into it.

Astraea perched on the bend of an enormous oak branch, her wings stretched out for balance. The Mapmaker stood below her on a wide path of packed earth covered with fallen leaves. Honorine padded her way across the cold forest floor on her bare feet, with Lux following right beside her.

"Where's the crow?" she whispered to Lux.

"Reconnaissance," he explained. "Looking out for Nautilus's men."

The Mapmaker leaned down, putting one hand on Honorine's shoulder. "Stay with Lux," he instructed as his eyes scanned the darkness around them. They were flashing from dark to light. Honorine supposed he could probably see much better in the dark, like a cat or an owl. "He will lead you back to the *Carina*. Astraea and I will take a higher route to keep ourselves between you and Nautilus. Move as quickly as you can without—"

A branch snapped with a dry crack that echoed through the woods. Before the sound had died, a rush of brilliant electric-blue sparks erupted underneath a tree a dozen paces away. They illuminated the outline of Corvus, no longer the size of an ordinary crow, but taller than the Mapmaker, with wings that reached out to a span of perhaps ten feet or more. The glow of Corvus, in turn, illuminated the silhouette of a person, slightly hunched over, with one foot balanced in the air, as if he were praying that no one had heard his very unfortunate encounter with the dry branch.

"Ah," the Mapmaker said. "And who do we have here?"

"Um, sorry!" said the silhouette nervously. "Didn't mean to interrupt! I heard some noise and thought I should check things over. Just for safety, you see."

"Oh, it's Sam!" Honorine said. He was just a bit older than Honorine herself and had worked in the stables for at least half a dozen years. "He's a stable hand. He's nothing dangerous."

"That's right," Sam said with an eager nod. "I tend the horses, keep watch on the grounds. Sometimes. As needed. That's all." His eyes moved from the wolf to the enormous crow to the winged girl, each faintly glowing. "So, none of this seems to be any of my business."

The Mapmaker stepped closer, offering him a hand. "And that's all you do here?" he asked as his hand closed over Sam's. Astraea's wings rustled, and she took a half step toward them. "You work only for Lady Vidalia?"

"And the lord, of course," Sam said. "Though we haven't seen him.... Well, I've never seen him. My, you have a very strong grip there, sir."

"Indeed," the Mapmaker said. The pointed blue star on his hand pulsed with light, and Sam tried to pull his hand away with a yelp.

"He's not dangerous!" Honorine repeated as Sam grew more frantic in his attempts to free his hand. The Mapmaker was still as iron, not flinching as Sam struggled and tugged, trying to escape. "Let him go! You're hurting him!"

Astraea swooped in on a trail of violet and silver sparks and stood behind Sam as he cried out and fell to one knee.

"Enough," Astraea said firmly. "This boy has done nothing wrong. Set him free."

The Mapmaker glared down at Astraea, gave Sam's arm a final twist, and then released him. The boy crumpled to the ground. Honorine rushed to him.

"Sam!" she said, picking up his hand. It was hot, his fingers a bit blue at the tips from the pressure. He flinched when she placed her hand on his shoulder. "Sam, are you all right?"

"I think so," he said, flexing his fingers. "That was terrible. Like I stuck my finger in a socket."

"Well, it's done now," Honorine said, offering him her other hand. Sam began to reach for her with his good arm, but when he looked up at her, his expression flashed from confusion to fear. He quickly drew his unhurt hand away as if she had shocked him just as badly as the Mapmaker, and scrambled backward.

"See? He's a quick learner, this one," the Mapmaker said with a nod. "Now he will stay away from us, which is the safest place for him to be."

"Sam!" Honorine said, taking a step toward him, which only sent him into an utter panic. He bolted away, pulling himself a few feet across the dirt and leaves before he managed to get his feet under him and take off running.

He had barely faded from view before a whistle pierced the dark around them, followed by a cannonball crashing through the trees and exploding in a blast of yellow sparks and green smoke.

The Mapmaker swung up onto the crow's back with one graceful leap. "Stay with Lux," he said, "and we will meet you on the ship."

Then, with a mighty lunge, the great black bird lifted into the sky, every feather outlined in glittering blue light and trailing a wake of shimmering sparks through the shadows.

A second thunderous boom of cannon fire echoed out over the forest, followed by an explosion of yellow-green light, like fireworks.

Lux nudged Honorine's hand with his nose. "Sam will be fine," he said. "The Mapmaker only gave him a warning. It could have been much worse. Now, follow me if you want to remain unexploded."

He nodded toward the trees and took off at a slow trot.

Honorine followed, but the way the Mapmaker had treated Sam had created a bother in her that curled up just under her heart. She had seen plenty of people being treated unfairly before, but as a maid, there was little she could do when someone was scolded too harshly. Perhaps this time, she thought, she could speak to the Mapmaker about it, when they had safely reached his ship.

The only light came from Lux's shimmering coat and his paws kicking up occasional white sparks. The rest of the forest was dark all around them, punctuated by blasts of yellow light from the cannon fire overhead. Amid the whistles and blasts was another sound, a low rumbling that rattled Honorine's ribs and ended in a wild growl.

"That wasn't a cannon!" Honorine said as she jogged a bit closer to Lux.

"No," he replied. "That was a lion. Nothing for you to be concerned about. He's really rather pleasant. You'll meet him when we get to the ship."

No matter how pleasant he might be, Honorine could not imagine that meeting a lion would not be cause for concern.

"About that ship," Honorine said as she ducked under a thorny branch. "We are quite a distance from the seashore."

"Ah, well," Lux said, "this isn't like any ship you would recognize."

"No, but I would," said a voice from the dark.

Lux's ears shot forward, and Honorine's eyes snapped to the tangled forest ahead, but neither of them located the speaker before they heard a crack of gunfire, followed by an explosion of white sparks so bright that Honorine shrieked with surprise and threw her arms over her eyes to shield them.

When she lowered her hands, there were still stray sparks floating down out of the dark sky, but the wolf was nowhere to be seen.

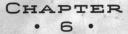

CHAPTER
· 6 ·

A Wolf, a Lion, and a Ship in the Sky

Lux?" she called. "Lux!"

"I did it!" said the voice from the dark. "I hit him!"

"Who's there?" Honorine shouted. "And what did you do to that wolf?"

"I shot him!" said a boy as he hopped down from the stout oak branches and landed on the leaf-strewn path just in front of Honorine. He held up an odd, clunky copper pistol, staring at it with both joy and bewilderment.

"I can't believe I hit him!" he said. "I've never done that before. And you're welcome, by the way." Then he looked away from the weapon and back to Honorine. He wore a small lantern on a copper chain around his neck that gave off just enough light so she could see his face.

"Francis!" Honorine shouted, both in greeting and surprise.

He had grown since she last saw him. He was taller and skinny, with shaggy hair and a slightly unkempt appearance, not at all like a boy who had been away at a very proper boarding school. He was dressed in black breeches and boots, a dark wool sweater with a high neck, and a snug black leather jacket, quite different from the tailored suits and cravats he had worn around the house. But it was unmistakably him.

"What are you doing out here," he asked, "wandering about in the dark with wolves?"

"*Me?*" Honorine asked. "What are you doing wandering about with guns? *You're* supposed to be at school!"

"Yes, well, let's not tell my mother," he said. "Are you all right? Did the wolf hurt you?"

"No," Honorine said with a quick shake of her head. "I'm fine."

"Well, we should get moving," Francis said as he reloaded the clunky pistol with round pellets made of glowing yellow-green stone. "These don't do much but distract them. Look, he's already coming back."

Francis was right. Honorine could already see Lux re-forming from the last of the white embers. They clung together along invisible ears, tail, and snout, illuminating the outline of a wolf. He gave a raspy, barking laugh and took a step forward, the little sparks multiplying and congealing to give him substance once more.

"It's like shaking up oil and water," Honorine said. As she was pondering the regenerating wolf, Francis tugged her hand, urging her to step back.

"Come on, then. We'll only have a few more minutes before he's all solid again."

Francis jogged off into the trees.

"Well, wait!" Honorine called, hurrying along after the bobbing light of the lantern around his neck. "You don't have to shoot him. He's not dangerous. He was trying to save me, actually."

"Save you?" Francis asked as he came to a stop near a particular oak so ancient that its lowest branches sagged all the way to the ground. "Save you from what?"

"Nautilus Olyphant. And his pirates."

Francis scrunched his nose in his familiar Francis way. And even if he had just shot a seemingly friendly, certainly magical wolf, seeing Francis again made her smile.

"So you're running away from Nautilus Olyphant?" he asked with a huge, goofy smile of his own. "Is that why you're out in the woods in a stable hand's overalls in the middle of the night, covered in mud and grease? And with no shoes to boot?"

Honorine looked down at her feet.

"Nope, no shoes or boots," she said, and started to giggle, then burst into an uncontrollable laugh that made Francis giggle, too. In moments, they were both snorting and laughing so hard they could barely breathe.

"A bunch of terrible brutes broke into your mother's house and tried to steal from your father's personal library," Honorine explained between bursts of laughter. "What about you? Is this how they dress you at school?"

"I wasn't *at* school," he replied. "I ran away with a band of pirates."

The laughter came to an abrupt end.

"Wait, pirates?" Honorine asked as cannons blasted again overhead. "Do you mean *those* pirates?"

"The very same!" Francis said proudly. "I came *with* Nautilus Olyphant, on a steam-powered airship, which is only about this much"—he held up his finger and thumb about an inch apart—"of the unbelievable things I've seen since I left. You have to come see it, Honorine. No one will ever appreciate this as much as you." He hopped up onto the lowest oak branch and reached out to help Honorine after him.

She had been warned that night that both the Mapmaker and Nautilus Olyphant were terribly dangerous individuals. She didn't yet know which side to believe. There was certainly nothing dangerous at all about Francis, though. So she took his hand and pulled herself up after him.

The branch was as wide as a forest trail and covered in a long mat of soft moss that made for decent footing.

"Did you hear what I said about Lux?" Honorine asked as she picked her way up the curve of the branch behind Francis.

"Who?" Francis asked as he reached the trunk of the tree and climbed across to a second, narrower branch leading toward an open patch of sky.

"The wolf," Honorine said. "You don't need to shoot at him. He won't hurt you."

She was answered by a deep, rumbling roar from somewhere in the darkness below.

"Oh right, but there is a lion," she added. "And I'm not entirely sure about him."

"Leo Major," Francis said. "Who else is out here tonight?"

"You mean what other Mordant?" Honorine asked as she pulled herself onto the higher branch.

Francis looked back, impressed. "How did you know they're called that?"

"Because your father wrote about them in his book." Honorine drew the little journal from her pocket. "The *Vidalia Field Almanac of the Celestial Constellations Both Known and Extinct.*"

Francis snapped to attention. "Where did you get that?" he asked as the branches rattled all around them. Honorine and Francis grabbed each other's hands for balance.

"I found it in the east parlor earlier tonight." She handed the book to Francis, who turned it over in his hands, admiring it as if it were a lump of precious gold before opening the pages.

"See?" Honorine said. "That's what he called them. 'Mordant.' Do you know what they are, exactly?"

"The Mordant?" Francis replied. "Eh...energy, like...electricity...a kind of spirit, I suppose."

"*Spirit* makes me think of ghosts," Honorine said, "or fairies. The Mordant seem to be something else."

"Muses!" Francis said, tapping the pages of the book. "That's what I meant. You've heard of them. In ancient myths, they inspired artists and scholars. They can show you anything, Honorine, about how the world works. People used to know them because they lived all around us, a long time ago. Now most people only know the names of their constellations."

Honorine stared up at the stars shimmering above, tiny diamond chips on a field of black velvet. Even though she had met them—a few of them at least—shaken their hands, touched their fur, spoken with them, it was still not quite believable to her. Could a constellation be a living thing? If it could, she was completely awed by the idea that on this very night, she had spoken with some of them in her own home.

"Ahoy, laddie!" a gravelly voice shouted. Honorine snapped out of her stargazing to see Nautilus's airship rise up over the trees, the great blue balloon hanging low in the sky, dappled with yellow light from the flames keeping the beast aloft. A stout woman in a blue coat, her long hair held back by a red handkerchief, leaned over the railing with a bundled rope ladder in her arms. "We're swinging around! Get ready to climb!"

Francis gave them a signal and then handed the little book back to Honorine, beaming with excitement.

"Are you ready to climb?" he asked as the ladder tumbled down off the railing of the airship and unfurled like a clumsy flag. He holstered his pistol and reached for the dragging lowest rungs.

"No, she is not," said the low, growling voice of Lux.

Honorine turned to see him standing on the branch behind them near the trunk of the oak, shaded from the view of the airship.

"Stay back, wolf," Francis said, reaching nervously for his pistol.

Lux ignored him, looking instead at Honorine.

"Come back down. Do not get on that ship with him."

She looked at the glittering white wolf. His eyes were wide and cold and yellow. He had absolutely no fear in him, not even after being shot by Francis only a few minutes ago.

"I'm not going to hurt you, Honorine," said Lux. "You know that." And she believed him.

"And you won't hurt Francis, either?" she asked.

Lux's nose twitched. He tilted his head.

"You have my word. I will not hurt—"

Right in the middle of his sentence, Lux burst into a cloud of white sparks. Again.

"Why'd you do that?" Honorine shouted at Francis. "I told you not to shoot him again!"

"I didn't!" Francis said.

"He was right in the middle of promising not to hurt you!"

"I didn't shoot him! Well, not this time!" Francis insisted, holding out his hands and letting go of the ladder. "I don't even have my weapon!"

"We got 'im!" came a gleeful, raspy shout, and Honorine and Francis looked down to see Salton and Bloom come tumbling out of the dark, right up to the base of the tree.

"What are you waiting for?" Bloom called. "Get up that ladder, boy!"

"Where is the lion?" Salton shouted. "We drove him this way. Have you seen him?"

With a roar so deep it shook the old oak from the roots up, the lion finally appeared from the dark forest, bounding toward Salton and Bloom as they scampered up into the refuge of the tree. Honorine stared in amazement.

It was three times the size of the Barbary lion in the parlor, which was already a formidable beast. His golden coat crackled with light nearly as blinding as the sun. Blazing orange embers burst out from the ground with each step he took, and tiny spots of fire dripped from the wild tangles of his mane.

"Leo Major," Francis said, his eyes wide in awe as his hand closed on the handle of his copper pistol.

"Francis!" Honorine shouted, feeling somehow offended that he would even consider shooting the gigantic, fiery lion, even though it also seemed like the reasonable thing to do in this very peculiar situation.

"Yeah, stow it for now, lad," Bloom agreed as he stumbled and wobbled up the tree. "That doesn't even knock the wind out of this one."

"We need something heavier," Salton said, indicating the cannons on the airship above. "But it's too close to fire now. They'll just hit this tree and knock us all right down into the beast's gullet."

"Just climb!" Honorine shouted as the rope ladder dangled within reach of Francis. "He's going to jump!" Even if she had never seen a gigantic lion made of fire before, she had seen ordinary cats, and she knew what it meant when Leo crouched down, the brush end of his long tail whipping through the air, his orange hellfire eyes locked on the branch above.

"You first," Francis said as he grabbed the lowest rungs and held the ladder as steadily as he could manage for Honorine.

Cannon smoke surrounded them, blinding Honorine, who coughed and gasped as her hands closed around the ladder rungs.

"Wait a bloody minute, you trigger-happy rat bag!" Bloom cursed, his hands flailing as he regained his balance on the branch.

"I'm trying to give you a bit of cover, you coopered old bludger!" shouted the lady at the top of the ladder.

"You'll blow the lot of us to hell!" Bloom replied.

"Climb a bit faster, would you, love?" Salton asked as Honorine pulled herself to the next rung, creeping up through the thick, sulfurous fog. The underside of the huge airship hung overhead, dripping more tendrils of the thick yellow-green smoke. Lights flashed and popped around them like fireworks, and the ladder lurched as the cannons were fired once more. Bloom shouted another garbled curse from below.

Then the airship began to rise, lifting Honorine suddenly out of the smoke, over the cloud of fog and the crowns of the oak trees. She looked down briefly, to confirm that Francis had not been left behind. He was on the ladder right behind her, and behind him, a few rungs farther, were Bloom and Salton, somehow climbing with pistols in their hands. Below them was such a dizzying sight as the trees fell away that Honorine thought she would be ill.

"Don't look down!" Francis warned. "Just keep climbing!"

The crew began hauling the ladder in from above. Just as she reached the railing, a callused hand grabbed Honorine by the straps of her overalls and dragged her aboard, where she landed in a pile on the rough wooden deck.

"Whoops," said a gruff voice, and she was pulled back up to her feet by the blue-coated woman with the ladder. "Hang on. The ride gets bumpy."

She moved Honorine toward an inner railing made of heavy rope strung between stout pine timbers that divided a small walkway along the outer railing of the ship from a slightly lower level in the center. Honorine grabbed the rope banister to steady herself as the ship bobbed and swayed on the wind. When she had caught her breath and managed to look around her, she instantly knew why Francis had run away from school.

The ship was a marvel of mechanics and sailing technology. Honorine looked up at the blue silk balloon, down silk lines strung with pennants infused with tiny yellow crystals, to the railing of the deck. Nearly every inch of the perimeter of the ship seemed to be packed with some kind of scientific instrument or mechanical contraption crafted from polished wood and brass and copper with touches of green patina. She was so busy taking in the sight of the ship that she didn't hear Francis, Salton, or Bloom rolling over the railing and flopping onto the deck behind her, where they lay for a moment like beached porpoises.

Francis was the first to recover, scrambling up to the railing beside her, then taking a moment to catch his breath after the long climb through the cold air and choking fog. "This is the *Nighthawk*," he finally said. "We use this when we have to travel inland, away from our main ship, or for communication when we're on a hunt."

"Uh-huh," Honorine muttered, enraptured with the airship. Her washing machine motors and clockwork elephants and battery-powered lanterns seemed a bit less fantastic now.

"And now who's this, then?" asked Bloom gruffly, before wiping a residue of green smoke from his nose with a ragged handkerchief.

"This is Honorine," said Francis, stepping in. "She's one of the most brilliant inventors and machinists you will ever meet, gentlemen."

Honorine smiled sheepishly at this introduction as she stood on the deck in her muddy bare feet and oily overalls.

"Is she now?" asked Bloom.

"Welcome aboard, then," said Salton in between rattling coughs. "Need all the help we can get."

Bloom dusted his hand on the soot-stained lapel of his coat and then thrust it out toward Honorine.

"Winston Rutherford Cornelius Bloom," he said. "Pleasure to make your acquaintance."

Since she was on their ship, it was no use being impolite, she reasoned. So Honorine took his offered hand and shook it firmly. Bloom looked surprised and snapped his hand away.

"Gave me a little shock, this one!" he said, then smiled with amusement as he shook his fingertips a bit.

Salton took her hand gingerly, as if he were being careful not to crush it in his massive mitt of a hand. "They just call me Salton," he said with a nod. "You can, too."

"It's nice to meet you both," Honorine said with a curtsy.

"Am I late? Have I missed the introductions?" asked an unfamiliar voice. Honorine turned around to see a gentleman walking purposefully toward them, his boots tapping boldly across the deck.

He wasn't a very large man. In fact, he was quite slim and short of stature, but there was an immense presence about him. He wore all black clothing, with silver-and-pearl buttons on his waistcoat. He had a short, neatly clipped beard, and very dark brown hair that fell in waves at his shoulders. He held one hand casually at his side, resting on the handle of a stout copper pistol in a tooled black leather holster. His fingers on both hands were covered in silver rings, much like the ones in his ears, and with one look at him,

Honorine knew exactly who he was. Francis introduced them anyway.

"Captain," he said to the man dressed in black. "This is my very dear friend, Honorine. Honorine, this is Captain Nautilus Olyphant."

Among the Sailors and the Stars

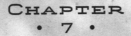

Nautilus Olyphant did not look particularly dangerous to Honorine upon first introduction. He seemed dignified and refined, and possibly a bit of a snob. But something about him reminded her of all the delicate yet deadly creatures displayed in the east parlor—the fragile butterflies and beautiful, spiny fish and charming little frogs that looked so harmless and alluring, but were in fact brimming with lethal poison.

"Welcome aboard…Honorine," he said. He did

not offer his hand the way Salton or Bloom or even the Mapmaker had done.

"Thank you," Honorine said without a bow or curtsy.

"So, you are a friend of Francis's?" Nautilus asked.

"I've known him my whole life," she replied. "That I can remember, anyway."

"Really," Nautilus said without making it either a question or a statement. "You must belong to the Vidalia house, then?"

"I am—or was—a maid for Lady Vidalia," Honorine replied.

"Really," Nautilus said again with a slight tilt of his head. "And before that?"

Honorine shrugged. "I don't recall anything before that. I was quite little when I started working with Agnes. She's the head parlor maid."

"Fascinating," Nautilus said drily. "Well, this is a scientific ship—"

A cannon fired, and Nautilus paused long enough for the echo of the blast to fade.

"So, Francis will be able to keep you from getting into trouble," he continued. "Just stay near him, and you shouldn't cause any problems."

Honorine frowned. This was a bit insulting, but

Nautilus was the captain of the ship, and they were flying five hundred feet or higher over the trees. She wasn't in a position to argue.

"Well," she said instead, "this airship certainly is magnificent."

"Thank Francis," Nautilus replied. "He helped build it."

Francis ducked his head humbly and nodded. "I did a little," he said.

"If by 'a little' you mean that you were instrumental in every aspect of design, fabrication, and experimental construction," Nautilus said. "Now, a report is in order. Who did you encounter on the ground?"

"Leo," Francis replied. "Major, I mean. And Lupus. I saw them firsthand."

Nautilus raised his eyebrows.

"At what range?" he asked.

"Oh... ten feet," Francis replied.

"That sounds like a confirmed identification, then," Nautilus said, looking impressed. "So, the lion and the wolf. What about Virgo?"

Francis shook his head.

"We found feathers," Salton offered.

Nautilus replied with a single raised eyebrow.

"I didn't spot her," Francis continued. "Though I still believe she's among the Mordant rebels, Captain."

"She?" Honorine asked. "Who are you talking about? What's a Virgo?"

"A girl," Nautilus explained. "About your size, but with black wings."

He was talking about Astraea. *Virgo must be the name of her constellation*, Honorine realized.

"You saw her, didn't you?" Nautilus asked. Suddenly, his full attention was focused on Honorine.

A little wriggling instinct deep in her gut told Honorine to be cautious, not to reveal too much information too quickly.

"Come, now, it's hard to forget something like that," Nautilus continued. "You don't remember a girl with black feathered wings, flying about your mistress's garden?"

She had to distract him with something more interesting than Astraea.

"No, just your men here," Honorine said, pointing over her shoulder at Salton and Bloom. "They were in the east parlor earlier today, looking for this."

She pulled the journal from her pocket and held it out to Nautilus.

He took it slowly, almost suspiciously, and stood for quite a while looking at page after page.

"Well," he said eventually, "I'm glad someone could complete the task. Even if it wasn't my carefully trained and well-armed crew."

He looked pointedly at Salton and Bloom. Then he turned to address the crew scattered over the rest of the ship.

"Good news, loyal crew!" he shouted, his voice booming out across the deck of the *Nighthawk*. It was a surprising amount of volume to come out of his modestly sized body. "We have confirmation of both Leo and Lupus on the ground this very evening! To your stations! Time to get hunting!"

A cheer went up as deckhands went immediately to work on various bits of equipment across the ship. Salton and Bloom disappeared into the bustle of the ship as well.

"Francis, Honorine," Nautilus said, "follow me."

He marched toward the forward deck, weaving among machinery and supplies and ropes with ease, even as the ship tilted and pitched on the wind. Near the front of the ship, on a little platform covered with an overgrown garden of telescopes and spyglasses and lenses of every color on poles of brass and copper, they met with a woman very much familiar to Honorine.

"Professor du Ciel," Nautilus said as the lady turned toward them, one half of her face covered with a rippling blue glass lens that made her eye look enormous and sideways. "Do we have a general heading on the *Carina*?"

Professor du Ciel lifted the blue lens.

"Southwest, outside town limits," she replied. "No movement since our crew landed, as far as we can tell."

"Very good," Nautilus said with a crisp nod. "You keep me informed of any changes."

There was no bother with introductions, and Honorine shuffled along behind Nautilus as he made his way to the next station, on the far side of the deck. This one featured a strange kind of desk, arranged in a wide arc. The top was covered in rows of what looked like fluted phonograph horns, manned by a scrawny fellow with spectacles and rumpled hair, wearing copper cuffs over his ears and moving vulcanized rubber-coated wires between countless tiny switches on the desktop.

"Jacques," Nautilus said, causing the scrawny fellow to twitch and pull off one of the copper ear cuffs. "Status?"

"Solid contact with the *Gaslight*," Jacques replied.

"Good," Nautilus said. "Are they ready to hunt?"

Jacques picked up a disk of silver metal with a patch of thick wire mesh in the center, and spoke into it. "Requesting status on the Sidus Apparatus."

After a short pause, he set down the disk and looked up at Nautilus.

"Full power, ready to go ahead," said Jacques. "Do we have a target?"

Nautilus looked out over the railing at the rolling sea of treetops lit yellow in the fading moonlight.

"We're going after the lion."

Jacques paused for a moment, his eyes widening.

"The lion," he repeated in a solemn tone. "Aye, Captain." Then he began relaying orders and moving wires and adjusting levers.

Nautilus turned back to Francis and Honorine. "This next part is going to get a bit rough. Francis, we need you at your post. And Honorine"—he looked down at her, brow raised and head tipped—"we need you out of the way."

And then he was off, calling out orders to another section of the ship.

"He's right," Francis said.

"Well, he was a bit rude about it," Honorine replied as she watched Nautilus vanish into the bustling, crowded deck. "I know how to stay out of the way, and I could probably be a bit of help around here."

"Yes, but he doesn't know that yet," Francis said. "Plus, he's the captain, and he has no manners when we're in the middle of a hunt. Which he's right about, you know—this is going to be pretty bumpy."

Just as he finished his sentence, the flames overhead blazed hotter, and the *Nighthawk* bobbed up higher into the night sky. Honorine was the only one on deck who wobbled a bit as the ship moved beneath her.

"We can watch from over here," Francis said as he led her down a short flight of steps onto the main deck of the airship. It wasn't a terribly large area to begin with, and space was tight. Most of the deck was covered with large machinery, larger guns, and thousands of ropes, many strung with hundreds of electric lightbulbs like drops of dew on a spider's web. Where there weren't machines and cannons in the way, there were crew members tending to them, both men and women, all in blue coats, and all working with single-minded determination. Some of them worked the machinery that kept the *Nighthawk* aloft and sailing; others were involved with charting measurements or tending to much more delicate machines that seemed to have no use for the art of sailing. Arms swung and boots stomped, and Honorine ducked twice to avoid being hit by large things on swinging booms.

"This ship is incredible," Honorine said as she watched ropes slide through pulleys and great brass dials churn like the gears of a clock. For a moment, she forgot to be overwhelmed by the sudden strangeness of her situation and was absorbed in wonder at the fantastical machine and the realization that she was, in fact, flying through the air under a great balloon.

"Don't get lost, now," Francis said as he made his way toward a raised platform surrounded by a wooden railing on the inner side. On the outer side, facing the open air, the railing had been fitted with a large panel made of a sheet of copper between two panes of thick glass. On closer inspection, Honorine saw that the copper was worked into little interlocked hexagons, like a honeycomb. In many of the chambers sat mechanical bees.

"This is my own little project," Francis said. "Nautilus didn't think much of it at first, but it's been very useful lately."

"*You* made these bees?" Honorine asked. "I've seen them before."

She drew the mechanical bee from her pocket and held it out on her palm. The little brass shell lay curled and still, with the legs drawn in protectively and the wings folded neatly behind it. "It's one of these, isn't it?" She pointed at the glass honeycomb.

"It is," Francis said. "Where did you get it?"

"I found it on my windowsill," Honorine said. "And it wasn't the only one. There was one in the east parlor a few weeks ago."

Francis looked completely stunned.

"*You* found it?"

"Yes," Honorine said with a grin. "It's incredible! It flies, Francis! I've never seen anything like it. You're a genius!"

"And you're a Mordant," Francis said.

The lower half of Honorine's face remained stuck in a bright, excited smile. The upper half went a bit scrunched with surprise.

"I'm what now?"

Francis shook his head and then put a hand to his mouth.

"You have to be!" he said. "But that's just impossible! But there's no other way!"

He was stammering a bit, holding his hands to his head and staring at Honorine as if she were a ghost.

"Francis, what are you talking about?"

"I made those bees to track the Mordant," Francis said. "That's all they do. We came here tonight because the bees came back with information—there was a Mordant here."

"But there is!" Honorine said. "You just saw Lux! Er, the wolf. I've seen others, too."

"Tonight you have. But you said you saw another bee weeks ago."

"Yes," Honorine said. "But I lost it. And then it turned up again outside my window."

Francis picked up the bee from her hand.

"That was a different bee," he said. "It came back with information that it had located a Mordant, one the bee couldn't recognize. A Mordant without a constellation. I was sure I knew who it was. You see, there's only one Mordant without a known constellation. He calls himself the Mapmaker."

"Oh!" Honorine said brightly, thinking she was about to say something quite helpful. "He *is* here."

Francis looked as if he might fall right out of his boots.

"How do you know that?" he asked, his eyes wide and wild.

"I saw him," Honorine replied, gesturing over her

shoulder in the general direction of the house. "Just before you found me with Lux. I spoke to him in that old greenhouse they use for making fertilizers."

"You saw him, face-to-face?" Francis asked, shocked, and then even more shocked still. "And you survived?"

"Well, clearly," Honorine said. "I'm not dead, am I?"

"The Mapmaker doesn't allow anyone to see him," Francis said. "He kills any humans who get a look at him. And you *talked* to him?"

"Well…yes," Honorine said. "So he doesn't kill everyone. He let Sam go, too. But maybe only because Astraea made him. Or because Sam didn't know who he was…."

"Why didn't you tell me?" he asked. "I've known you my whole life—I thought we were friends."

"We are," Honorine said. "You're my dearest friend. Francis, I'm not a Mordant."

"But the bee found you." He turned it over in his hands, making painstakingly light adjustments to minuscule controls in the mechanical insect. "The Mapmaker talked to you and let you live. That's why he came here. Not to find some old journal of my father's. You're…one of his kind."

Honorine began to shake her head, but Francis held the bee out to her.

"Take it," he said when she hesitated. Honorine held out her hand, and Francis set the little copper bee back in the middle of her palm. The yellow stone eyes immediately shone with light.

"You see?" Francis whispered. Then he took her other hand and pressed it to the glass covering the copper honeycomb. The bees inside immediately began to move, vibrating in their individual compartments, starting with the ones closest to her hand. The eyes of every single one began to shine.

Honorine pulled her hand away and furrowed her brow.

"The eyes," she said, pointing at the glowing bee in her hand. "Are they made of the same stuff as your mother's omen stones?"

"Yes," Francis said, with a nod. "But—"

"You're wrong, then," Honorine said, with a swift shake of her head. "Those stones don't glow around me. I've never seen them glow before tonight."

"You didn't let me finish," Francis said, returning the bee to the hive. "Yes, this is the same kind of stone. Part of one I...borrowed...from Mother, even. I've been working with it, refining the properties, to make it more reactive. Whatever it is the stone detects in you may be faint, but it's there."

Honorine stepped back from the hive, and the bees grew quiet, though their eyes continued to glow. Then she leaned closer again. The bees, in unison, began to buzz until they shook the glass panes around the hive itself.

"Why don't you sit up here with me," Francis said, "before someone else sees this." He climbed up onto the railing of the platform and gestured for her to come sit beside him. "Just...stay here, out of the way, and enjoy the view for a moment. I have to think."

Honorine needed a moment as well. What Francis was saying couldn't be true. And yet, the Mapmaker had said that Nautilus would be looking for her once he figured out who she was. And Nautilus *was* hunting the Mordant....

With all the events of the night so far, this was just a bit too much. While Francis stared at his bees, Honorine took a moment to clear her mind, looking up from the blinding light and overwhelming clutter of the ship out over the dark, calm landscape.

From this height, the whole country below looked like a great map. The dizziness and the ill stomach

Honorine had felt on the ladder had vanished. She felt strangely comfortable at this precarious height and exhilarated by the view. She had never seen so much of the world all at one time, roads and forests and towns rolling out ahead of them, topped with endless black sky to the west.

In the distance lay a stony ridge where the ground suddenly fell away into a steep seaside cliff. Beyond that, there was nothing but rolling ocean all the way to the end of the world.

"The sea," Honorine whispered. Her heart trembled in her chest. She hadn't expected to be so drawn to the sight of the ocean, but there it was, as big and dark and endless as the sky.

Farther out on the calm water sat a massive, idling steamship, rising from the water like a sheer black cliff. The railings were lined with lights in glass globes, and from the center of the deck rose a huge, glittering crystal dome, lit from within by sparkling golden light.

"That's the *Gaslight*," Francis said. "Our main ship."

He looked perplexed, and anxious and just a bit angry, staring down at the floor with an expression of deep thought.

"Francis, what's wrong?" Honorine asked. She stood up and leaned against the railing. "I'm telling you the truth. I'm not a... I'm not one of them."

"But what if you are?" Francis asked, looking around suspiciously at the rest of the crew. "And I brought you here!"

Honorine's heart tensed in her chest.

"Why shouldn't I be here?" she whispered. "What are they doing on that ship?"

Francis's eyes looked pleading, apologetic, and even a bit scared. He was still fumbling about for a reply when something moved over his shoulder, out in the sky past the rear of the ship. Something even more impossible than all the impossible things she had already seen that night.

"Francis?"

"Yes?"

"Is that... a... What is happening...?" She couldn't even get out all the words she had intended to say. All she could do was point toward a particular spot off to the northeast, where the forest they had just passed over a moment ago was now, unmistakably, rising up from the ground and floating into the sky.

CHAPTER
· 8 ·

The Lion Hunt

Maybe step back now," Francis replied, reaching out toward her. But she gripped the railing tightly, unable to look away as the patch of woodland—trees, roots, and all—continued to rise above the rest of the forest until it was completely silhouetted by the faint violet light of dawn just starting to break on the distant horizon.

"*Carina!*" shouted Salton from across the ship, and the *Nighthawk* lurched once more, sending Honorine crashing to the deck.

"What...is a *Carina*?" Honorine asked, wide-eyed, as Francis reached out to help her up once more.

"The *Carina*," Francis replied. "The Mordant ship."

The mood on the *Nighthawk* changed at once from excitement to high alert. Crew members rushed about, turning levers, adjusting dials, spooling and unspooling lengths of rope. They were moving swiftly forward, past the forests and farms, over the last proper town before there was nothing but black water on the horizon. But the *Nighthawk* started sinking. Behind them, the patch of forest in the sky was moving unmistakably in their direction. As a shadow passed over them, Francis and Honorine looked up at the same time to see the gas flames begin to dim and sputter.

"We're losing heat," Francis said, and the *Nighthawk* dropped lower still.

"Bloom!" Nautilus called from somewhere near the front of the ship. "Why are we losing altitude?"

"Fuel lines are good, Captain!" Bloom called back. "Might be close to your lion."

"What's happening?" Honorine asked as the ship dropped again. She and Francis both hung on to the railing to keep from being tossed about by the careening airship.

"Well," Francis said as he hugged the banister, "Leo Major can have a curious effect on fire. If he's nearby, he's probably trying to bring us down."

"The lion is putting out the fire?" Honorine asked as the flames above dissolved into a faint flicker.

"LION!" came a sudden bellow from across the ship, just as a roar like thunder rumbled below them, rattling pennants on the *Nighthawk* and shaking Honorine's bones.

A blaze of golden light shot into the fading night as the form of the gigantic lion rose up at the edge of the cliff, directly between the *Nighthawk* and the *Gaslight* out at sea.

"We're going to fly right into him!" Honorine said.

"No," Francis said, shaking his head, his mouth breaking into an eager grin. "Keep looking! You don't want to miss this!" He leaned out to get a better view, letting go of the railing in his excitement.

"Leo Major, sighted!" Jacques shouted from his station of Victrolas. "*Gaslight* confirms Sidus Apparatus coordinates!"

"We've got him now!" Francis shouted.

The lion moved along the cliff, its golden light spilling out over the black ocean like a sunrise. A cold sense of panic slipped down Honorine's spine, tightening every muscle in her little body.

"Wait, what are you going to—" she began to ask, but her voice evaporated into the wind as a sudden bright light burst forth from the *Gaslight* ahead. Between the burning glow of the lion and the sharp rays of electric light flashing through the ship's greenhouse dome, Honorine could hardly focus her eyes to watch. The light from the *Gaslight* grew brighter, and suddenly the lion began to flicker, his tail, then his paws, then his mane dissolving into bursts of golden sparks that swirled frantically on the wind, as if trying to stay together.

"Hold steady!" Nautilus ordered as the *Nighthawk*'s flames continued to sputter and the lion's shape did likewise, evaporating into a cascade of sparks that were quickly snuffed out by the draft of the *Nighthawk* as it raced through the space that had been full of fiery lion only a moment before.

"Sweet merciful heavens," Honorine sputtered through her shock and surprise. "What on earth was that? Where did he go?"

"To the *Gaslight*!" Francis replied excitedly. With the lion subdued, the flames of the *Nighthawk* roared back to full power, and the ship began to rise at once, nearly tipping Honorine over the side.

"Hang on," Francis said. "All we have to do now is get back to the ship before they can catch up with us."

Honorine turned back to the impossibly levitating forest ship, which was now looming larger and closer to the increasingly small-feeling *Nighthawk*. As they sailed over the edge of the cliff and out toward the open sea, struggling to move faster and gain back some altitude, Honorine caught a glimpse of the crow sweeping overhead, a bare blue outline against the sky.

"Corvus," Honorine said, tugging at Francis's sleeve. "Crow, right ahead of us!"

"Salton!" Nautilus called out from the front of the *Nighthawk*. "Ready the guns!"

"Why guns?" Honorine asked. "Can't they do whatever they did to the lion?"

"It's too soon!" Francis shouted. "The *Gaslight* can't adjust for the crow that quickly!"

"He's right above us!" Salton announced, reaching for a rifle mounted on the railing.

They could hear feathers and claws brushing against the balloon silk.

"Steady, men! Stay on course!" Nautilus called out.

The airship was very close to the water, which at first was a relief to Honorine, for it seemed safer to crash into the sea than onto the dry, hard ground. Then the dark water began to bubble and churn as something huge and glowing faintly red slithered up from the depths.

"Francis!" Honorine said, hanging dangerously far over the rail. "There's something down there as well!"

"Nautilus!" Francis shouted. "I think we also have a sea serpent!"

Nautilus rushed across the deck to confirm Francis's sighting.

"Bloom! More altitude!" he barked.

"Aye, Captain!" Bloom replied.

"I don't have a clear shot, sir," Salton warned, his hand on the trigger of the rifle.

"Take any shot you get!" Nautilus directed. "Bloom! *Higher!*"

Salton called out an order, and a row of cannons exploded at once, sending a barrage of yellow stone cannonballs toward the sea serpent. They created a tremendous blast of smoke and steam as they hit the water, sending spray in all directions and creating a strange flash of red light under the rippling waves.

The rising smoke created a brief screen from the approaching *Carina*. Bloom called out a second order, and the crew braced themselves as all power was momentarily diverted to gaining altitude.

Flame exploded into the balloon chamber, and the airship bounced higher into the sky like a cork shooting up through water.

"Ready a second volley, Salton! Now for speed, Bloom!" Nautilus ordered, gripping the wheel of the airship. Bloom gave a signal to the crew members working at the set of turbines that provided acceleration for the airship. The *Nighthawk* raced forward, rising up and out over the black water below.

"Five hundred yards, Captain," called Professor du Ciel from the bow as the *Nighthawk* raced onward and upward toward the *Gaslight*, waiting in the dark sea. A shot of light streaked by overhead, spitting out arcs of fire that flew like arrows and then dropped like rain. More cannons blasted stone and smoke into the air and the water around them. The *Nighthawk* rose just high enough to clear the upper railing of the *Gaslight* for a landing on the main deck.

Honorine anticipated the touchdown. Her eyes darted from the cannons along the lower decks, much larger and more powerful that the ones on the airship, to the crystal dome, to the stairs twining up to spindly lookout platforms tangled overhead. She wanted to explore it all, every inch of this marvelous ship and how it was built. She nearly had one leg over the rail, ready to climb out, when she was startled by a hand closing on the back of her overalls and hauling her back onto the airship.

"Just what do you think you are doing?" Nautilus asked.

"I was just—"

"About to fall overboard," Nautilus said. "You have to be more care—"

There would have been more lecturing, which Honorine was used to, but instead, Nautilus gave a strangled shout as he looked at something over her shoulder.

She turned back around, expecting to see the sprawling deck of the *Gaslight*, but instead she saw only glittering black feathers, a coal-black eye, and curved black talons.

"Get down!" Nautilus commanded. He drew a short copper pistol from his belt and leveled it at the crow.

Honorine ducked and hid her head under her arms as the crow reached out, brushing her side with his talons. Nautilus fired his pistol, but the crow was agile for so large a creature. The shot sailed off into the dark like a shooting star and fell harmlessly into the ocean below.

"Salton! The guns!" Nautilus cried.

"We're too close for cannons, Captain!"

"I'm telling you to fire, gunner, so you obey my order and *fire!*"

With a quick nod and a muttered "Aye," Salton obliged. He aimed the cannon and fired a single, perfect shot.

The crow was caught in midflight, straight through the heart, and burst into sparks along with the cannonball, which exploded into a million shards that flew in every direction. A great deal shot straight through the blue silk chamber of the *Nighthawk*'s balloon, creating tiny, raw punctures on one side and blowing an explosion of flaming gas out the far side. A blast of green fire and glittering sparks blinded the crew below and choked them with a cloud of rancorous smoke.

The once magnificent airship quickly lost all buoyancy and plummeted like a comet toward the water below, leaving a trail of fire and blasting embers.

"Honorine!" Francis shouted, diving toward her.

"Francis!" Honorine shouted back. She felt his hand close around hers and tried to hold on, but she'd caught only the tips of his fingers before something else exploded, ripping the deck free from the remains of the balloon and tossing crew members, equipment, and bits of the ship in every direction.

"Honorine!"

She heard him call one last time as she fell. Looking up at the sky, at the last twisting knot of fire that had been the balloon, the tiny bright stars in the distance, and the great black cliff of the *Gaslight*, she filled her lungs with a tremendous breath, intending to shout out for Francis, but instead she plunged into the cold black water.

The Forest in the Sky

The last thing she saw before the dark water covered her completely was a flash of silver light, and then she was submerged, fighting against the cold, choppy water, struggling to keep her head above the surface. Despite her desperate efforts and much flailing about, one little maid—who had never been in deeper water than a bathtub—was swallowed by the sea like a tiny stone.

She closed her eyes tight against the sting of the salt water and held her breath as the cold entombed her. As she continued struggling and sinking, something brushed her hand. Her eyes opened in surprise, but before she could feel relief, she saw what was lurking under the water.

Beneath the paddling arms and kicking feet of the crew at the surface lurked the sea serpent, a huge snake gliding through the water, glowing with dim red light under its rough black scales. Its sides were lined with long, curving spines like strange fins.

It curled under the wreckage, slipping between the sinking bits of ship and around the thrashing feet, all the while keeping its big, glowing green eyes locked on Honorine.

She couldn't swim away. Even if she knew how, she could never move as swiftly as the serpent through the briny deep. She braced herself for a strike, but instead the serpent lowered his head and slipped beneath her, catching her gently against the long spines rising from the top of its head. It then began to swim from the wreckage site, carrying Honorine far away from the sinking airship before lifting her toward the surface, where she broke through the water, riding on top of the sea serpent's scaly black head.

Back on the proper side of the water, she coughed and spat until she could breathe again and tried to wipe the wet hair from her face, but just as she reached up, the cold talons of the crow closed gently around her arms and lifted her into the air. Through the salt stinging her eyes and the hair flying in her face, Honorine saw a glimpse of the *Gaslight* and, beside it, a sudden explosion of red sparks at the surface of the water, followed by a trail of red flashing light that snaked down into the dark sea.

Was that the sea serpent? she pondered as the crow sailed over a patch of floating fire that must have been the remains of the *Nighthawk*. Then, in a few beats of its wings, they were flying through trees into a thick forest, and the crow set her down amid a tangle of roots on a carpet of moss speckled with patches of white sand and curious red-capped toadstools.

Honorine sat up, shivering in her wet clothes, her left arm beginning to feel not at all right. She thought she must have been brought all the way back to shore, until the ground dipped beneath her, and cold, salty seawater sprayed across her face.

It was the patch of forest she had seen rising up into the sky. But now that she was seeing it from the other side, it wasn't entirely a forest at all. It was a ship...made out of forest. A few scattered planks of true deck wood peeked out between the roots of tall, slender pine trees and knotty, curling junipers. Their branches were lined with thousands of tiny lanterns giving off gold and silver light that trickled through the thick leaves and speckled the root-covered deck like snow. Instead of sails, the tallest trees held out oversized leaves that caught the wind, and instead of railings, the perimeter of the main deck was surrounded by tangles of grapevine and blackberry brambles, all heavy with hanging fruit.

"Are you all right?"

Honorine looked up to see Lux standing over her, his coat ablaze with cold illumination, his eyes glowing intensely yellow. In the glittering forest, he looked much less like a mangy old wolf and much more like a constellation come to life.

"Were you hurt in the fall?"

She felt dizzy and confused, still coughing salt and seawater. She shook her head no and tried to reach up to Lux, but when she lifted her left arm, a pain overtook her like she had never felt in all her life. She cried out, even before looking down to see the sleeve of her shirt gone and the skin of her shoulder blistered and torn.

"You've been burned," Lux said as he leaned down to examine her. "Try to be still."

The numbness from the cold of the ocean was wearing off, and Honorine began to feel the useless pain of a burn that lingers and swells long after the source of the heat has been removed. She twisted away as if something hot were still pressing against her skin.

"Honorine, be still," said a second voice. Astraea landed beside her, black wings cutting through the lantern light, creating a tiny breeze that was like knives on Honorine's raw flesh. "Sirona will help you."

A woman appeared between Lux and Astraea. She was pale, with short dark hair that bounced up in loose curls around a fine circlet of silver set with gemstones. They appeared to Honorine as tiny, hovering lights. Sirona was dressed in leggings and a sleeveless tunic tied with a wide silver sash. Her arms, from her shoulders to her fingertips, were covered with tattoos of snakes, coiling and slithering over her skin.

"Honorine?" said Sirona as she knelt down on the sandy deck. "It's lovely to finally meet you. I understand you've had quite an eventful journey to be with us tonight."

Honorine nodded and then felt her head go wobbly with pain as Sirona lifted the ragged edge of her shirt from the damp open wound on her shoulder. She turned her head and squeezed her eyes shut, as if that would provide some escape from the pain.

"Oh yes, this won't do," said Sirona. "Lux, take her other hand."

Honorine felt the brush of bristly wolf fur under the hand of her uninjured arm. She opened her eyes briefly to see Lux lying at her side, her arm draped over him.

She heard the others talking and the tearing of fabric, and at the point where she felt she couldn't take it any longer, there was a cool, immediate relief, starting between her shoulder blades and then spreading, as if someone were draping a cold cloth up and onto the back of her neck, over her shoulder, and down her injured arm all the way to her elbow. She slumped forward, feeling at once utterly relieved and overwhelmingly tired.

"There, that's all," Sirona said. "Your wound will heal, and there will be no more pain. Though you do need to rest."

Honorine nodded, her eyes opening only enough to see hazy lights all around her. Sirona said something further as she pressed a hand gently to Honorine's forehead. Then she felt she was being lifted up, but she couldn't be certain if that happened before or after she had fallen into a deep, silent slumber.

* * *

She awoke lying on her back, swaying gently from side to side, and looking up into a bough of reddish pine branches swarming with spiders. After a short screech of alarm and a brief struggle with an unexpected blanket, Honorine tumbled to the ground, landing with a thump directly on top of Lux, who had been lying quietly beside her as she slept.

"Feeling better?" Lux said, ears pinned back, as he stood up and shook out his glistening white fur.

"Spiders!" Honorine shouted in reply.

Lux raised his wolfy brow and tipped his head to the side. "Yes, of course," he said. "The ones that spun your hammock."

She looked over at a swinging, tangled net of silvery silk containing a few fat pillows and a thick blanket, all bundled and hanging from the trees like a strange mess of fishing tackle.

"Oh," Honorine said, managing to catch her breath, though her heart still hammered in her chest.

"Did you sleep well?" Lux asked.

Honorine looked around, taking in the trees and the lanterns and the dark sky above them. She started to remember all the events that had happened, and the order in which they had unfolded, that led to her sitting on a pile of white sand, under a fleet of spiders, surrounded by pine trees and toadstools.

"How long did I sleep?" she asked.

Lux scrunched his nose. "Time is a very hard thing to keep track of up here," he said. "Do you feel rested?"

"I think so," Honorine said.

"Then you slept the usual amount, I suppose. And your arm?"

Honorine sat up sharply, remembering the burn, particularly the pain. When she looked down, she saw she was wrapped in a thin, shimmery gauze like a mummy, completely covered from her ribs all the way up to her neck and back down her left arm to the elbow. She stretched her shoulder, waved her arm, wiggled her fingertips.

"It doesn't hurt at all!" she said. "Though my head feels a bit...fuzzy."

"Well, that happens, I'm told, when Sirona works an especially intensive amount of healing on a person," Lux said with a look of amusement. "And also, you fell out of an exploding dirigible from an impressive height."

Honorine nodded as she turned her arm about and ran her other hand over the soft bandages around her neck. She realized that something was missing when she reached up to the back of her head.

"Oh yes, the hair," Lux said. "A fair bit of it seems to have been... well, burned right off, I'm afraid."

Honorine patted her head. Her hair was now no longer than her chin in the front, and chopped roughly in the back. There was barely enough left to run her fingers through. Her hand came away a bit sooty.

"Well," she said with a shrug, "I'd rather lose my hair than an arm, I suppose."

She tried to pry the gauze back to take a look at the skin underneath.

"Leave your bandages for now," Lux said. "Sirona will want to check them and see that you've healed properly. In fact, she'll probably want to see you right away."

"But I can't have healed already," she protested, trying to reconcile how long she had slept. The last few moments before she fell asleep were a bit of a jumble, and before she could puzzle out what had happened, she noticed that her overalls and shirt were gone and she was sitting on the ground in only her bandages and bloomers.

"Well, this isn't proper at all," she declared, waving a hand over her unacceptable lack of attire. "Could I get the rest of my clothes back?"

Lux pinned back his ears and shook his head.

"You won't want those any longer," he said. "We'll get you something better to wear."

He growled up at the trees, and then stood back as the spiders descended and began to spin a very dense web, which, curiously, included a tunic, a pair of leggings, and a long sash, all in the palest peridot green and embellished with fine, sparkling silver. In barely a moment, they were finished and retreated back into the branches above.

"Well?" asked Lux, staring expectantly at her. "Don't you like them?"

"They're...lovely," Honorine said. "I was just a bit surprised at how they were...woven."

"Spider silk makes the finest garments in the world," Lux said frankly, as if this were a well-known fact among people who didn't travel on flying forests and leave trails of sparks everywhere they stepped. "Though they are nearly impossible to come by, as only spiders themselves can work with their silk in such an elegant manner. And sadly, nearly every human weaver has forgotten how to work with spiders. So put them on, unless you'd prefer to go about in bandages and your underthings."

"No, of course not," Honorine said, getting unsteadily to her feet to reach the clothes. The fine silk was impossibly light and stronger than any fabric she had felt before. It came down off the line the moment she touched it and felt like liquid between her fingers. She pulled the tunic over her head. The loose silk fell a little above her knees, and the sleeves were the perfect length, a bit baggy at the shoulders and fitted from her elbows to her wrists, as if they had been woven right on her body. She pulled off her old bloomers and then slipped on the leggings, which also fit as if she were putting on another layer of skin. The spider silk was the softest, most comfortable fabric she had ever felt— light, yet so warm that even in the cold air, she felt as snug as if she were wrapped in a thick fur stole.

"Much better, isn't it?" Lux asked.

Honorine smiled as she tied the silk sash around her middle. "Yes. Very much."

A trill of cold wind cut through the pine boughs, rattling the lanterns and creating a soft whistling music through the trees. Honorine looked up to see the branches part, giving her a brief glimpse of dark sky. Her head began to clear, and she was overcome with the notion that something was missing.

"It's night again," she noticed.

"Well, it's always night here," Lux replied.

"But we're on a ship, aren't we?"

"Yes, the *Carina*. The ship of the stars. She has the largest constellation in all the night sky, Argo Navis, though she is now considered three separate constellations by modern astronomers. Vela, Puppis, and, of course, Carina, are all part of the same magnificent ship."

Honorine made her way across the sandy, root-tangled deck. She stepped up to the grapevine railing and leaned out cautiously, expecting to see ocean spooling away underneath the ship. There was nothing below them but stars and thin silvery mist.

The *Carina* wasn't sailing across the ocean, but soaring through the air.

"We are currently sailing just between dawn and dusk on the Sea of Ether, a place only Mordant can travel," Lux replied. "And, thankfully, a place where Nautilus cannot find us."

At the mention of Nautilus, the image of the

Nighthawk ripping apart and plunging toward the sea suddenly flashed through Honorine's memory.

"Francis!" she said with a gasp. "Lux, where is he? Did you bring him here, too?"

"No," Lux said, shaking his head. "He did not come here. Only you, Honorine."

"Well, what happened to him?" Honorine asked, dread falling over her. "Where is he?"

"I'm afraid I don't know."

Honorine thought of Francis still in the water, sinking into the depths, never to be found. The dread began to crush her heart against her chest with a pain more intense than her burned shoulder.

"I have to know where he is," she replied. "I have to know if he's all right."

Lux looked at her with calm golden eyes and nodded.

"Someone here will know," he said. "We need to find the Mapmaker and Sirona anyway and let them know you're awake."

Lux led the way through the pine boughs toward the back of the ship, where a grove of black oaks grew over a gentle slope of rising steps, their ancient roots curling tightly into tiered levels and curving branches forming arches draped in moss. Tiny white moths flitted about the grove like little fairies. The hum of crickets settled in the air like a soft fog, but it wasn't a usual rhythmic insect chirp. There was a faint melody to the sound.

"Ah, the crickets," Lux said. "That means Scorpio is about somewhere."

Honorine waited under a mossy oak arch as Lux trotted around the grove, sniffing at the roots and the air.

"No use hiding," he called into the trees. "You have to come out and meet her eventually."

There was a long pause, and then a rustling of branches as Lux retreated to the middle of the grove, followed by a scorpion so enormous that his great barbed tail hung as high as the treetops, with huge black claws and eight glittering, lidless black eyes over a grotesque mouth of pincers and fangs.

"There you go," said Lux encouragingly. "Nothing to be worried about."

The scorpion turned toward Honorine, which required moving his entire enormous body on eight monstrous legs that gouged the deck with each step.

"Honorine, this is Scorpio," Lux said, nudging his nose toward the towering arachnid, who stopped just in front of her and raised his great claws. Green embers crackled and drifted from the creature's black armored body.

Honorine winced as the embers drifted toward her. She had been hit by popping sprays from the fireplace before and was especially wary after the burn to her arm and shoulder. To her surprise, the green embers brushed over her face like falling snowflakes, nothing more.

Scorpio's claws clicked softly. Something about his quietness made him much less frightening, and though Honorine was not exactly comfortable in his presence, she was not inclined to run screaming into the forest, either.

"He wants to know if you're feeling better after that terrible fall," Lux said.

"Yes, I'm feeling much better," she replied.

"And the clothes," Lux interpreted. "Are they to your liking? It was his spiders that wove them for you."

"Um…yes. They're wonderful. I love them."

The scorpion's upper half raised up in what could only be interpreted as a nod of thanks, or as close as he could get.

"Honorine is eager to know what happened to Francis Vidalia," Lux said to Scorpio.

There was a pause as Scorpio's strange insect mouth moved about in unsettling directions. He didn't seem to make a sound, yet Lux nodded.

"He does not, unfortunately, have any information for you about the boy."

"Oh," Honorine replied. "Well, thank you for asking."

Something rustled the treetops, and Honorine tried not to cringe at the thought of another huge insect appearing in the grove. But it was only Astraea swooping in, windblown and trailing violet sparks.

"You're awake," she said. "Good. Now, brace yourself. The Mapmaker is on his way."

"And he's in a pleasant mood?" Lux added hopefully.

Astraea folded her wings and sent back a withering look just as Corvus came flying through the trees like a comet, trailing blue sparks before landing abruptly in the oak grove. The Mapmaker leaped to the ground before Corvus's wings were folded and advanced directly toward Honorine. He gave Lux some manner of signal to retreat, which the wolf did, but only a few steps.

"Honorine," the Mapmaker said in a tone that made her own name sound like a curse. "What have you done?"

She was too frozen in surprise to come up with a reply. The Mapmaker leaned down until he was so close he could have bitten off the tip of her nose. The rage in his eyes was painful to look at, though she didn't dare turn away.

"I told you what he was doing," the Mapmaker said. "I told you he was hunting us. I asked you to come with us, to help us. You *agreed*. And then"—he took a long, angry breath—"then you ran off with *Nau*tilus *Oly*phant!"

"No! I didn't!" Honorine shouted in defense. "I didn't leave with Nautilus. I left with Francis!"

"Oh, so it's acceptable to break your word and abandon us as long as it's for Francis, is it?"

"I...I'm sorry," Honorine said. She had learned through experience in dealing with the staff of the Vidalia Estate that sometimes taking blame and making amends was the safest course of action. "I didn't mean to leave with Nautilus. I was just happy to see Francis. I just wanted to—"

"What?" the Mapmaker asked. "Wanted to join up

with Nautilus, tell him all about us, help him hunt us down one by one while we run for our lives?"

Honorine shook her head furiously. "No! No, certainly not!" she insisted. "I just wanted to know where Francis had been all this time. And now I just want to make sure he's safe."

"Safe!" The Mapmaker reeled back with a snort of laughter, raising his hands to the heavens in disgust. "The world is full of fire and rats, my dear girl. And wolves and sea serpents and snake charmers and girls with wings who look like angels but most certainly are *not*. Nothing is safe. The closest you will ever get to it is on this ship, and you chose . . . someone else."

The Mapmaker's rage seemed to crest in his glowing blue eyes, like a wave about to crash down over her.

"You betrayed us."

"No, she did not," Astraea said, her wings rising over her shoulders as she took a step forward, forcing a bit more space between Honorine and the Mapmaker. "She acted out of loyalty to Lord Vidalia's son."

"Nautilus's protégé! Hardly any better."

"But nevertheless, someone very important to her," Astraea said. "A boy she would never abandon."

The Mapmaker fumed. He frowned and squinted

and blew out a long breath like an angry bull. But gradually the rage quieted, and he looked highly perturbed instead of murderous. His eyes calmed from a hurricane to a rolling thunderstorm, and he finally nodded at Astraea, who folded her wings and took a seat on a low-hanging oak branch.

"The girl wants to know about her dear friend Francis," the Mapmaker said. "So, what do we know about Nautilus's ship and the status of his crew?"

"The *Nighthawk* is destroyed," Astraea said. "All the equipment and the balloon are gone."

Honorine felt the breath rush from her lungs and her skin prickle with cold, as if she had just fallen back into the crushing black sea.

"But no souls were lost," Astraea continued. "Every member of the crew was recovered. They are all back aboard the *Gaslight*."

The breath rushed back. The cold evaporated, lifting the crushing feeling off Honorine's chest. The Mapmaker, however, didn't seem so pleased.

"Wonderful," he said. "We've lost Leo. And can anyone confirm if Hydra escaped?"

Astraea shook her head. The Mapmaker crossed his arms.

"So, until further notice, we assume he's gone as well. That's two captured in one night, and they have just as many men left to hunt us." He turned back to Honorine. "Do you know how valuable Leo was to us? A lion that can control fire?"

"It was hardly her fault," Astraea said from her perch. Scorpio seemed to click his claws in agreement.

"And Hydra?" pressed the Mapmaker. "How long has he managed to evade Nautilus, only to be captured trying to save her?"

"It's the risk we all take, every time we leave this ship," Lux added.

"A risk we can no longer afford. If Leo had come back to the *Carina* instead of chasing after that airship, and Hydra hadn't come to the surface to save *you*"—the Mapmaker pointed a sharp finger at Honorine—"we wouldn't have lost them."

"All right," Honorine said, standing up as straight as she could and crossing her arms. "They're gone, and it's partly my fault. So I apologize, I suppose, even if I don't know what for, exactly. I'm sorry the lion got captured. Now, how do we get him back?"

Every eye on the ship turned toward Honorine. Lux's eyebrows rose. Astraea tilted her head and almost smiled. Scorpio's body lifted slightly on his jointed legs. And the Mapmaker's eyes turned a burning, intense shade of blue.

"How do we indeed?" he asked.

Astraea held out her wings and dropped from her perch onto the sandy deck. "We lost Leo, yes, but for the moment, we have an advantage," she said, drawing the Mapmaker's attention back to her. "Without his flagship dirigible, Nautilus won't be able to follow us so easily over land."

Lux nodded in agreement. "If Nautilus can't follow easily, we might be able to get the rest of them before he can."

"Exactly," Astraea said. "The first step, I think, is to gather every remaining hidden Mordant."

The Mapmaker rubbed a hand across his chin as he considered.

"I'd like nothing more," he said. "But there are so few of us left—and so scattered. As you just acknowledged, it's a terrible risk every time we leave this ship."

"But we have to try," Astraea said. "This is our last chance."

The Mapmaker turned back to Honorine. "Before we do anything, though, you must answer this question,

Honorine. Where do you *want* to be?" he asked. "On Nautilus's ship? Or here with us on the *Carina*?"

Honorine looked up at the Mapmaker. His eyes burned so brightly they illuminated his face, making him look different, wilder. She was suddenly aware that though he looked like a man and spoke and dressed and moved like a man, the Mapmaker was not human. He was something else. Something powerful. She had seen him hurt Sam with only a touch of his hand. What was he capable of doing if he truly got angry?

But she certainly did not want to leave the *Carina*. She had only seen a tiny sliver of the Mordant world, and it was already the most fascinating experience of her life—even more than sailing on the *Nighthawk*, which was saying something. The constellations had come down from the sky to find her, had told her she belonged among them, and now she was beginning to feel it. Astraea, Lux, and even Scorpio, in his own way, had stood up for her. They were claiming her as one of their own in a way no one had ever done before. And perhaps there might be answers here about her past that only these creatures could give.

"I want to stay here, with you," she said.

The Mapmaker took a breath, then nodded.

"You will have a chance to prove your loyalty to us," he said. "After what I've already seen, I'm not entirely sure I can trust you. So my offer to let you join the crew has been amended. You will have to earn a place aboard this ship."

The sound of footsteps made the Mapmaker turn toward an arch of oak branches, where a man was struggling a bit with his cane and the tangled roots in his path. Not a monster, not a beast, not an ethereal mythological creature. Just a man. He wore very elegant but old clothes that hung loosely off his frail shoulders. His short beard was pure white, and tufts of fine white hair rose like mist around his head.

Honorine took in a sharp breath. Of all the wild and fantastic things she had seen that day, this might have been the most unbelievable.

"Lord Vidalia!"

Chapter
• 10 •

The Lost Mordant

Lord Vidalia gazed down at Honorine with the same bright, sharp eyes that stared out from his portrait over the mantel in the east parlor, though the face around them had weathered over the years. He reached a thin, knobby hand out from the sleeve of his once splendid jacket, and Honorine stepped forward to shake it. She could feel every knuckle and tendon under his brittle skin, but his hand felt like a human hand, of a regular temperature, with no uncomfortable electric twinge in her own bones.

"Pleased to meet you," she whispered, forgetting to bow or curtsy or do anything other than stare. Lord Vidalia had been missing for so very long that he seemed more like a myth than a real person. Now that he was standing in front of her, it was somehow even more surprising than meeting a talking wolf or a ten-foot-tall scorpion.

"And you as well," Lord Vidalia replied with a stiff nod. He smiled quickly, then drew his hand back and leaned heavily on his cane, his expression keen but also melancholic.

"How nice that we're all acquainted," said the Mapmaker. "Honorine, I'm sure you don't remember meeting the long-absented Lord Vidalia, but he has seen you before, haven't you, Bernard?"

"Well, yes," Lord Vidalia conceded. "When she was just a newborn child. I haven't seen her since."

"And yet," the Mapmaker continued, "she was raised by your wife alongside your only son, who currently sails with Nautilus Olyphant."

"Yes, that is true," Lord Vidalia replied, a flash of feistiness in his sagging eyes. "And I have expressed my concern and disapproval over that many times. *And* you will remember our arrangement—I work for you, so long as you do no harm toward my son."

"And I would never have dreamed of breaking that agreement," the Mapmaker continued, "until I learned that you have been keeping this from me for a very long time."

"I did," Lord Vidalia said. "But only with the best of intentions. What have we been doing here all this time? Protecting you. Protecting the Mordant. Trying to keep them out of Nautilus's reach. *All* of them." He nodded unsteadily toward Honorine. "What better way to keep her protected than to keep her hidden, even—for a time—from you?"

The Mapmaker's eyes tumbled from light to dark like waves crashing under flashes of lightning. Lord Vidalia, stooped and feeble as he seemed, stood up as tall as he could manage, for a moment taking his weight off his cane. He looked the Mapmaker square in the eye.

"The girl needed a home and care, so I sent her to Josefina," he continued. "And I sent along my very last journal, so that one day, if I never did see her again, or her parents never did find her, she would know at least a little bit about who she was and where she came from. And that is all. A full confession. There is no reason to punish Honorine or my son for my actions."

"Well, for all your noble efforts, it was only by chance that we found this girl when we did. She almost succeeded in running off with Nautilus."

"I did not!" Honorine insisted, tired of being spoken of as if she weren't there. "I was with my friend *Francis*. I never even heard the name *Nautilus* before last night, when his crew showed up at the Vidalia Manor looking for *you*." She waved her hands toward the Mapmaker, and also Scorpio and Astraea and Lux, who were standing in the oak grove around them. "And then Francis turned up on the same night we get pirates in the house, and he was leaving on the airship, and I've known him my entire life, and Francis has always been my friend. So when he thought—"

She paused, uncertain of how to explain the next part. She wasn't sure she believed what Francis had told her, but she wasn't sure she didn't believe him, either. The Mordant seemed to think she belonged with them. It was all very confusing, which might have been an effect of the healing sleep, or because it was actually rather complicated to puzzle out.

"Francis thought I was one of you," she said finally. "He said he thought I was a...Mordant."

The Mapmaker leaned back. Everyone else stared at Honorine.

"Is it true?" she whispered. "But I can't possibly be...."

Lux, sitting closest to Honorine, tilted his head and opened his mouth to speak. "It's—"

"You're telling the truth," the Mapmaker interrupted. "You really don't know who Nautilus Olyphant is."

"He's a man with a ship," she declared. "That's all I know. Promise."

"Well, I'm inclined to believe you," the Mapmaker said. He stepped closer to Lord Vidalia and clasped his shoulder in one ink-stained hand. "If Honorine is going to help us stop Nautilus, then she is going to need to know everything about Nautilus Olyphant. And don't spare her. We do not want her to underestimate the danger we *all* face."

Lord Vidalia was silent for a moment while the crickets sang their eerie song and the wind rippled through the oak leaves. Then he nodded, slowly looking up from the knotted roots along the ground to the Mapmaker.

"I understand," he said. "I will teach her. As long as Francis is safe."

"Your boy will remain under my protection as long as the girl is loyal to me," said the Mapmaker.

Astraea's wings bristled, but she remained silent for the moment as the Mapmaker turned to Honorine. "She can start by telling us everything she knows about Nautilus. For instance, where he's headed next."

Honorine shook her head. "I don't know. They were going back to that great, gigantic steamship, but after that…" She shrugged. "I promise, if I knew where they were going, I would tell you. I wouldn't do anything to hurt Francis, or any of you."

"I hope that's true," the Mapmaker said. "Because at this moment, there are at most three Mordant left, aside from those presently on this ship, who have not been captured by Nautilus."

"Good lord," muttered Lord Vidalia. "Only three?"

"Yes. He's gotten to the rest of them at a surprising rate. The three who remain are on opposite sides of the ocean, and if we make the wrong move, Nautilus will have them before we can blink. So, Vidalia, take your charge back to your study. Get her started on her task. Maybe get her something to eat. That's probably in order."

He marched across the deck toward Corvus and gestured for Astraea to follow.

"Since we don't know where Nautilus is headed, we have a bit of scouting to attend to. I'll call on you when I return to see what progress we've made."

Astraea took a step toward Honorine.

"Listen to this one," she said, patting Lord Vidalia on the shoulder. "He is wise beyond his years."

Then, they were off. The Mapmaker, Corvus, and Astraea launched into the sky, sailing over the oak branches until they were little more than shooting stars. Scorpio scuttled back into the trees.

Only Lord Vidalia, Lux, and Honorine remained on the quiet deck of the ship.

"Well, we'd best be getting to our work, then," Lord Vidalia said as he turned to navigate the trails of oak roots laced across the deck. "I'm sure you have questions, so let's see if we can find you some answers."

"You go ahead," Lux added, shaking out his shimmering white coat. "I'll be along in a little while to check on you."

Honorine and Lord Vidalia made their way to his study, which comprised a large collection of alcoves formed by walls of tangled roots, down in the belly of the ship. There were a few pieces of proper furniture—chairs, desks, bookshelves, and even an old potbellied stove tucked against a wall. The room smelled of paper and sweet tobacco and sand, and was lit with lanterns hanging from the dangling roots along the ceiling and glowing shelf mushrooms of every color, clinging to the walls. The floor was a bit smoother, carpeted with worn silk rugs and dusted with glistening sand that gathered in piles in the corners.

"This is beautiful," Honorine said, gazing at the odd treasures scattered about the room: a globe dotted with stars rather than continents, a black stone obelisk carved with images of stargazers looking up at a sky full of flying creatures, a tapestry woven with black wool and silver threads, depicting what must have been Lux running across a field of stars, among dozens of others. "So this is where you've been all this time?"

"Well, I've been here..." he began as he lowered himself into an old armchair beside his desk, "ten... eleven... twelve years. It doesn't seem so long. But then it's been your entire life, hasn't it?"

"As far as I know," Honorine said, settling herself onto a fat, puffy ottoman. In her days at the Vidalia

Manor, there had been many hundreds of questions she had wanted to ask him, but now she couldn't think of one. There was nothing she wanted to know about further back than the previous day. "I don't remember anything before living in your house."

"Well, you would have been far too small," Lord Vidalia said with a nostalgic smile.

"You knew I was there all this time?"

"I was the one who sent you there."

Now the many hundreds of questions flooded into Honorine's skull, along with a hundred new ones, but she could only come up with a single word.

"Why?"

Lord Vidalia began to rummage in the drawers of his desk. He pulled out a battle-scarred cheese board and a dull-looking paring knife with a bone handle and a broken point, followed by a flat basket stacked with an array of fruits.

"Well, where shall we start?" Lord Vidalia asked with a deep breath and a long sigh. He cautiously split a fat yellow apple and offered her a slice. "Let's go back a bit further. You've seen my collections, the work I brought back from my travels?"

Honorine nodded and took a bite of the apple. It was tart and juicy and somehow tasted like pale morning sunlight.

"When I was younger, I studied ancient civilizations. Egypt, Mesopotamia, the Incan Empire, and many other grand, old societies that have since crumbled into ruins or vanished into folklore. Along the way I met many fellow explorers, most of them crackpots or treasure hunters out for their own glory or to make their fortune robbing graves and desecrating temples. It was on my travels that I met Nautilus. And he was different from the rest of them... at first."

Lord Vidalia handed her a section from a dark green fruit mottled with stripes of red. It tasted of sweet apple but also cinnamon and a hint of buttery crust like a whole slice of fresh apple pie.

"Nautilus was brilliant," Lord Vidalia said. "I suppose he still is. When I met him, he was already an inventor, full of grand ideas. He wanted to build things that would advance the world's capabilities with communication, education, nutrition. He wanted to help people. He traveled the world, gathering information from every culture he could find. We were very similar in that regard, except he was studying living cultures, and I was focusing on those from the past."

He cut into a fruit that looked citrusy, but the flesh inside was very dark. It tasted of orange and also chocolate when Honorine bit into the offered slice.

"Do you like these?" Lord Vidalia said, gesturing to the various pieces of fruit.

"They're unbelievable," Honorine said, taking another eager bite of the apple pie–flavored slice.

"It's the trees," replied Lord Vidalia. "Mordant trees hold a curious kind of…I suppose you'd have to call it magic. Though that's not exactly the right word."

He took a bite of apple, the crisp fruit snapping between his teeth, then rubbed the tired knuckles of his frail, old hands.

"Let me help," Honorine said, pulling the old cheese board across the table. She eyed the dull, chipped blade of the bone-handled knife. "Haven't you got any other?"

"Hmm? Oh, certainly, somewhere around here," Lord Vidalia said, puttering through drawers and producing wooden pens with no nibs, chopsticks, coins from around the globe, spare bits of string, tattered playing cards with curious symbols, and a few large brass buttons, along with a scattering of unrecognizable parts of other things. Finally, a much larger knife with a stout wooden handle and a curved blade appeared.

"There's this," offered Lord Vidalia. "But it's uncomfortably heavy for me, I'm afraid. Now, where were we?"

"You were telling me about when you first met Nautilus," Honorine said as she lifted the heavier-but-sharper knife.

"Right, right," he said, nodding. "We spent years together traveling, researching, gathering knowledge while I compiled a great history of the ancient world and Nautilus made advances on the great machines he would create to change the world. And then...we discovered the Mordant. Or *rediscovered* is more correct. The constellations are so important to every culture, you see, past and present. We found mentions of them everywhere. But we didn't truly understand until we finally made contact with one. Only then did we realize how important they are. How powerful, and also how dangerous. It was the discovery of a lifetime...but it was also the beginning of the end."

"Why?" Honorine asked as she tinkered with the other detritus on the desk. "The Mordant seem so...

amazing. All I had to do was touch Lux to feel brave, and Sirona healed my arm in moments!"

Lord Vidalia looked up at Honorine from under his bushy white eyebrows. "That reminds me. Are you thirsty?" he asked, getting up from the desk and shuffling into an alcove to retrieve a kettle, a tray of cups, and a tin of loose-leaf tea. He took them to the wood-stove. "Sirona brought this particular blend. It works marvelously for my arthritis." He rubbed his knotty hands again.

"Can't Sirona do anything else for you?" Honorine asked. "If your hands hurt, can't she heal them?"

Lord Vidalia shook his head. "By now you must realize how powerful the Mordant can be," he said. "But there are limits. Sirona can heal the body, and teach others to heal, but she cannot stop time. Only ease it as we pass through."

"And she can teach others?" Honorine asked. "Francis said the Mordant are muses. But...I'm not sure what a muse does."

"Well, they aren't exactly teachers," Lord Vidalia said as he carefully portioned out the tea leaves into little silver diffusers shaped like fish, "though one can certainly learn from them. They provide inspiration, and understanding of possibilities. They heighten one's own abilities and natural inclinations, but each in their own ways. Lux can inspire courage, Astraea justice. Scorpio can both instill fear and take it away, and Sirona, as you saw, can heal."

"Can she inspire anyone to heal?" Honorine asked as she began to assemble the stray items on the desk into something new.

"She can inspire those with an inclination toward biology and physiology, certainly," Lord Vidalia said. "But hers is an art that requires a specific temperament and intellect. Not everyone can learn, but not everyone would like to, you see. Societies need practitioners and specialists in many areas in order to thrive and grow. There are many others, with many other wells of knowledge to share with us. You've barely met a fraction of them. For instance, Sirona is not the only one with knowledge of healing. Serpens is stronger with medicines. You haven't met him, though. He was one of the first ones Nautilus captured."

"So, while he's been missing..." Honorine said, fitting the thoughts together in her mind as she fit buttons and wood scraps and bits of string together in her hands. "Has no one been able to learn to make medicines? Are the sick going without remedies?"

"Well, without inspiration, superstition can take over," Lord Vidalia said. "The world is a darker and more dangerous place without the Mordant in it."

"Then why would Nautilus capture them and take them away?" Honorine asked.

Lord Vidalia looked away from Honorine.

"Something in him has changed," he said, holding his hands near the steaming teapot to warm them. "When I knew him, he was tenacious, but also clever and kind. Now he has become...ruthless. Though perhaps he always was, and I just chose not to see it.

"We were working together for...it must have been five or six years, before we finally contacted a Mordant. And after that, the whole world seemed to change. We met so many of them. Eventually, they brought us to their city, a place only the Mordant can find. That was the most productive and inspiring time of our lives. Both of us were working like madmen, I on my historical records and Nautilus on his inventions. We were finding ways to record the wisdom of the Mordant and channel their power into the most comprehensive catalog of technology and history ever compiled in the modern age. Until, of course, the Mapmaker found out."

The kettle began to whistle. Lord Vidalia poured the water, disappearing in a cloud of fragrant steam.

"The Mapmaker, you see, has different objectives than we did," Lord Vidalia said. "He's been around for too long to count, I imagine. He's seen the world through a hundred cataclysms and apocalypses. All those societies I had found decaying in the jungle or the desert or under the foundations of new societies— he had watched them fall. All the current, flourishing societies that Nautilus was studying—the Mapmaker knew they, too, would someday disappear from the world."

Lord Vidalia picked up his tray and shuffled toward the desk, the cups wobbling and tinkling, threatening to spill with every step.

"Are you sure you don't want me to carry that?" Honorine asked.

"No trouble at all," he replied as he finally made it back to the desk, setting the tray down on the only available bit of space. "My word, what have you got there?" He nodded at the growing structure in front of Honorine.

"Oh, I like to work with my hands while I think."

"What a lovely habit," Lord Vidalia said. "Sugar?"

Honorine nodded, and Lord Vidalia dropped a cube into her cup. The tea was faintly lavender in color and had a scent like flowers blooming on a spring afternoon.

"The Mapmaker did not like finding mortal people in the Mordant city," Lord Vidalia said after a long pause. "He's weary from spending centuries guiding civilizations to their peak, only to see them destroyed by those who become too ambitious or greedy and the people he cared for left suffering. And he never could come to terms with how short mortal lives can be. Now he's decided that he wants to simply fade away into mythology, for the world to forget about him completely. Some of the Mordant agree with him. But not all."

"But couldn't some of them stay?" Honorine asked. "And the Mapmaker go away?"

"Ideally, yes," Lord Vidalia agreed. "But the Mapmaker doesn't see it that way. The Mordant can teach you anything. Music, language, agriculture, architecture—everything about the natural world. But the Mapmaker...he has talents that are even more prized."

"Why?" Honorine asked. "What can he do?"

Lord Vidalia looked uncomfortable. He leaned closer, his eyes sweeping the room, as if the walls themselves were listening.

"Well, even I don't know the full extent of his power. But I know what I have seen these past dozen years. He can kill a man with a touch. He can shake the very fabric of the earth. Tsunamis, mudslides, avalanches—I've seen them all happen at his command. I've seen a volcano erupt, and I suspect it had something to do with him. He has a connection to the earth itself. But none of that is why people seek him out."

Honorine stopped tinkering with her invention and looked up at Lord Vidalia.

"The Mapmaker can tell what you want most in the world," he said. "But even more important, he can show you exactly how to get it."

Anything you wanted. And exactly how to get it. Honorine immediately pictured herself with her mother and father. Could the Mapmaker tell her who they are?

"And now you're thinking about what it is you want most, aren't you?" Lord Vidalia asked.

Honorine nodded. "My parents," she said. "He could tell me how to find them?"

Lord Vidalia took a long breath and then a longer sip of tea before he answered.

"Indeed."

"But if he can do that..." she said, "he could help so many people."

"Ah, but not everyone wants to protect their children or find their long-lost families," Lord Vidalia said. "Not everyone's goals are so noble. Or noble at all. Many people have to hurt others to get what they want, and what has broken the Mapmaker is how many people are willing to do it."

He paused to refill his teacup.

"He doesn't want to see into the dark hearts of any more evil men. It took me a long time to understand him. But when I finally did, I agreed. He should be able to vanish, even if it would make the world a lesser place. By the time I realized this, though, it was too late. Nautilus had already done something irreversible."

Again, Lord Vidalia paused, taking a long sip of tea and looking at the few remaining pieces of fruit in the basket.

"Would you like another?" he asked, reaching toward the basket, but Honorine held up her hand.

"Let me try this," she said, picking up a rust-red apple striped with orange and placing it in her mostly finished machine. Then she pressed her hand on a paddle fashioned from a pair of wooden pens secured with twine. These attached to the handle of the curved, heavy knife on its own little easel structure, which held it steady as the blade bobbed downward, slicing cleanly through the fruit before it made a quarter turn to be sliced again. Honorine offered a slice to Lord Vidalia before popping another in her mouth. It tasted slightly of cheddar cheese.

"Well, isn't that delightful!" Lord Vidalia said, eating his own slice, and then eagerly loading another crisp green fruit to test out the contraption for himself. He smiled with amusement as he dipped a freshly cut piece of fruit into his tea, and motioned for Honorine to do the same. This fruit tasted of peppermint. "Forgive me, but where were we again?"

"You were about to tell me what Nautilus did," she said. "The reason why the Mapmaker despises him."

"Well, there's more than one reason for the Mapmaker to be a bit sore with Nautilus now. But the first thing, the one that started all this nonsense, seemed so innocent at the time."

Lord Vidalia put down his cup and took another long breath.

"Nautilus had a child," he said finally. "A child with a Mordant mother."

"Who—" Honorine began to ask, but Lord Vidalia shook his head and held up his hand.

"The Mapmaker was trying to separate from the mortal world, to erase himself from mortal history, and cut the connections between Mordant and humans. But a child—this child—half Mordant and half mortal, would do just the opposite. In his mind, it would bring the two worlds closer than ever, make the ties stronger, and make it impossible for him to escape it."

Honorine put her hand to her forehead. "But what could he do?" she asked. "If Nautilus already had a family, what could the Mapmaker do about it?"

Lord Vidalia's expression grew very grim. "Well, you see, he could... eliminate... Nautilus and his family before anyone in the mortal world ever knew about them."

"Eliminate?" Honorine asked quietly. "You mean... murder...."

"The possibility was considered," Lord Vidalia replied. "I don't know if he ever would have actually

 • 149

gone through with it. The rest of the Mordant intervened before the situation grew any more perilous."

"What did they do?"

"A very delicate kind of truce was reached," Lord Vidalia explained. "The Mordant convinced the Mapmaker that Nautilus would cause no further harm, that he would leave the Mordant city and never contact them again, and that his child was to be raised never knowing of Nautilus or the Mordant. And I agreed to travel with the Mapmaker, erasing every trace of him from human history so that he could fade away and live in peace. We spent ten years gathering every ancient scroll, every carving, anything that might lead someone to find him again. The Mapmaker was satisfied with the arrangement. He promised not to pursue Nautilus any further. But as you now know, that arrangement didn't last."

Honorine shook her head. "What happened?"

"A few years ago, we learned that Nautilus had built a new ship. That he was possibly trying to contact the Mordant once again. And then, only a short time later, the Mordant began disappearing."

"Nautilus was capturing them," Honorine added. "But why?"

"For information, most likely. Whatever his true intentions may be, once Nautilus started hunting, we began trying to gather up the Mordant to protect them, while also trying to devise a way to stop him. And of course, there was still the child. Nautilus broke his word to stay away from the world of the Mordant, and so the Mapmaker felt no obligation to hold up his end of the agreement—to keep his distance from Nautilus's child. Which is why he was a bit cross with me when he found out I had known your whereabouts all this time."

Honorine sat back on the ottoman, her skin prickling as if she had been dipped in ice.

"Me?" Honorine asked.

Lord Vidalia nodded solemnly.

"Nautilus Olyphant," Honorine said, "is my father?"

"And the Mapmaker's enemy. And that puts you in a difficult place."

As the Crow Flies

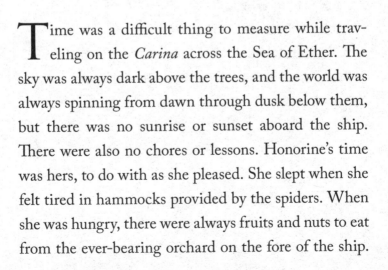

Time was a difficult thing to measure while traveling on the *Carina* across the Sea of Ether. The sky was always dark above the trees, and the world was always spinning from dawn through dusk below them, but there was no sunrise or sunset aboard the ship. There were also no chores or lessons. Honorine's time was hers, to do with as she pleased. She slept when she felt tired in hammocks provided by the spiders. When she was hungry, there were always fruits and nuts to eat from the ever-bearing orchard on the fore of the ship.

And in between, she explored the forest, studied the Mordant, and asked questions. Many, many questions.

From the moment she was told that Nautilus was her father, the very next question was, of course, "Then who is my mother?"

When she had first asked, Lord Vidalia had patted her hand and shaken his head.

"I'm afraid I cannot tell you yet," he said. Honorine had never been so infuriated by an answer in all her life. But the soft sadness in Lord Vidalia's eyes told her that it pained him to give her such a cruel answer. "I made a vow to protect you, and part of that agreement was to keep her identity a secret until she chose to reveal herself."

"But she *is* a Mordant?" Honorine asked.

"Well...yes," Lord Vidalia replied.

"Which means, *I'm* a Mordant," Honorine said. Francis had been right! But Honorine still did not quite believe it. "So, I have a constellation? Am I a muse? I don't feel like I could be. And I don't make the omen stones glow. Or make sparks, for that matter. I bleed like any ordinary person when I'm hurt...."

Lord Vidalia nodded along until she took a breath.

"You are half Mordant, to be sure," he said. "But also still a child. Someday, you may have a constellation, but not yet. If you had a constellation already, made stones glow with light, and inspired brilliance in human people, Nautilus would have been able to find you quite easily. And we never could have kept you hidden from the Mapmaker."

"Someday I may?" Honorine repeated. "Does that mean...I might not be a Mordant like they are?"

She pointed toward the ceiling. Somewhere on the other side were the rest of the *Carina*'s crew, the true Mordant.

Lord Vidalia sighed.

"All in due time," he'd said, and filled her cup with more lavender-colored tea. "When this problem with Nautilus is resolved, you will know everything, I promise. For now, you have one parent back. That must be enough."

This was followed by Sirona arriving to remove Honorine's bandages and proclaim her healed, and Lux inviting her on a tour of the ship to see the orchards and the giant redwoods, the curious baobabs with their stout trunks, and the maple trees always in autumn shades of red and gold, growing from gentle dunes of snow-white sand. Honorine asked about all of them, about the age of the trees, and where they'd come from, and how they could grow on the ship, with no earth to hold their roots.

"They are like us," Lux replied as he and Honorine made their way through an oasis of palm trees, some impossibly tall and slender, some short and positively primordial, gathered around clear, shallow pools of warm freshwater. "They look like trees, but they are much more than that. We plant them all around the world, in places that are distinctly important to us, and they can live for thousands of years."

"There are trees in the world that are thousands of years old?" Honorine asked as they ducked under a spray of hanging palm fronds.

"Indeed there are. And this is as far as we should go, for now."

Beyond the palm oasis, at the farthest end of the *Carina*, was a dark, silent swamp crowded with cypress trees, their branches dripping with gray spanish moss, their trunks surrounded by rounded spires like crocodile teeth rising from shallow, tea-stained water. There were no lanterns in the swamp. Light seeped in from the palm oasis and was quickly smothered in the quiet dark.

"What's in there?" Honorine asked as she peered around the gently swaying tendrils of moss. Her feet sank into wet sand, leaving footprints filled with brack-ish water.

"The Mapmaker's quarters," Lux replied. "That's where he stays when he requires peace and solitude. I suggest you respect his wishes."

Lux was not alone. Sirona, Astraea, and even Lord Vidalia all advised her to keep her distance from the cypress swamp. Corvus, though he never spoke, cawed harshly at her when he happened upon her wandering a bit too close. Scorpio expressed no opinion on the mat-ter, but he was also the only one ever to go into the swamp besides the Mapmaker himself, when he hap-pened to be on the ship.

The Mapmaker, Corvus, and Astraea were very often away, trying to keep track of Nautilus and deter-mine where he was moving to. They returned regularly, but again, with no clocks and no sunrise and no sunset, there was no way to tell how long they were gone, and how long they stayed when they returned. The immea-surable time aggravated Honorine. When she found Lord Vidalia's old pocket watch, which had long since stopped working, it was simple enough to fix, but with no other clocks around to set it, it was impossible to keep the thing properly wound.

"You must let go of this attachment," Lord Vidalia said after Honorine marched into the study, dropping the puttering, old pocket watch onto a table with a clunk and an irritated glare. "Time is going to be different for you than it has been before."

He rubbed his sore hands and sipped his therapeutic tea, and then rummaged about for a very old book, which he pried down from the bookshelves, causing the ancient leather binding to groan.

"Here's something you could devote your attention to," he said as he brushed off a layer of dust and opalescent spider silk from the gilt-edged pages. He tapped a gnarled finger on the cover, which had the same tooled crown of stars as his little journal. "Much more comprehensive than my field journal. They're all in there. And you will meet them one day."

While Lord Vidalia shuffled off to brew another cup of tea, Honorine curled up in a chair with the heavy, musty old book. She realized, when she held it in her hand, that her mother was among the Mordant listed in that book. But it was an impossibly dense volume, the pages filled with tiny handwritten script, often with passages in foreign tongues, and footnotes and annotations that interrupted proper reading. She found she could rarely get through more than a few pages in a single sitting, and there were far too many distractions aboard the *Carina* to allow enough time for quiet studying.

There were the other Mordant, of course. Lux was constantly wandering about the ship, as if he was patrolling it, and always glad to have company. Sirona had endless macabre yet fascinating stories of the way mortal bodies could be injured or sickened and then healed. When, in the deepest hours of night, the *Carina* would sail lower, near the sea, Sirona would perform healings on injured seabirds, turtles, squids, and even once a young whale with a shark-bitten tail fluke.

Astraea rarely spoke to her, but Honorine discovered that she was interested in games of any kind, as long as there were clear, uncomplicated rules. When she was aboard the ship, Astraea would always agree to a game of chess or cribbage or a quick round of knucklebones, just to pass the time. Though Honorine would attempt to ask her questions, Astraea made it clear that she preferred to play in silence. So Honorine wasn't quite sure if Astraea was pleasantly surprised or annoyed to return from a long flight to find Honorine waiting in the oak grove with a satchel of game pieces.

"What do you call this?" Astraea asked as Honorine scattered a little haystack of finely carved wooden instruments onto a table made from an oak stump.

"Jackstraws," Honorine replied. "Haven't you ever played it?"

Astraea shook her head as she picked up a piece from the table. It was a miniature spade, about four inches long, carved from pale white wood. The other pieces were fashioned into tools as well, among them a rake, a hoe, a broom, a saw, an ax, and even a tiny ladder.

"It's very simple," Honorine said, picking up a long, thin stick with a tiny hook at the end. "You pick them up one at a time, without moving the rest of the pile. If you succeed, you get a point. If you move the pile, you lose your turn."

Astraea loved the game.

"Did we have this somewhere down in the depths?" Astraea said, indicating the cabins belowdecks. "Or did one of the trees make it for you?"

"The willow made them for us," Honorine said as she gently freed a miniature pickax from the pile. That had been another delightful surprise about the *Carina*. Just about anything one could want the trees could grow, as long as it could be made from wood. The chairs and desks and furniture down in Lord Vidalia's study had all been grown like fruit from the buds of the pine and oak and walnut trees, and then plucked when ripe and ready for use. They could do the same with croquet mallets and bowling pins, playing cards and paper dolls, violins and the sheet music to play with them. All that was needed was a written request on a square of parchment, folded and slipped into an open knothole on a hollow branch.

Things that could not be grown from the trees were a bit harder to come by. But after scavenging in the darkest, dustiest corners down in the roots of the ship, Honorine had collected a surprising amount of materials: some glass, leather, iron, assorted ceramics, a few bits of jewelry, and even a jar half-full of omen stones, though the rest of the crew called them starglass.

"The only one who ever called them omen stones was my dear Josefina," Lord Vidalia explained as Honorine inspected the collection. There were all sizes from pebbles as small as her fingernail up to hunks the size of a croquet ball. All of them gave off a faint, consistent glow here aboard the *Carina* but grew intensely bright near any of the Mordant crew.

Honorine kept her small hoard of materials in a far

corner of Lord Vidalia's study, where she went to tinker with ideas for new inventions and improvements to old ones when she needed a break from the rest of the ship and its inhabitants.

The Mordant, she had noticed, had the ability to inspire moods. Spending a lot of time around Sirona made her very analytical. Being with the healer for too long would make Honorine start to pick apart every story she'd read down to the sentence and try to reason how all the parts worked together. Spending time around Scorpio, however, made her cautious. He could amplify fears. Too much time around him made her anxious.

Astraea would make her feel melancholy or even angry and, at her worst moments, a bit hopeless.

"Justice is a tricky thing," she told Honorine one day before flying off with the Mapmaker for another scouting expedition. "When it seems near, it can be most powerful and uplifting. But when it is denied, it can eat away a person until they are nothing but bitterness and regret."

Honorine did feel a bit bitter for all the Mordant being trapped on Nautilus's ship; for herself being separated from Francis; and for her mother, still unknown, her identity kept hidden. She grew a bit relieved when Astraea was away from the ship.

Lux usually made her feel bold, strong, and curious. But too much time around him also made her anxious and frustrated. He often spent time at the edges of the ship, in places he could look down over the world. He wanted to go back there. Being stuck on the *Carina* for so long was turning him into a ball of nervous energy.

It seemed they could all use a break from the endless sailing. While Honorine waited for the *Carina* to arrive at a destination—*any* destination—she kept herself busy turning the old bits of clockwork and worn instruments in the study into new gadgets and inventions.

She made two important discoveries fairly quickly. First, the starglass, aside from glowing around any particular Mordant, had another, even more curious property. If aligned in a pattern that matched a constellation, the stones would glow brightest when the corresponding Mordant was nearby.

Second, the ironwood tree, though it grew at the very edge of the forbidden cypress swamp, provided spectacular tools for working on smaller, more meticulous projects. After braving the darkest parts of the ship to retrieve them, she took apart the old pocket watch with ease and fashioned instead a kind of bracelet with a thick leather wristband. She reworked the round ebony watch face with tiny, polished chips of starglass arranged in the pattern of the five constellations representing the Mordant aboard the ship. Whenever a Mordant was near, the glowing chips gave her a bit of warning if she was just about to run into Scorpio in the dark woods or if Corvus was swooping in overhead.

She was wandering through the pine trees, nibbling on a meringue-flavored lemon with a hint of graham cracker, testing her Mordant watch, when something buzzed by her, brushing back her hair with a flutter of wind.

There were insects on the ship—moths and glowworms and beetles and, of course, spiders—but this was something else. Her watch didn't react to it in any way. Honorine looked up to see a tiny flash moving swiftly through the trees, and she followed it to the redwood forest, where the very tallest of the redwoods stood at the precise center of the ship, acting as the mainmast. Somewhere near the crown was the crow's nest—not just the lookout spot on a traditional ship, but an actual nest, where Corvus rested when he wasn't ferrying the

Mapmaker. Corvus actually made Honorine a bit nervous, but his nest seemed to be where the little light was headed, racing upward into the mist and the feathery needles of the tree.

Honorine dashed up a tight spiral staircase in the center of the mast tree. She reached a narrow opening at the top that led into a shallow dish of moss and sticks resting between the trunk of the mast tree and the forks of a stout branch. The tiny, sharp light she had seen below was nowhere to be found. She considered climbing back down, but as she raised her hand to reach toward the trunk of the tree, she glimpsed her Mordant watch, secured to her wrist. According to her new invention, and assuming it was working correctly, Corvus was somewhere very near....

The rush of wind as he landed shook a spray of dew from the branches, pelting Honorine with cold droplets. Corvus ruffled his feathers and turned about on the nest, until his black eye reflected Honorine in the nook of the tree trunk. He took a step forward, his hooked claws sinking into the soft moss, and reached toward her.

In the tip of his pointed beak he held a tiny speck made of cold brass and bits of copper, with crystalline wings and round stone eyes. It was one of Francis's bees! The eyes were still glowing, the wings trembling. Corvus dropped it into Honorine's hand, and she quickly closed the other one over it to keep the bee from flying away.

"This is from Nautilus's ship!" she said. "He must be nearby!"

Corvus nodded.

"We should bring this to the Mapmaker," Honorine said, but this time Corvus shook his head in disagreement. He leaned down and stretched out one wing, as if inviting her to climb onto his back. "You want to go now? To look for the ship?"

Corvus cawed at her, a sound that rattled in her chest and stung her ears, and shook his wing impatiently. She hesitated for a moment, wondering if this was some breach of etiquette, but the thought of flying with Corvus and getting off the ship was much too tempting. She tucked the bee deep into her tunic pocket and climbed aboard, settling onto the crow's back, her legs tucked under his wings, a handful of feathers in each fist.

"All right," she said, and the next second they were off, so fast that all the breath was drained from Honorine's lungs. She took a huge gulp of air and crouched as low as she could over his neck as they rocketed across the sky.

Flying on the *Nighthawk* was exciting. Flying on the *Carina* was amazing. But flying on the back of Corvus, looking out over the whole of the world, with only the force of the wind to tell her how fast they were racing, Honorine had never felt such freedom or such joy in all her life.

Corvus bolted across the sky. Each wingbeat might have propelled them a hundred miles—she couldn't be sure from that height. It was difficult to see where they were going, as the wind and the cold made Honorine's eyes water, and she dared not let go of a handful of feathers to wipe them. The world became a swirl of silver and violet as they raced across the Ether in a streak of blue.

Eventually, Corvus slowed a bit, and Honorine felt her stomach lift as they began to descend toward the earth below. After managing to rub the water from her eyes on the sleeve of her tunic, Honorine looked down to see the clouds and the ocean coming up to meet them. The entire world was somewhere below them, the whole spinning globe, with every city, river, church, dairy cow, wild tiger, butterfly, and living person upon it. She wondered if anyone could see her and the crow, and if to them, she was nothing more than a glittering star sailing across the black of the night sky.

Corvus banked to the left, dipping below the clouds, and there, under his wing, Honorine saw a curious line of white mist hovering very low over the dark water.

"The *Gaslight!*" she said, leaning farther over Corvus's rising and falling wing, until she could make out the sparkling outline of the ship far, far below, at the head of the trail of steam clouds.

They were headed for Francis. Corvus seemed willing to take her all the way there. All the way to the *Gaslight*.

"No," Honorine warned. "We can't go that far. Don't fly too near the ship. They'll catch you!"

She desperately wanted to see Francis again. Even though Astraea had insisted that all aboard the *Nighthawk* had been saved, Honorine still wanted to see him, alive, with her own eyes. And Nautilus. She remembered something of his appearance, enough that she would recognize him if she encountered him again. But she hadn't looked closely enough before. She hadn't committed his face to memory, the way she felt she should have for Nautilus to truly feel like her father. At least she knew what one parent looked like.

Corvus swooped in a wide arc, as if asking one more time if she was certain she wanted to turn back.

"We have to tell the others he's close by," Honorine said, pointing back up toward the *Carina*. It was no more than another point of light in the starry sky. Though she wanted nothing more than to fly on and find Francis and her father, instead, she and Corvus soared back into the Ether.

Honorine clung on like a burr as Corvus set down at the edge of the redwood forest, where the Mapmaker, Lord Vidalia, and the rest of the Mordant crew had gathered at the base of the mainmast tree.

"Nautilus!" Honorine blurted out as she slipped less than gracefully from Corvus's back onto the mossy deck. She took a moment to draw in a breath, her heart pounding with the excitement of the flight and from nervousness at having seen the *Gaslight* so close by. "He's right down there, right this moment!"

"Did you see an airship?" the Mapmaker asked at once.

Honorine shook her head. "No, just the *Gaslight*," she said. "And I thought the *Nighthawk* sank."

"That was his flagship," the Mapmaker continued. "But he has others. No doubt they are already deployed, seeing how close we are to a possible destination. He's been making his way across the Atlantic, but recently his ship has changed course. The only logical destination is South America."

"And who do we think is still there?" asked Lux.

"There are two who I think we can reasonably say are still there, and still free," said Astraea. "Libra and Eridanus."

Scorpio shifted about on his eight scuttling legs. Lux nodded. Sirona crossed her arms.

"He's going there for both of them, we assume," said the Mapmaker. "And here's the sticky bit. Libra is most likely in the Andes, on the far western coast. Eridanus is on the other side of the continent, in the Amazon River Delta."

"Which one is he going after first?" Lux asked.

"Well, if he's in the southern Atlantic," Honorine piped up, "then the Amazon is closer."

"And how would you know that?" the Mapmaker asked.

"He had an absolutely gigantic map of the whole world on his library wall," she said, gesturing at Lord

Vidalia sitting on a stump across the grove. "I had to dust it for years. The Amazon River runs across the continent, but the delta bit is on the eastern coast. So that would be the first place Nautilus will reach when he gets to South America. And if I were him, I'd go to the closest place first."

As soon as she said it, she felt her stomach churn nervously.

If I were him.

The Mapmaker rubbed his chin, the blue of his eyes dark and rolling, like deep ocean waves. Eventually, he shrugged and dropped his arms to his sides.

"It makes sense, I have to say," he said. "Though Libra is much less protected in the mountains than Eridanus is in the delta. Still, we'll sail for the Amazon and make our way from there."

He nodded at Honorine, and she nodded back.

"Fast as we can manage," the Mapmaker instructed. The Mordant began to disperse back into the woods with the meeting at an end.

"Honorine, please stay," he politely requested, taking a seat on a mossy stump. Over his shoulder, Honorine spotted Lux's pale white silhouette, watching for a moment before disappearing into the trees.

"It's machines with you, isn't it?" he said aloud, though he seemed to be asking himself and not Honorine. "Or perhaps technology in general."

Honorine tucked her hands into the pockets of her tunic, her fingers folding over the mechanical bee.

"It's what I'm good at," she said. "Always have been."

"Just like your father," the Mapmaker said with an implied *that's what I was afraid of* at the end. He leaned back, drawing a long breath before he spoke.

"You saw what happened to Leo," the Mapmaker said, "when he was captured by Nautilus's great machine. And you've been on his airship. You've seen his creations. What did you think of them?"

This was a dangerous question. Honorine thought of the *Nighthawk* with all of its gadgets and instruments.

"I'm asking for your honest answer," the Mapmaker pressed. "You liked what you saw? You found it interesting?" His eyes were nearly glowing with furious bright light.

Honorine's cheeks flushed. Her fingers tangled nervously on her lap.

"There's no need to be afraid," he said, though his posture and his stare indicated that there was every reason. "I want you to be honest with me, Honorine. Tell me what you thought of Nautilus's work."

"It is…fascinating," she replied. "I've never seen anything like Nautilus's machines. They are incredible."

The Mapmaker nodded.

"That is no fault of your own. And there was a time when even I saw his work as no more dangerous or threatening than a steam engine or an electric lantern or a windup toy. But now…he has built something new. He has something on that ship that is not just a curiosity or an advance in technology. It is a weapon."

"He has cannons," she said quietly. "And bullets made from the same stuff as Lady Vidalia's omen stones."

"No, nothing like that," the Mapmaker said. "Those novelties of his are an annoyance, but they cannot do any real damage to us. His new creation, though, is something entirely different. Lord Vidalia warned me that Nautilus had envisioned such a weapon. Something he could use not to track us down, but to capture and imprison us. I never thought it would be possible to build. But he did, and he has it on the *Gaslight*. Because ever since that ship began sailing, the Mordant have begun disappearing."

"Well, he's not the only inventor in the world," Honorine said. "If he can build a machine to fight you, perhaps we can build a machine to defeat him."

The Mapmaker sneered, though he tried to hold it back.

"No," he said forcefully. "No more *machines*. Not now, anyway. Use what you know to help us, Honorine. You've seen what he builds, and how they work. Now think of a way to stop him."

"Without using any new machines?" she asked.

The Mapmaker drew a long breath and rose to his feet.

"I would prefer that we just worry about the ones already out there for now."

The Eternal Lightning

Honorine sat on a white sand dune with the little copper bee lying quietly in her hand. She lifted it up to her eyes, waiting for it to twitch or glow, or make any sudden motion at all.

"I don't know what that is, but I suspect it has something to do with your remarkable discovery of Nautilus's ship," said a lupine voice.

Startled, Honorine looked up and saw Lux walking slowly up the dune toward her. His white coat reflecting off the pale sand made him so bright she could hardly stand to look at him. She shaded her eyes as she held up the bee.

"It came from his ship. They track down Mordant," she said, "and report back to . . . a hive."

"And can you tell how long that one was on our ship, before you found it?"

Honorine shook her head. "I don't think it was long, but I don't know for sure," she said. "And I can't tell if this is the only one."

"Well, Scorpio should be able to help with that," Lux said. "And what are you going to do with the one we know about?"

"I'd like to study it," Honorine said, turning the bee over and examining its stone eyes. "But the Mapmaker does not seem to like that plan."

"He's wary of anything with a hint of Nautilus's hand in it," Lux said, his ears splaying back in distaste. "And I can't say I blame him. But I do think that continuing your studies could be helpful. Just . . . be discreet."

"You want me to lie to him?" Honorine asked. "That seems pretty dangerous, too."

"There is a difference between lying and simply not speaking about something."

"It doesn't seem much different," Honorine said. Lux tipped his head and squinted, then padded across the white sand and stopped very close to her. Even though he was kind and clever, and slept by her side while she was in her hammock, it was still intimidating to look a wolf in the eye.

"I shouldn't tell you that there's nothing wrong with lying. But I will tell you that I find no harm in lying to the Mapmaker in certain instances. Because I didn't come along with him for his sake. I came to find you."

Honorine frowned. "You came where to find me?"

"On the *Carina*," he said. "Two years ago, when the Mordant first began disappearing. The Mapmaker began a mission to gather us all up, but most of the others didn't want to come along. A few came out of loyalty to the Mapmaker, but as for myself and Astraea, we came because we had promised to keep you safe if you ever turned up again. And I knew as soon as Nautilus was back on the trail of the constellations that you were out there somewhere, and you needed someone to protect you."

Honorine looked down at the sand shyly. "I suppose there's none better than a wolf," she said, staring down at her feet, drawing little crescents in the dry sand with her toe.

"And as it turned out, the Mapmaker was right," Lux said. "Those who stayed out there were quickly captured."

"What do you think happened to them?" Honorine asked. "Are you sure they are still alive? Could Nautilus have...killed them?"

Lux shook his head. "Even with all his tricks, Nautilus cannot kill a Mordant. There is only one thing that can. A Bellua."

He said the word with a growl that made Honorine's skin prickle.

"What is that?" she asked. "It's not in any of Lord Vidalia's books."

"He knows it is far too dangerous even to mention the Bellua." Lux paused every time he said it, as if the word curdled in his mouth. "They are very ancient and very dangerous. In the way that the Mordant can inspire learning and art and culture, the Bellua inspire war and destruction. One of the duties we perform has been to keep watch over them so that they stay in a place where humans cannot travel to, where they will never be found."

"Like the Sea of Ether?" Honorine asked.

Lux curled his lip as he considered.

"No, nothing like this place. Where the Bellua reside is dark and deep, one of the oldest and most dangerous places in any world. People once called it Hades."

"The underworld," Honorine said.

"But not the land of the dead of the old myths. The true Hades is a place only the Mordant and the Bellua can go. There were once a handful of gateways between this world and that one. Over the millennia, we've managed to destroy most of them. But one still remains, and that one we guard."

"Then what happens if Nautilus captures all of you, and there's no one left to guard the gateway?"

"That...is exactly what we're trying to avoid," Lux said. "And there would be consequences far beyond the Mordant. Nautilus may have machines that can stop us, but I am certain he has nothing that would work against a Bellua."

Honorine felt something on the ship change, as if the *Carina* herself didn't like the mention of the Bellua, either. First, the deck bobbed a bit, sending dry leaves scuttling and the lanterns overhead swaying. The *Carina* had never so much as quivered before. Then a wind rushed over the ship, not from the sides, but from below, rising up through the trees, as the *Carina* descended. Honorine's stomach lurched as she rose to her feet, wobbling about as the deck trembled.

"Ah, there you are!" called the Mapmaker, striding through the trees toward her. "Come this way! You'll want to see this!"

He waved for her to follow as he marched toward the front of the ship. The sinking slowed as Honorine picked her way through the pines and into the orchard. The *Carina* began to glide again in a more forward direction, and thunder began to rumble in the distance, growing louder as she approached the pointed prow of the ship. There stood a slender maple tree, its trunk twisted into a spiral from growing against the wind, its branches curved up around a large, single lantern.

The Mapmaker and Lux stood under the tree, looking over a rising landscape of tumbling black clouds and flashing lightning. Far in the distance, a tiny sliver of a moon cut a shimmering gash in the night sky.

"That's quite a storm!" Honorine said, hanging on to the twisted maple tree with one hand while peering over the railing of the ship as far as she dared. A ghostly coastline stretched out before them, covered in mossy green. It was dark and silent up and down the coast, except for a wide bay straight ahead, where water from a rambling river poured out of the jungle and into the ocean. Huge, stony mountains rose up on all sides of the bay like a wall.

The constant thunder intensified, rattling her bones.

The sky above the treetops flashed with shots of white and blue light, over and over again, barely spaced enough to tell one flash from the next. The thunder and lightning never ended, but the air was dry and warm. No rain fell from the flashing, thundering clouds.

"Does the lightning ever stop?" Honorine called.

"No, not while Eridanus resides in the river," said the Mapmaker.

"So this is a good sign?"

"Very good indeed," the Mapmaker said as the *Carina* dropped again in altitude. "But we will still have to be swift. When the *Carina* touches down, we will be vulnerable to Nautilus's attacks. We must find Eridanus, get her on the ship, and get back in the air as quickly as possible, which won't be easy, as she might not want to come along."

"Why not?" Honorine asked. "Doesn't she know what's happening? What Nautilus is doing?"

"I only know she is stubborn, and she's never really seen eye to eye with me on many matters. This one being no exception. That's why I'll need you, Honorine, to help me."

Honorine looked up nervously. The Mapmaker's eyes were pale and stormy, reflecting the flashing lightning.

"This is your chance," he said, "to prove that you are on our side in this fight."

Honorine nodded and wrapped her arms around the slender maple. She would do everything she could to rescue Eridanus before Nautilus could find her. She didn't want the Mordant being imprisoned. But she still wasn't sure, even as the *Carina* rushed toward the sea, that she truly was on the Mapmaker's side. He had a temper. He could be cold, and vindictive. Lord Vidalia sailed with him, but only to keep the Mapmaker from harming Francis. Lux generally stayed out of sight when the Mapmaker was around and had told Honorine directly that he wasn't there out of loyalty. Astraea spent much of her time challenging or outright arguing with the Mapmaker. And it was hard to tell with Sirona and Scorpio. She wondered if he had any true companions at all.

"Brace yourself," the Mapmaker warned as the keel of the ship brushed over the water. It was a jarring transition, slipping through the air to cutting through the waves. Salt water splashed up and over the deck as the ship settled firmly on the water, racing directly toward the bay and the sharp mountains and the storm, which was now above them in the sky.

Honorine had never been terribly concerned about thunderstorms or lightning, but then, she had never seen a thousand bolts of lightning striking the earth every minute as she sailed directly into them.

"How close are we going to get, exactly?" she asked, having to shout a little over the building roar of thunder.

"Pretty close," Lux said as the ship cruised directly toward a curtain of endless lightning shooting straight into the water, churning the muddy waters of the river and the blue water of the ocean bay into a wild froth.

Honorine clung harder to the tree. Lux sat down beside her.

"Don't close your eyes," he said. "You won't want to miss this."

When the ship grew close enough, the endless lightning began to spread out over the sky, grasping the tips of the branches as if it could feel. The curtain of lightning then began to part, surging up and down all around them, arching over the ship to allow it safe passage through.

Honorine let go of the tree. Her hair flew out around her, the electricity in the air making everything feel fragile and brittle. The hem of her silk tunic fluttered in the delicate wind generated by the flashing lightning.

In a moment, they were through. The curtain closed behind them, cutting off the view of the river and the forest and the towering mountains.

Behind the wall of electric bolts, the water was a calm and flat pool, and the light inside was strangely steady and pale, the thunder outside muffled. Honorine could still feel the low timbre rattling in her ribs, but she could also hear the water flowing around them and the Mapmaker speaking to Lord Vidalia somewhere at the port-side railing.

At the center of the pool stood a mound of huge, rounded granite boulders flecked with clear crystal and carpeted with cascading moss that was in turn speckled with tiny white star-shaped flowers. Among the stones grew a small cluster of hemlock trees with great, drooping branches, laden with brilliant green needles, each one tipped with a point of faint silver-white light. From the center of the mound of stones bubbled a spring of clear water that trickled down through the moss into the pool within the lightning.

The *Carina* came to a gentle rest at the edge of the stones.

"Be quick," said the Mapmaker as Lux jumped up onto the railing of the ship, balancing on his white paws. "We don't know how close Nautilus may be."

Lux looked back toward Honorine. "Perhaps she should come with me," he suggested.

The Mapmaker furrowed his brow.

"Eridanus will not want to leave," Lux added. "But when she sees the girl is with us, she may be more agreeable."

Astraea ruffled her feathers. "You're sure?" she asked.

"I want to help," Honorine said. "Isn't this an opportunity to earn my place on your ship?"

Then she gave the Mapmaker a beaming smile. He looked back at her quizzically, then gave a short, amused laugh.

"Right this way," Lux said as he bounded from the ship to a round boulder over Honorine's head.

The Mapmaker helped her up onto the railing near the closest mossy rock, and she hopped across, putting her feet down on solid ground for the first time in weeks.

The stones were large and quite rounded, and also very wet from the trickling water. Honorine managed to struggle gracelessly upward, crushing the delicate flowers and scraping swaths of moss from the granite stones. When she arrived at the summit, her hands were covered in grass stains, and bits of moss and hemlock needles were mashed into the knees of her leggings. At the top of the pile, she found Lux waiting next to a basin of dark stones and a pool of perfectly clear water filled with bright white water lilies.

The air crackled, and the water rippled. Then, with a rush, the water began to rise over the boulders, fast and wild, splashing with silver light and sending a spray of droplets and sparks out over the pool. Through the spray rose a creature unlike anything Honorine had ever seen before.

She resembled a horse, mostly, with long legs, an arched neck, a tail like an ox, and a wet, dappled gray coat that danced with light. Instead of hooves, she had three wide, webbed toes. Her face was long, with huge, dark eyes, no visible ears, and a tapered snout with nostrils on the top, like a crocodile's. But her most surprising features were curving golden horns covered in blunt spines like coral, and a spiny fin, jet black and speckled with silver spots, running down her neck and along her spine all the way to the tip of her tail, which raised and lowered like the dorsal fin of a fish.

She was one of the most beautiful creatures Honorine had ever seen. She seemed to be made of raw power, but also gentleness, as if she could be quiet as a summer morning or wicked as a thunderstorm, depending on her will. She was the living embodiment of water.

"Eridanus," Lux said with a bow of his head.

The beautiful water horse nodded back.

"Lux," she replied before turning to Honorine. "And who might you be?"

"Honorine," she replied, remembering to give a little curtsy.

"Nautilus Olyphant's daughter," Lux said very plainly. Honorine almost blushed. She had never really been formally introduced to anyone before, and never as anyone's child. It still didn't seem true, even though Eridanus nodded again in agreement.

"And she came here with the Mapmaker," Eridanus said, looking down the rolling mound of granite boulders toward the *Carina*, where the man stood with Sirona and Astraea.

"Scorpio and Corvus are with us as well," Lux said. "And we are nearly the only ones left."

"Left where?" Eridanus asked.

"In the world," Lux replied. "It seems that Nautilus has found a way to track us down and capture us."

She did not seem surprised. "That would be why it has been so quiet lately."

"And why you need to come with us now," Lux said.

Eridanus raised her head, the fin along her spine rising as well.

"I don't ever leave," she replied. "This is my home. And I protect this place."

"But Nautilus is on his way," Honorine said, then leaned closer and lowered her voice, as if it was dangerous to speak of such things out loud. "I've seen what he can do."

But Eridanus looked calm and unconcerned.

"He can't enter this grotto," she said as lightning crashed all around them. "I'm perfectly protected here. There is only danger in stepping outside."

Lux pinned his ears back and looked up at the boiling clouds overhead. Honorine could feel his restlessness bubbling up again, making her anxious. They couldn't waste time here, and they couldn't leave without Eridanus.

"It's lovely that you're protected here," Honorine said, looking back at the elegant water horse. "But what about the others? Nautilus has them captive on a great steamship, and he'll never let them go. We need help to set them free."

Something small and bright splashed into the pool behind Eridanus, sending a tiny ripple under the water lilies. Eridanus glanced back with a twitch of her head.

"She's right," Lux said as yet another something fell from the sky, this time missing the pond and cracking on the rocks. "There are only two others left, besides those gathered here right now."

"Two?" Eridanus asked. Her head rose, but her fin folded tightly to her body. "You must be mistaken."

Lux shook his head. "At the very best, Libra and Sagittarius remain, but we might not even have them before the day is through."

"Even more reason to stay here," Eridanus said. "Where we will be safe. All of us… and let the Mapmaker sort out this business with Nautilus once and for all."

"The Mapmaker said there was no such thing as safe," Honorine replied. And then a third object fell from the sky, bouncing off the rocks at the rim of the pool and tumbling across the moss to rest right at Honorine's feet.

It was another of Francis's bees.

"And maybe he was right," Honorine said as she picked up the little copper machine, hot from the lightning. Its tiny crystal wings fluttered, too cracked to fly.

"That's from his ship!" Lux growled as Eridanus stared down at the mechanical bee. "He knows you're here."

"He's always known that," Eridanus replied.

"He has other machines," Honorine said urgently. "Ones he's using to hunt down the Mordant, and he's building new ones all the time. Maybe he has a way around your protections now."

"You made promises long ago," Lux said. "Now it's time to keep them."

Eridanus looked almost annoyed with him and then looked back at Honorine.

"I did," she said finally. "So I will go. But *not* to help the Mapmaker."

"Of course," Lux said. "And you have me as your ally. I am not here for him, either. Now, there's no more time to waste."

They started back toward the *Carina*. Though she was much more agile and better at climbing, Eridanus went slowly, patiently waiting for Honorine to keep up. That was, until a swarm of bees came falling through the dome of thunderclouds overhead. They fell broken to the ground like hot copper buckshot. Honorine yelped angrily as one hit her shoulder, and covered her head as she and Eridanus rushed the final few feet to the *Carina*.

Eridanus bounded gracefully over the railing. Lux grabbed Honorine by the back of her tunic and lunged onto the ship, where she tumbled to the floor, landing in a puff of white sand and dry leaves.

"Nautilus is here," Lux said. "Just as Honorine predicted."

"We can see that," Astraea said. "Hold on to something, and get ready to fly."

The *Carina* began to slowly ease back from the fountain of stones, turning about to sail the way they'd come in.

"When we get into the open, we're going to move quickly," the Mapmaker warned. Honorine grabbed hold of the railing.

The curtain of lightning began to part to let them out to sea. But instead of open ocean and a path back to the sky, they saw the shining black broadside of Nautilus's steamship idling in the water—directly in their way.

CHAPTER
• 13 •

The Flight on the Amazon

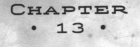

The *Carina*, already building up speed to take off on the open water, slammed to a halt, tossing Honorine to the sandy deck again. As she pulled herself back to her feet with the help of a handful of Lux's fur, she caught sight of the Mapmaker, his hands held out to his sides, palms angled toward the sea. He gave a short, powerful wave of his arms, a gesture that looked like half a wingbeat, and the water rose up before them, reflecting the flashing lightning as it swelled, lifting the entire bulk of the massive steamship and pushing it far out to sea. Honorine watched the ship sway and tilt as it was carried away on the crest of a wave that towered like a mountain rising from the black water, until the curtain of lightning closed again, sealing the *Carina* on the other side.

"Well, now we know Nautilus's whereabouts," Lux said as the Mapmaker turned back, his face dark in the shadows, but his eyes bright as two chips of ice shining in a northern sea.

"We're not going that way," the Mapmaker said.

"The river," Eridanus said.

"It's the best course," Astraea said as the *Carina* swung around, skirting the edge of the rock pile and sailing away from the ocean, toward land. The lightning parted, revealing a wide, snaking river of dark water, twisting away into a chasm between soaring mountains covered in dense jungle. Creatures moved up and down the riverbank, revealed only by rustling leaves and swinging vines. Things breached in the water, creating sprays of mist before disappearing back into the darkness. On a deep wash of pale sand, a band of black caimans rested, perfectly still, until they sensed the *Carina* nearby, then they bolted into the water.

"Are they coming for us?" Honorine asked as she watched the reptiles slither through the brackish river, only eyes and snouts and the tip of a waving tail cutting above the water.

"Don't worry about the caimans and the crocodiles," said Astraea, her wings rising over her shoulders. "Worry about that."

Around the bend, the broadside of an airship hovered just above the water, its name visible in looping gold script that reflected the light from the *Carina*'s lanterns. The *Black Owl*. They were staring down a deck lined with cannons, so close that the starglass ammunition was already glowing in the round mouths of the barrels.

"Duck," Astraea commanded as the cannons fired near-simultaneously, heaving a dozen shots toward the *Carina*. They ripped through leaves and branches, knocking down one knotted old apple tree and blowing a hole in the railings at the front of the ship.

"Eridanus!" Astraea shouted as the *Carina* plunged into a wall of thick yellow-green smoke.

She stepped into a little clearing among the trees, lowered her head, and raised her spiny fin. The air trembled and came crackling to life as a controlled thunderstorm began to form ahead of them, only as wide as the river.

"Scorpio!" Astraea called next. Honorine barely dove out of the way in time as the huge arachnid charged out of the trees and crashed into the water before scuttling off into the jungle.

"Will he be all right out there?" Honorine asked as he faded into a trail of bowing treetops.

"He'll be fine," Lux said.

Up ahead, the thunderstorm sent down a sheet of rain that cleared the green smoke, revealing the airship with cannons already reloaded.

"Watch your heads!" Astraea shouted before the second volley of shots screamed past, taking out more branches and crashing through the deck. The *Carina* sailed through another wave of smoke as the airship attempted to turn away and lift higher over the river. But Eridanus sent her storm to hover above it, drenching it and forcing it lower, away from the blinding lightning.

"If that strikes the balloon, it'll explode," Honorine warned.

"Yes, we've seen that before," said Lux as they chased the airship around a bend in the river, headed toward what looked like a huge white sail floating eerily in the distance. As they drew closer, Honorine realized that it was, in fact, a gigantic web being woven by thousands of huge spiders.

"That is going to keep this ship busy while we make our exit," Astraea said.

As the airship hit the web and stuck fast, the *Carina* began to lift out of the water. The storm, full of momentum, rolled on, dissolving into a patter of rain.

Honorine held her breath as the *Carina* soared up into the air, then shouted in delight as they cleared the top of the airship and sailed past it. Even Lux gave a short howl of approval as they continued to rise over the river.

Just as they rose above the treetops, a last volley of cannon fire shot toward them, hitting the underside of the ship and blasting through the deck. One shot came up through the deck at a strange angle, taking out a railing, and Sirona along with it.

The rest of the crew gasped as shards of broken cannonball turned her into a burst of green sparks. Honorine leaned over the side, watching them drift back down into the jungle.

"It's all right!" Astraea called. "We'll pick her up when we come about!"

The ship was starting to turn, to bank away from the river and head out over the jungle. They dipped low again to gather up Scorpio as he raced out of the trees and onto the riverbank, and then leaped aboard the ship.

"Tell the Mapmaker to turn back to starboard!" Astraea said. "To recover Sirona."

Scorpio scuttled away immediately, back into the forest of the *Carina*, toward the helm of the ship.

"Stay back from the rail!" Astraea instructed, though it looked more like a hole to Honorine. But the grapevines were already growing back, curling over themselves and twisting along the outer edge of the deck, which filled in with tree roots that rose up to meet the vines.

The ship pitched suddenly as it banked hard toward the fading cloud of green sparks that had been Sirona just a moment before. Honorine slipped on the sandy deck, sliding right toward the hole in the railing, which finished closing just in time to keep her from tumbling over the side.

"Keep an eye to starboard!" Astraea shouted.

"There!" Honorine shouted back, pointing at a glowing green light shining through a fan of huge green leaves.

Lux leaped over the side of the ship, landed with a spray of sparks, and took off at a gallop, turning into a bluish-white streak crashing through the trees.

"Wait!" Honorine said as she flung one leg over the rail, her heart thumping. It was too dangerous for him to go, too! He could be captured by Nautilus any time he was off the *Carina*.

"Honorine, don't you move!" Astraea shouted, which wouldn't have stopped her. What did was a blinding flash of golden light, followed by a burst of huge green sparks that blossomed out of the jungle like a firework. It looked almost exactly like when Leo had been captured.

"Sirona!" she shouted into the jungle. And then, "*Lux!*"

For a moment, there was only silence. Then, from under the trees, Lux came bounding back, ears flattened to his head.

"Up!" he shouted. "Take us up!"

He made a mighty leap and landed on the deck, skidding to a halt and leaving long burn marks on the wood. The *Carina*'s nose swung up sharply, just in time for a perfect view of a charred patch of ground a few feet from the riverbank, where Sirona had been standing just a moment before.

"He has her," Lux said. "Nothing we can do now. We have to get away."

While Eridanus called up another storm to shield them as they launched into the sky, the *Carina* and its passengers left the jungle behind.

The Abandoned Temple

The Mapmaker was right. Nowhere was safe. And now Honorine was aware of it with every breath and every thump of her heart. Even tucked away aboard the *Carina*, thousands of feet above the earth, curled in a plump armchair in Lord Vidalia's study, she still felt as if she were down on the banks of the river, searching for Sirona, always too far behind to save her.

The crew had scattered the moment they were out of Nautilus's reach in the Sea of Ether. There was little to say as they focused on sailing for Libra before it was too late.

Honorine spent nearly all her time in Lord Vidalia's study. She hadn't seen the Mapmaker since they left the Amazon, and she was growing ever more anxious about the next, inevitable encounter with Nautilus. Lux and Lord Vidalia assured her that there was little she could have done to prevent losing Sirona. But Honorine felt there must have been some way she could have helped. And the next time, she was going to be ready. She wasn't going to watch anyone else be stolen away.

They needed her. And she needed them. What would happen if one of Nautilus's cannonballs or Francis's stone bullets hit *her* instead of a full Mordant? She wouldn't just burst into sparks like Leo or Sirona. She couldn't be sure she would survive the way they could.

How could she stop Nautilus? Did she even have any ideas on how to begin?

In any tally she took, the answers were no. At least, not while she was on the *Carina*. She couldn't stop Nautilus from using a machine she had never even seen before. The longer she sailed with the Mordant, the more she began to think—though she would never tell the Mapmaker, or Astraea, or even Lux—that the only way for her to be useful was if she was on the *Gaslight*. Time, measured or not, was running out, and it wasn't just Honorine's own life on the line. It was Francis's, if the Mapmaker decided not to protect him any longer. It was the rest of the *Gaslight*'s crew, if Nautilus couldn't be stopped. It was any chance to one day be reunited with her mother, or even know her name. And if there were murderous beasts lurking behind a fragile gateway that only the Mordant could guard, it was the lives of everyone on Earth.

When they landed to look for Libra, Honorine wanted to be ready. She wanted to take action and be useful. And the only way she knew how was to start building something. The Mapmaker might not like the idea of more machines, she thought, but he could hardly object to anything she made that could prevent Nautilus from capturing another Mordant. The first step was to take apart one of Francis's bees and figure out exactly how they worked.

She was deep into the project, surrounded by a table of dissected copper insect carapaces, when she heard a familiar but unexpected fluttering from across the room.

"Ah, there you are. Hard at work."

Honorine looked up, past Lord Vidalia asleep in his armchair, to see Astraea at the bottom of the steps, staring uncomfortably into the room.

"Astraea," Honorine said, setting down a disarticulated bee wing. "I've never seen you down here before."

"This place reminds me of being underground," Astraea replied. "I don't like being underground."

She stepped cautiously up to the table, examining the bits of wings and legs and striped copper abdomens arranged in neat little rows.

"What are you doing here?" she asked, holding her wings stiffly and her hands tight to her chest as she leaned in as close as she dared.

"I'm trying to find a way to help," Honorine said. "We'll reach Libra soon, and if Nautilus is there—again—I want to be able to do something this time."

Astraea raised an eyebrow. "And this is going to help?"

Honorine sighed and let her hands drop to her sides. The bees were surprisingly complicated in their construction, and she did not have the energy or the inclination to try to explain any of it, especially to Astraea, who not only had no interest in machines, but she also seemed to distrust them quite thoroughly.

"These came from Nautilus's ship," Honorine said. "If I can at least figure out how he's using them, then maybe I can find a way to use them to our advantage."

"That seems reasonable," Astraea said with a nod. "Use his own weapons against him. Are you going to be able to do it?"

Frustration bubbled up in Honorine's stomach, rising through her chest and into her shoulders, before causing her cheeks to flush bright pink.

"I don't know," she muttered.

Astraea looked around uncomfortably, tilting her head, which made her look more birdlike. "You seem discouraged," she said.

"Of course I am!" Honorine replied. "I can't help you. I can't help Francis. We're running out of time to catch Nautilus!"

Astraea nodded again, her face remaining blank. She was never particularly warm or comforting, and her attempts to be helpful or supportive only made her seem more rigid and difficult to talk to.

"Perhaps this isn't the way," she said, narrowing her eyes at the field of little copper bodies and jointed brass legs.

"This is the only way," Honorine said, pushing back from the table and crossing her arms. "For me, I mean. I don't know what else to do, besides try to work out how to stop Nautilus's machines. But this is the closest thing I have to Nautilus's machines, and he didn't—"

She stopped herself. She was about to say *he didn't even build these*, but no one on the *Carina* besides herself knew that these bees had been made by Francis, and something in her warned, harsh and stern as Agnes ever was, to keep that information to herself for the time being.

"He didn't…make these very…easy to understand," Honorine finished, fumbling through an obvious lie.

Astraea's eyes remained as cold and steady as ever, as her brow slowly crushed together in an uncomfortably suspicious expression. She seemed about to ask further questions that Honorine most likely couldn't answer, when a tremendous crack of thunder rang outside the study walls. Lord Vidalia stirred in his chair, waking with an interrupted snore.

"What was I saying?" he mumbled, sitting up and patting the desk in front of him, as if having woken from a dream of filling out paperwork.

"You weren't saying anything," Astraea replied. "We're descending, and we should probably assemble upstairs to see why."

Astraea flitted ahead, swooping up the stairs and out onto the deck. Honorine lagged behind, waiting for Lord Vidalia to rise unsteadily from his chair and make his way up the stairs with stiff, labored steps. His health seemed much worse without Sirona around to provide tinctures and remedies, but he rarely complained. This time he seemed particularly slow, his steps dragging, his grip unsteady on the handle of his cane.

"Have you had your tea today?" Honorine asked, reaching out a hand to help him over a rather tall root at the foot of the steps.

"Yes, I have," he said, taking her hand instead of waving her away. His fingers felt brittle and weak. "Two cups."

"Perhaps you should have another," Honorine said.

Lord Vidalia shook his head, then stepped up close, his gaze shuttling from the stairway back to Honorine several times as he spoke.

"Remember what I said when you first arrived. You do not want the Mapmaker as your enemy. He may be away from the ship for long stretches of time, but he keeps a keen eye on us. Don't let him see what you're doing down here."

Honorine frowned. "I'm just trying to be helpful."

"Oh, you have been, and now he trusts you, I think," Lord Vidalia continued. "Don't give him a reason—*any* reason—to doubt you. It'll be the end of you."

Honorine wanted to protest, but Lord Vidalia wasn't scolding. He was warning. He patted her on the shoulder as he started up the stairs, taking each one with careful steps.

The *Carina* was sailing quite low when Honorine and Lord Vidalia stepped out onto the deck. Eridanus was already assembling a compact thunderstorm, the dark clouds flashing with lightning just off the port side of the ship. Below them was a sea of soft, fat clouds, huddled together and barely drifting, blocking out the world. Astraea peered down over the railing, her wings dark silhouettes against the bright clouds.

"Where are we?" Honorine asked as a flash of pale lightning brightened the forest. Eridanus's storm was drawing closer.

"It should be the eastern Andes," Astraea said. "Ah yes, look up there."

Straight ahead, a sharp, dark ridge rose up through the clouds like a jagged black eyetooth. The mountain peak was capped with a temple built from huge beams of dark wood covered in fine golden moss and skirted by wide, grassy paths cutting back and forth across the steep grade of the mountain slope, down into the valleys below.

"That's Libra's temple," Astraea said.

"Already?" Honorine asked. "It seems like we just left the river."

The bees weren't ready. She didn't know what she would do when Nautilus turned up again. She needed just a little more time.

"We're not terribly far from the coast," Astraea said, raising her wings to shield Honorine and Lord Vidalia from a spattering of rain.

The *Carina* slowly circled the temple on the mountain peak. Honorine thought of the images of Libra from Lord Vidalia's books and journal. She was depicted differently in each illustration, with clothing and features familiar to the people of whatever region she was in at the time. Her constellation was described as the scale, but she was portrayed as a woman in human form.

Though she hadn't shared her suspicions with anyone else on the ship, Honorine had begun to harbor a small seedling of hope that Libra might be her mother. And from that seed a little sprout began to burst up as the *Carina* slowed and approached very near the temple where Libra might be living that very moment. The sprout lasted until the ship came to a hovering halt. Even from above, Honorine could see that something was wrong.

Gathered around the temple, on narrow, flat terraces carved along the slope of the mountain, stood elegant houses with stone foundations, beautifully carved timber walls, and windows of wavy glass, each surrounded by little yards of stubby mountain plants. Water flowed down through carved stone channels, filling the reservoirs for the houses along the way. This was not just a monument, but a proper city, built for people to live and work.

Yet there was no one to be seen.

The Mapmaker arrived at the side of the ship.

"Are we setting down?" Astraea asked. "It doesn't look as if anyone is here."

The sprout of hope began to wilt and curl, but Honorine took a breath and stared out hopefully over the ominous landscape.

"We need to at least have a look," the Mapmaker countered. "Libra might very well still be here, holding out against Nautilus. Perhaps she sent the villagers away for their own safety."

"I don't like the look of it," Astraea said, shaking her head and stepping back from the railing. "This could be another ambush."

The Mapmaker nodded. "I will go this time. Nautilus can't do a thing to me, even if he were standing right out there in the courtyard."

Honorine looked up sharply. "I'll come as well."

"No need," the Mapmaker said, shaking his head. "Nautilus can't catch you with his machine, but that won't stop his men from picking you up and carrying you off."

"But I want to help," Honorine said, struggling to come up with an excuse to get onto the mountain and see Libra for herself. If she was there but wouldn't come with them, Honorine might completely miss a chance to meet her mother. "I don't feel like I've done enough yet. I want to be useful. I persuaded Eridanus to join us. I could do the same with Libra."

The Mapmaker took in an impatient breath.

"Fine, then. We're already wasting too much time. But hurry. This will be just a quick look around. We'll know if Libra is here as soon as we get into that temple."

The *Carina* drifted toward the jutting rooftop of a house near the peak of the mountain. They hopped across from the ship to the roof, and then made their way up a short rise to the foot of the temple. It was as quiet and dead as the rest of the town. The ground was covered in a great circular wash of burned grass and ash, spreading up the steps to the temple's open arched doorway. Lines of flags strung over the courtyard still fluttered in the thin air, their edges singed and blackened.

In the precise center of the great circle of ash, two small footprints stood out, the grass dead and white beneath.

"Well, I think we can stop looking," the Mapmaker said. His eyes flashed the color of lightning, and his fists tightened at his sides, the blue star pulsing on the top of his hand. "This is the last place she stood upon this earth."

He stepped cautiously around the perimeter of the ash, careful to keep his boots from touching the singed grass. Honorine briefly explored the courtyard and the steps to the open door of the temple. Inside, she could see gray stone statues and brilliantly colorful weavings hanging on the walls and across the ceiling. But there was no Libra. A tug in her heart told her the place was barren and deserted.

"How very curious that Nautilus managed to get all the way here and then back to Eridanus before we could even reach the coast," the Mapmaker said, standing at the foot of the temple steps, directly in front of Honorine.

"That airship of his must be very fast," she replied.

"Or he knew where we were going," the Mapmaker continued. "But how could that be possible?" He reached out toward Honorine and opened his hand, revealing a copper bee resting on his palm. "Maybe this had something to do with it?"

It suddenly felt very cold on the mountain, and it wasn't the altitude or Eridanus's storm rolling overhead. It was a fear shooting through Honorine from the inside out, threatening to swell into a panic.

"Could be," Honorine said, trying to look as if nothing was wrong, while her heart pounded so anxiously that she began to feel light-headed.

"And what does it do?" the Mapmaker asked.

"It...it finds Mordant," Honorine said.

"Do you know how?" the Mapmaker asked. "I know you've been tinkering with these, down in Lord Vidalia's study. And I'm guessing you don't want to tell me what you know."

"But I *do*," Honorine said, taking a half step back from him. "I only wish there was something to tell. Nautilus uses those to track Mordant, but I don't know exactly how he uses them. I've been trying to figure out—"

"And what if you're wrong?" the Mapmaker snapped. "What if you've made a mistake, and these are telling him everywhere we've traveled, and where we are right now?"

"Well, I suppose I could be," Honorine said. "But then he already knows. So we might as well try to figure out how he's doing it so we can find a way to fight back, right? Isn't that what we're trying to do?"

"Of course," the Mapmaker said, and his tone made Honorine pause, just for a moment. His eyes had returned to a calmer blue. "That's a perfectly reasonable plan. But you see, I am responsible for everyone on the *Carina*. Which means I need to know what's happening, because I can't protect us from what I don't know. Do you see?"

Honorine swallowed, her cheeks still flushed and warm, and nodded, looking down at the charred ground and the stark footprints in the pale grass.

"Someone else is telling you not to trust me," the Mapmaker said. "That wolf and I have never been square."

Honorine shook her head. "Lux hasn't said anything against you. No one has. I just haven't had much occasion to trust anyone, in my life. It's as new to me as flying forests or talking wolves or mechanical bees."

The Mapmaker, after a pause, gave her a faint half grin.

"Yes, well, I suppose being raised as you were, there wasn't much around that couldn't be taken away. But I would never take anything from you, Honorine, to be petty or controlling. I would never keep you from something, or someone, without reason."

The heat flushed hotter in her cheeks, and she looked away again.

"What, the boy? Francis?" the Mapmaker asked. "I haven't done a thing to harm him, Honorine, I swear—"

"No, I know that," Honorine said. "You're right, you haven't kept anything from me. But the others have."

The Mapmaker looked from Honorine to the ground with a puzzled expression that eventually faded into realization.

"Ah, your mother," he said. "Yes, I suppose that is something you would want to know."

"Of course," Honorine said.

"I can tell you this. She is not Libra."

The seed of hope withered, but it was almost with relief. If Libra wasn't her mother, then her mother could still be out there, somewhere in the world.

"Does that help?" the Mapmaker asked. "Do you trust me, just a little bit more now?"

Honorine nodded. The Mapmaker nodded in reply.

"Well then, I feel I can trust you with this," he said as he handed her the bee. Honorine clutched it in her hand and nodded again.

The Mapmaker pointed at the footprints outlined in the ash. "With Libra gone, there is only one left. Sagittarius, the archer. The muse of Defense. The good news is I believe I know exactly where he is. The downside, however, is that if Nautilus gets to him before we do, he can use the archer to defend his ship, and we won't be able to stop him."

"Well, the longer we stay on this mountain, the farther Nautilus gets from here," Honorine said.

"Quite right," the Mapmaker replied. "So we'd best get going. We are now in a race for our lives."

A Key from the Ironwood Tree

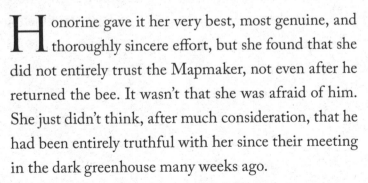

Honorine gave it her very best, most genuine, and thoroughly sincere effort, but she found that she did not entirely trust the Mapmaker, not even after he returned the bee. It wasn't that she was afraid of him. She just didn't think, after much consideration, that he had been entirely truthful with her since their meeting in the dark greenhouse many weeks ago.

She did not say this to the Mapmaker, nor anyone else on the ship. Instead, while the *Carina* raced to reach the archer first, Honorine settled back into the study to work on the mechanical bees and her own personal theories on what exactly was happening around her.

Her first concern was the Mapmaker himself. She believed he was rightly alarmed about Nautilus's ability to hunt and capture the Mordant. She also believed that he wanted Nautilus stopped, yet she had seen him send a wave high and strong enough to nearly capsize the *Gaslight* with only a gesture of his hands. An ability of that kind could surely stop Nautilus cold, if that was what the Mapmaker wanted. It almost felt as if he was biding his time, waiting for a specific moment, but she could not begin to imagine what that would be.

The other bit she did not completely believe was that the archer was the last Mordant left on Earth, aside from the handful of passengers on the *Carina*. He might have been almost the last, but there had to be at least one more....

Her mother.

She had thought about it for hours, down in the study. She didn't understand exactly why Nautilus would want to track down all those Mordant. Except if it was to find his lost love. This thought buoyed Honorine when she was feeling frustrated with the increasingly uncooperative bee project. Lord Vidalia watched her work intently, though often from a comfortable chair near the woodstove, with a thick blanket tucked over his legs and a cup of tea within reach. Sirona had been doing much more for him than he would admit, but Honorine could see it, as he moved slower, slept more, and tried unsuccessfully to hide the increasing winces and grunts when he moved his old joints to lift a pen or a book or his ever more stooped body.

He was curled in his chair, asleep, and looked more like a knotted length of wood than a man, when Honorine managed to get her first taken-apart-and-repaired bee to fly. Unfortunately, it was in a straight line right into his crown, the little copper projectile striking him just above his right eye before dropping onto his blanketed lap.

"Hmm?" he mumbled as he stirred, his eyes each prying open in their own time. "What's this, then?"

With some difficulty, he picked up the bee from his blanket.

"This seems so familiar," he said. "Like I've seen it before."

"You have," Honorine said. "I've been working on them right over here for some time."

Lord Vidalia's memory seemed faulty at times, and he would ask odd questions or suddenly look quite confused about where he was, or whom he was with. Honorine wasn't sure how much more serious a symptom this was than stiff hands or an unsteady gait, so she tried to help him along as best she could.

"You made these?" Lord Vidalia asked. "How remarkable."

"No, I did not make them," Honorine explained. "Actually, Francis did."

"Ah, Francis," Lord Vidalia said with a nod. Francis he always remembered.

"He's a very good inventor, it seems," Honorine said.

Lord Vidalia smiled. "He should be," he said. "Growing up with you. I do hope I might see him again one day."

"When this bother with Nautilus is over, you will."

"I'm sure I will," said Lord Vidalia. "Though he'll hardly know me. I only saw him as a wee baby. So he's never really met me."

"I've only met my father once," Honorine said. "And I didn't know he was my father at the time, so I suppose it almost doesn't count, now, does it?"

She imagined that Nautilus would have been much different if he had known who she was when he first met her.

"Well, if you do see Francis before I do," said Lord Vidalia, "tell him to look up the story of the Stolen Fire. From mythology. If he's read anything from my study, he'll know it."

Honorine looked up, suddenly hit with a strong but cloudy memory.

"I've heard of that before," she said. "You wrote it in your—"

She was about to say *journal*, but Lord Vidalia interrupted her.

"And do give your mother my regards, if you should see her first," he said as he set the bee down, pulled off his blanket, and prepared to get to his feet.

"I will, if I ever meet her," Honorine said as she took his hand to help him up. "I don't even know her name, you know."

"Oh, well, I do," Lord Vidalia said absently as he shuffled around gathering teacups left around the room.

Honorine's heart nearly stopped.

"Or, I used to know," he added, stacking cups with the soft clink of delicate china. "The Mapmaker knows.

And Astraea and Lux, I'm fairly certain. Oh, and the ship, of course."

"The ship?" Honorine asked.

"Well, yes," Lord Vidalia said. "It's a living thing, isn't it? The ship of the stars. Living things have knowledge, even if it's locked up in a form we can't quite understand."

Locked up.

Honorine's heart came to a full stop this time, before starting up just quickly enough to keep her from fainting dead to the floor. But she composed herself, brought Lord Vidalia a chair, and prepared his tea. When he finally settled back in with a book and some blank pages, Honorine scribbled a note on a scrap of parchment and slipped out onto the main deck of the ship.

It was empty and quiet, apart from the chirp of crickets. Scorpio was somewhere among the trees.

She had asked every one of the Mordant about her mother, and each of them had refused to tell her a thing. But she had never thought to ask the ship herself.

But how did one ask a ship a question?

If she wanted food, she went to the orchard. If she wanted a game, she went to the pines or the willows.

What she wanted now was a secret. And secrets were kept in the cypress swamp.

She worked her way along the edge of the ship, through the pines, past the redwood forest and oak grove, and around the edge of the palm oasis. With a quick look around and a check for any indicators on her watch, she slipped into the forbidden swamp.

She reached the edge of the brackish water but found her courage flagging with each step into the wet sand and deepening water. Among the tall, straight trunks of cypress, she spotted the ironwood tree, on a tiny hill at the edge of the swamp.

It stood out, its shape more bent and bushy, its black bark streaked with rust-colored moss, and no lanterns at all in its sparse, twisted branches, hanging low enough to reach.

Honorine snuck up to the tree, just as she had when she'd asked it for her tools, the little scrap of parchment clutched too tightly in her hand. This time, instead of a request for an item, she had written on the little scrap, *The name of my mother.* She wedged the parchment securely in the trunk, under a lower branch, and then took a step back. It disappeared, as if melting into the wood, and a little rustle of wind shook the leaves high overhead. And then another noise, much closer and much more alarming, reached her ears. Footsteps, splashing through the silty water. Honorine pressed herself against the ironwood's trunk and looked back into the swamp, even though she already knew who was coming.

The Mapmaker.

She couldn't run. The water around would splash, giving her away at once. With few other options, she grabbed the lowest branch and swung up into the ironwood tree.

Within moments, the Mapmaker passed directly under the tree, heading toward the palm oasis.

Honorine stood up on the branch, trying to see where he'd gone. When she turned back around, she saw something hanging on the next branch over, quite near the trunk.

A key.

It was small and dark, and shaped like an old iron skeleton key, though it was made of pure black wood. She plucked it down, holding it for a minute while her heart pounded again, all the way up into her ears.

But what was she supposed to do with a key? There were no locked doors on the *Carina*. She had never encountered anything, not even a chest or cupboard, that required a key to open it. Once again, she quickly realized, the thing she hadn't yet found would be in a place she hadn't looked before. The swamp.

She checked briefly for the Mapmaker. Then she slipped from the tree and waded in deeper as quickly as she dared.

To her relief, the swamp did not continue on very far past the ironwood tree. The water receded as fast as it had deepened and rose back up to a bank of dark sand and a second tier of deck. It was thick with vines and moss hanging over a solid wooden wall with a single small door right in the center.

She paused in front of the door, expecting to be discovered by someone, anyone, lurking about in the dimly lit swamp. But no objection came as she fit the key into the lock under the silver doorknob.

It turned almost without effort. The door swung open, leading into a low, rounded room, the roof barely higher than Honorine's head. It was impossible to see what the walls were made of, for it was nearly pitch black. The only light came from tiny incandescent points of clear crystal embedded in the domed roof. At first, it seemed like a random scattering of lights. But as her eyes adjusted, Honorine noticed a pattern, a slightly misshapen hook outlined in spots of light.

It was the constellation of Scorpio. Nearby, she found Virgo (for Astraea), Lupus (for Lux), Corvus, Eridanus, Sagittarius, one she did not recognize at all, and finally, the long sprawling formation of Andromeda.

All of these were constellations of Mordant who Nautilus hadn't captured yet. Six were on the ship. One was probably the Mapmaker's unnamed constellation. And the last one was Andromeda.

It had to be her. Honorine's mother.

Honorine wanted to stay there, in that dim little room, staring at those tiny spots of light, but she didn't dare linger much longer. She locked the door on her way out and tucked the key in her pocket.

She had to go right back to Lord Vidalia's study, to his old almanacs, and confirm that she was right about the constellation. If she wasn't, she would have to come back and check again, and it would be too dangerous to keep sneaking in and out of the swamp.

In her excitement, she was much less cautious on the way out. There was much more splashing as she rushed back toward the palm oasis, and she had nearly reached it when a voice stopped her, dead as stone, in midstride.

"And what might you be doing so near to my quarters?"

The Mapmaker.

He took a step forward, extending his hand with the star-shaped mark embedded under the skin. It wasn't exactly a tattoo, though that would be the closest description. This looked more like veins, Honorine realized as the Mapmaker approached.

"I don't fault you for being curious," the Mapmaker said. "Everyone has their secrets, and their darkest wishes."

He seemed tired. His eyes were very dark and still. His steps slow and deliberate.

"What did you find in there?"

He nodded toward the swamp behind her. Honorine did not look back.

"What is it that you want most in the world?"

As soon as he asked, she knew, as if he had unlocked a door long closed off in her mind. She saw herself, and, to her surprise, Nautilus, and also a woman, though her exact features were hazy and undefined. Honorine was with them, together. It was a mother and father, a real family.

The Mapmaker took her hand, the way he had the very first time she'd met him. His skin was uncomfortably warm and unusually dry. The blue mark began to glow once more.

"What a perfectly reasonable wish," the Mapmaker said. "A family for a girl who always believed she was an orphan." He shook his head. "And now the difficult part. Let me show you what you must do to make your vision come true."

The Mapmaker and the trees and the world around her faded out, as if a curtain had just dropped in front of Honorine's eyes. A moment later the curtain rose again, and an image appeared, like watching a dream playing out in front of her.

She was on the deck of the *Gaslight*, dressed in a finely tailored blue jacket, just like the rest of the crew. She walked into a laboratory, under a beautifully monstrous machine made of glass globes on slender copper pipes, hanging inside that huge greenhouse dome on the deck of the ship. Honorine watched herself walk to the controls, turn the dials with precision, and pull the switch that brought the smoldering globes overhead to life. In the vision, the machine flared with a crash of electricity and wild sparks. When the blinding light settled, Honorine was holding a globe containing the tiny form of the Mapmaker under a shell of marbled amber.

Then the image shifted, and she was standing on top of a mountain, her face lit by the glow of the amber globe in her hands. Inside, the Mapmaker pleaded silently with her, but she ignored him, looking down into a wide hole in the ground at her feet. Far, far below, a pool of monsters writhed in a lake of lava. Spines and horns and thorny claws reached up toward her from somewhere deep below the earth.

Honorine held out the globe. She looked one last time at the Mapmaker. Then she dropped him, still in his golden prison, down into the waiting jaws of a slithering beast that swallowed him in one hungry snap.

Over the mountain, a collection of stars flickered and failed, growing eternally cold and black, disappearing into the velvet darkness. And the Mapmaker was never seen, never written of, never spoken of for all the rest of time.

The vision faded. Honorine was back on the *Carina*, her arm tingling and lifeless. She looked up at the Mapmaker, still standing before her, but with his hand at his side. "That is the path that will bring you what you desire."

"I wouldn't do that," Honorine said.

"Not to be with your mother? Your father?" he asked. "You would sacrifice your own family for me? You would live out the rest of your life as an orphan, at least in practice, to spare *me*?"

Now she was terribly conflicted and confused.

"You saw Nautilus's machine," the Mapmaker said. Honorine nodded. "I saw it, too, when it was just an idea. A little kernel of inspiration in his mind."

"You knew he would try to capture the Mordant?" Honorine asked.

"I knew he could, if he wanted to," the Mapmaker said. "He had the ability. It was just a matter of whether he would use it. I'm not surprised that he did."

"And you think I'm the same?" Honorine asked. "You think I would do that to you, just to get what I wanted?"

"I've seen men and women do far worse things, for far less reward," the Mapmaker said. "And you see now why it is such a risk for me to trust you. I've known this from the moment we first shook hands."

Honorine did not know what to say. There was no way to convince him that she wouldn't betray him, especially if he was right. What if the only way to get her mother back was to help Nautilus? To capture the Mapmaker? Could she give up the chance to have her mother and father back just to let the Mapmaker go free? She wanted to believe that she would. At least, she wouldn't throw him into a pit of monsters.

"I don't believe I would do something like that," she said finally.

"Remember that, when the time comes," the Mapmaker replied. "And remember this—an ironwood key will unlock any door. But you might not like what you find on the other side. Some doors are locked for a reason."

Honorine barely left the study for the rest of the trip, working at a hurried pace as the *Carina* flew across the sky in a race against Nautilus, sailing on the sea below.

They were nearly halfway across the Atlantic Ocean when she figured out the last bit of the bees' function, and called the Mapmaker down to the study to demonstrate.

"It's fairly simply, really. Each bee is assigned a location with this mechanism here."

She pointed to the first of three bees arranged on a little scrap of velvet. The back half of its abdomen lifted up to show a simple system of three tiny tumblers, with numbers and letters that could be arranged in different patterns.

"The next step is the trigger, here." Honorine pointed to the second bee. The top of the head was lifted up, revealing a little switch connected to the bee's starglass eyes. "If these come in close-enough contact with a Mordant, it triggers this switch on the inside, and the eyes light up."

"So how does this tell Nautilus where we are?" the Mapmaker questioned.

"That's the best part," Honorine said, moving on to the last bee. "The bees will fly over any location in a pattern, for a set amount of time, and then return back to the hive. So you pick a code for the location, you send the bee out there, and if it comes back with the switch triggered, there's a Mordant in that location."

The Mapmaker nodded.

"I assigned each of these bees to a part of the *Carina*. One for the orchard, one for the pine forest, and one for the oak grove. Look, these two bees lit up."

She picked up the two bees with lighted starglass eyes.

"That means there was a Mordant in the orchard and one in the oak grove when the bees were there," Honorine said. "And—if this worked—no one in the pine forest. Shall we check?"

She led the Mapmaker to the orchard, where Lux was waiting under a pear tree, and then to the oaks, where they found Eridanus standing stoically under the mossy boughs.

"Okay, I admit I asked them to wait here for the bees to find," Honorine said.

"But it worked just as you predicted," said the Mapmaker.

"There's only one thing I haven't figured out," Honorine continued. "Somehow, Nautilus knows which Mordant the bees have found. I can't get them to be that specific. They light up for any of you. But I still have an idea about how we might use these. We could trigger some bees in the wrong place and send them back to Nautilus, to distract him while we go after the archer."

"Are you sure that will work?" said the Mapmaker. "Wouldn't he know they've been tampered with?"

"Maybe," Honorine said. "But maybe we'll hit a correct code just by chance, maybe we won't. But at least we'll confuse them. At best, they might think every bee is malfunctioning, or that there is another Mordant out there they've overlooked. That machine of his takes time to operate. After they caught Leo, they couldn't go after Corvus right away. So maybe we can trick them into hunting a Mordant they can't catch. At the worst, if they're distracted trying to sort out the accurate bees from the inaccurate ones, maybe that gets us a little extra time."

The Mapmaker nodded again, then scratched his chin, and finally broke out into a wide grin.

"Well, let's give it a try," he said. "Honorine, prepare your bees."

It took her the rest of the journey to get the bees ready to fly. Only the first one she'd disassembled and accidentally set on fire couldn't be salvaged. By the time the Mapmaker gave her fair warning that they would be making landfall, she had eleven fully functioning bees, and only one left that was giving her problems.

The mechanism that opened the rear part of the bee seemed to be jammed. She had left it for last, thinking that there were already enough, if she couldn't get it to work. But now she decided that any extra help they could get was worth the trouble. She tried it one more time.

The bee finally opened. And inside she found not a set of tumblers like in the other bees, but a tightly curled bit of paper. She rolled it open to reveal a note. A note written to her.

Honorine,
If you find this, look for me in the dunes.
—Francis

The Gates Beneath the Sand

L ord Vidalia did not join them on the deck for the first flight of the bees. His health was growing grave enough that he couldn't navigate the stairs. He slept more often and seemed confused for long stretches when he woke. Sirona was the only one who could help him now, and Honorine felt the added weight of his worsening condition as they approached the eastern African shore in search of Sagittarius. She couldn't let anything happen to Lord Vidalia before he had a chance to see Francis again.

The *Carina* was already below the Sea of Ether, back in the proper earthly atmosphere, when Honorine emerged on the deck.

Eridanus and Astraea were standing under a clump of birch trees near the rail as Honorine approached with Lux and the basket of bees. The landscape ahead of them was very different from the last places they had visited. Stretched across the entire length of the horizon was the ocean breaking on a land of frozen red waves of sandstone that rolled away for miles, before rising into sand dunes as tall as mountains.

"Where are we now?" Honorine asked.

"The oldest desert in the world," Lux replied.

"How do you find anyone in there?" Honorine asked, looking up and down the endless, empty coast. There were no houses, no roads, no towns, just a repeating landscape of rock and sand. She was thinking not of the archer, hidden somewhere in the dunes, but of Francis, out there possibly all on his own.

"First, you set your bees loose," Lux said, pointing his nose toward the basket. "Nautilus is here already, and we need to distract him."

"What?" Honorine said with a gasp.

"I spotted his ship off the coast as we came back

down from the Ether," Eridanus said. "I sent a small thunderstorm to slow him, but he will most likely make landfall today."

"Which means we need to be back in the sky before the sun rises," Astraea added. "Are you ready?"

Honorine nodded. The full moon was setting swiftly beneath the black ocean, which meant that sunrise was soon to follow. There was not much time. She took the lid off her basket of bees, humming with the vibrations of their little wings, and leaned it onto the railing. One by one, they rose and disappeared into the night, green eyes glowing with sabotaged news.

With the bees set in Nautilus's path, the *Carina* banked and began to sail south, riding along the frothy white coastline where the blue-black sea met the deep red shore.

"I haven't seen daylight in . . . I don't even know. But it feels like a very long time," Honorine said to Lux as they sat on a little rise of tufted grass in the orchard, where they had a clear view off to the east. She watched the horizon, hoping for just a glimpse of sunlight before their task was complete.

"It's all very bright," he said with a bit of a growl. "I never really understood the appeal of daytime."

"Yes, but you're just an old grouch about some things," Honorine said.

"Indeed," Lux said. She patted him on the shoulder. For a moment, she considered telling him about the note from Francis, but there were already enough distractions. Nautilus was headed straight for them, and there wasn't much time to find Sagittarius and get safely back into the sky.

The *Carina* banked again and headed inland, setting down at the foot of a mountainous sand dune that looked like every other spot up and down the coast. The Mapmaker came down from the wheel of the ship when they were settled.

"All right," he said as he adjusted his jacket sleeves. "Nautilus was a little too close for my comfort as we came in. For safety, Honorine and I will go fetch the archer. The rest of you wait here, to move the ship if we have to."

"But this should be quick," Lux said, his fur rippling a bit with light. "I can help you with the archer if he's reluctant to come along."

"We cannot risk it," the Mapmaker said. "Nautilus knows you're with us, after that last encounter in the jungle. We need you on this ship when we return."

Lux reluctantly agreed, giving Honorine a quick look of concern, or perhaps warning, before she slipped over the railing of the ship and dropped down onto the sand. It was bone-dry and slipped away from her feet, but the landing was still hard, and she toppled over into a dusty cloud of fine red grit.

"Careful," the Mapmaker said, helping her up. "It doesn't take much to stir this up, and it'll be difficult enough to find the cavern without a face full of sand."

"It doesn't look like there's anything here, though," she said, getting to her feet.

"Oh, it's here," said the Mapmaker. "It's just very hard to find. Now, I haven't done this in a while, so forgive me if I'm a bit rusty."

Then he held his arms straight down, palms flat and facing the ground. The sand beneath him began to tremble and vibrate. The blue star on his hand glowed. Then the ground gave a quick but violent shudder, knocking Honorine down again and sending a tremor right toward the sand dune. It began to crumble and slide, the sand rolling away until it revealed what looked like a tiny stone archway.

"Ah, I've still got it," the Mapmaker said, shaking out his hands and adjusting his sleeves again.

Honorine looked into the dark hole leading into the earth and felt her nerves quiver.

The Mapmaker looked back toward the coast, scanning the horizon.

"I don't see a ship," he said. "The timing should work out perfectly."

"We'll have just enough time to get the archer before Nautilus gets here?"

"We'll have enough time to get the archer and still be here when Nautilus arrives," the Mapmaker corrected.

A faint chill brushed down Honorine's spine. "Don't we want to be gone by then?" she asked.

"Not anymore," said the Mapmaker. "After this, we can finally stop running. With the archer to protect our ship, we'll be able to lure Nautilus out to open waters."

Honorine's heart began to race, though much of the rest of her went numb.

"And then what?" she asked, rising.

"Then we finally get rid of Nautilus," said the Mapmaker. "We take over that ship and sink it, if we have to."

"But what about the Mordant on the ship? Or the people?"

"The Mordant can't be hurt by a shipwreck," said the Mapmaker. "And as for the people, well, they don't appreciate their own mortality. They put themselves in harm's way. And I, unlike most of the others, respect their decision."

It was unbelievable, and yet she was surprised that she was surprised. The Mapmaker had said all along that his plan was to stop Nautilus. He never actually said that he didn't plan to do so by killing him.

"But...Francis," Honorine said. "You gave your word that you wouldn't hurt him if I helped you. And I'm helping you."

"Ah, but there's every possibility that he could survive. He has before, hasn't he?"

Honorine leaned back from him. She was in the wide-open desert, yet she had never felt so cornered.

"That's not what you promised," she said. "And you know it."

"Are you saying you'll stop helping me?" the Mapmaker asked.

"I think it's only fair that you promise that Francis will live," she said.

The Mapmaker laughed. "Honorine, he's a human being. No matter what I do, Francis is not going to live. Not forever."

"Maybe not," Honorine said. "But you don't have to go out of your way to make it happen any faster."

She felt anger building as she thought of everything she'd done to try to help the Mapmaker. He had never really offered her anything in return. And now, it seemed, he wouldn't even help her protect the people she cared about most in the world, even though he had the power to do so.

A dry breeze whistled out of the entrance to the cavern. Off in the distance, a storm cloud rumbled over the sea. Eridanus had sent a storm—that was probably it. Nautilus was racing toward them, toward his doom, and the possible death of everyone on his ship.

"You don't have to do that," she said. "We'll figure something out to get the Mordant off that ship and stop Nautilus from hurting them ever again, but *without* killing anyone."

"And if that's not possible?" the Mapmaker said. "If you have to choose between saving your father or protecting the Mordant, which would it be?"

Honorine shook her head. "But we don't have to choose! There's still time to save everyone."

"There it is!" the Mapmaker shouted, so loudly that his voice echoed down the hollow stone tunnel before them. "You're not here to help me. Or even to help Francis. What you really want is to save Nautilus. Your *father*."

"I want to help you all!" Honorine insisted. "Yes, even Nautilus, if I can! You made an agreement with Lord Vidalia when he helped you. Why not help me, as well?"

"I offered to protect his son," the Mapmaker replied. "An arrangement I would never extend to Nautilus. I shouldn't have to make deals with you, Honorine. You belong with us; you should be working in our interests, no one else's."

"I am!" Honorine shouted. "Do you still need me to prove it after all this?"

The Mapmaker smirked.

"Fine," he said, pointing into the void under the arch. "Go down into the darkness, bring the archer back ready to defend the *Carina*, and I'll believe you."

A cold breeze whistled up from the stone tunnel. Honorine's bluster and anger suddenly ebbed.

"Alone?" she squeaked. "What's down there?"

"I have no idea," the Mapmaker said. "I haven't been down there in centuries. Could be snakes, scorpions, corpses, the whole place could be collapsed into a bottomless pit. And the archer doesn't like visitors. Really anything could happen."

Honorine felt her heart thundering again.

"All right," she said, drawing up every bit of stubborn courage she had to spend. "I'll bring him back. And we will find a way to do this without anyone getting killed." Then she spun on her heel and walked through the arch.

The air smelled of wet stone and very, very old earth. It took Honorine's eyes a moment to adjust. Ahead of her was a narrow, worn trail scattered with white sand that glowed in the light of starglass fixed into the walls.

This place was rougher than the others. There was no elegantly constructed masonry or delicate pools of clear water. This was hard stone, ancient earth, and the faint scent of decay seeping out from the cold rock all around her. Honorine remembered Astraea's opinion of being underground. Astraea didn't like it one bit, and now Honorine understood why.

The narrow trail eventually widened into a broad path through a wide cavern. The walls and ceiling were covered in drawings, etchings, and paintings of antelope, scorpions, lions, and elephants in exquisite tones of yellow, red, and sandy brown. In the flickering light of the starglass, the images seemed to move across the walls. The herds of antelope galloped; cheetahs seemed to crouch and pounce.

At the farthest end of the cavern, a set of ancient, crumbling steps led up toward great, sprawling gates of thorny, twining iron vines. She was only halfway across the cavern when a sound rang out, hooves hitting stone, followed by a low, rumbling grunt that echoed through the hall, shaking the tiny pebbles on the floor.

The gates creaked open and fell forward, sending a cloud of sand out over the steps and across the cavern. Honorine ducked her head behind her arm as she heard a bellow, like that of a bull, but mixed somehow with the angry shout of a man. The galloping animals on the walls froze in place.

And then a horrifying silhouette appeared in the light.

He was immensely tall, an honest ten feet from the floor to the tip of the stout, curving bull horns sprouting from his head. His upper half was of a man with blue-black skin covered in a pattern of glowing, script-like tattoos. His lower half was like a black goat with thick fur, grotesquely bent legs, and cloven hooves shod in silver. His face was somewhere in between with a thick brow, a wide cleft nose, and very large, dark eyes. He wore a quiver of arrows on a leather strap over his shoulder and a string of luminous blue and white beads around his thick neck. He marched toward her, his hooves spitting out blue-white sparks as if they were striking flint with each step.

Honorine felt her hands trembling as she looked up into the black eyes of the archer.

"You must be Sagittarius," she said, trying to stand up tall and look him straight in the eye. "I'm Honorine."

The archer snorted. "And how, may I ask, did you find your way down into this cavern?"

"I came with the Mapmaker," she said.

"Oh?" said the archer, lifting his head. His horns left trails of sparks in the air. "Why would the Mapmaker bring a child all this way?"

"Because I am a Mordant, apparently," Honorine said. "At least half, because my mother is Andromeda."

It was the first time she had spoken the name out loud to anyone, or had claimed herself to truly be one of the Mordant.

The archer furrowed his brow and tilted his head in a posture that looked distinctly like a bull about to charge. The cavern was utterly silent for a moment as he studied her and cold enough that his breath sent up a plume of pale steam. Finally, he took several crashing steps forward and dropped to one knee. He bowed his huge head, his great, curving horns cutting through the air on either side of Honorine, surrounding her for a moment in a curtain of silver sparks.

"Long ago I vowed my allegiance to your mother," he said, holding his hand out toward her. "And so, by extension, it is yours as well."

"Thank you...?" Honorine replied, a bit stunned, as she reached out toward him, expecting perhaps a formal handshake. Instead, he clasped her tiny hand between his huge ones in a shake that might have seemed gentle to him but felt to Honorine as if it would rip her arm from its socket. "Well, then maybe you would be willing to help me. You're the defense...

person.... That's your specialty, or talent, right? Well, I need something defended."

"Do you now?" asked the archer. Over the points of his horns, Honorine caught sight of the gates at the top of the crumbling steps.

"Unless you can't leave," she said. If he truly was the muse of Defense, set to protect things, then perhaps he could not leave the gates at all. "Do you have to stay near the gates?"

He rose back to his full height, which seemed even bigger when he stood so close.

"No," he said with a shake of his head. "There's only one gateway that still requires a guard. But that is in the ruins of the Mordant city of Possideo. That gateway can still be opened. This gate"—he gestured over his shoulder—"is closed now. No one comes here."

"Then why do you stay?"

"Because *no one comes here*," he replied, his voice rolling across the floor, echoing off the walls. "I prefer to be left alone."

"Like the Mapmaker," Honorine said.

The archer's head reared back. He looked at her from the corner of his eye, the white showing, his nostrils flared.

"Nothing like him," he said in a low, rolling tone.

The archer did not care for the Mapmaker. This was even better.

"Good," Honorine said. "Because the thing I need you to protect is a ship. A great big steamship that the Mapmaker is going to attack. I need you to protect it from him, just long enough so that I can get everyone off it."

The archer nodded his horned head. "That sounds perfectly reasonable," he said.

"There's a bit more," Honorine continued with a wince. "The Mapmaker is going to expect you to protect *his* ship while he attacks the other one. So I need you to, well, seem to agree with him, while I try to figure out how to get this resolved without anyone getting killed."

The archer raised his brow. "This other ship," he said slowly. "The one you truly want protected—why? Whose ship is it?"

Honorine took a breath. There was no use hiding this from him.

"Nautilus Olyphant," she said.

The archer's eyes widened. "He's still around?" he asked. "He must have done something very clever to avoid the Mapmaker's wrath all these years."

"Well, he's built a machine," Honorine said. "And he's using it to capture the other Mordant."

The archer drew up to his full height. His tattoos pulsed and shimmered with blue light as he crossed his arms and let out a long, angry breath. For a second, Honorine could see the entire plan coming to an unpleasant end.

"He's capturing Mordant. For what purpose?"

"We don't know," she replied. "But I'm going to put a stop to it. I just need a little bit of time before the Mapmaker sinks Nautilus's ship and the captured Mordant and everyone else on it."

"So you want to double-cross the Mapmaker?" the archer said with a wicked grin.

"I...suppose so...?" Honorine said, looking up at the archer.

The archer laughed. A deep, hearty, booming laugh that bounced around the chasm.

"Then I suppose there's no time to waste," he said. "Let's be off, then."

He started down the trail toward the entrance to the cavern, his silver shod hooves creating a flurry of sparks with each step. Honorine followed quickly, her heart pounding with the fear that this was never going to work, but her mind slightly at ease with the hope that it would. She soon smelled the fresh night air drifting down into the stale cavern. She would be glad to be aboveground again. And then she saw pale daylight shining on the other side of the stone archway.

It was just past sunrise.

The archer somehow maneuvered through the narrow entrance. Honorine was just about to follow when she heard a blast, loud and sharp, that shook the ground and sent sand trickling down from the stone arch. She had heard that sound before. Cannon fire.

They were too late. Nautilus was already here.

Sandstorm

Honorine huddled in the doorway of the stone arch and peered carefully out into the morning sun shining off the red sand dunes. She could see the black clouds of the thunderstorm over the ocean and two rippling black shadows on the red stony ground. Inching farther out, she found the Mapmaker and the archer standing a dozen yards from the archway. They were looking up at the *Carina*, hovering low over the ground, and Nautilus's airship, guns firing in the *Carina*'s direction.

The cannonballs that hit the ground sent up blasts of sand, which were in turn being picked up by a building wind. Eridanus was calling the thunderstorm in from the ocean, sending it after the airship.

Then the cannon fire sputtered a bit as the storm raced up onshore in a crash of thunder and a blast of wind that at once stirred up huge clouds of sand and dust. The airship wobbled about, trying to regain its equilibrium under the storm, but in a moment, the sand and green smoke had been whipped into a thick fog that blocked everything from view: the ocean, the ships, even the Mapmaker and the archer only a few feet away. Honorine untied her silk sash and wrapped it around her nose and mouth in an attempt to keep out the flying sand, but some still managed to work its way in, sticking in her teeth and the back of her throat.

She could hear voices shouting, but she could not tell who was speaking or what they were saying. She contemplated setting out for the *Carina*. Then her thoughts jumped to Francis. If he really was out there in the dunes, he could be trapped in the mess as well, with cannonballs and lightning flying all around him.

The explosions and thunder blended together into one unending roar of noise. She could see nothing but the occasional silhouette of the ships amid the flashes of lightning and cannon fire and the gusts of flying sand. Nothing but the hands in front of her face, and her Mordant watch, secured on her wrist, with one faint spot of light in the dusty darkness.

"Lux!" Honorine shouted through her improvised face mask.

"There you are," he said as a shining white wolf outline trotted toward her. "Hurry, we have to get back to the ship."

"No! Not yet! Francis is out here!"

"In this storm?" he asked. "He'll be killed!"

"I know!" Honorine shouted back. "We have to find him! He can't stay out here alone!"

Lux's ears twitched. "All right. Hold on to my coat. And don't let go, or I won't be able to find you again."

Honorine put her hand on his shoulder, grasping a thick handful of his wiry coat. Then she pulled the end of her scarf around her head to shield her eyes and began to walk beside Lux as they picked their way across the desert sand.

With her head down and the silk whipping about her face, Honorine could see nothing but Lux's paws and her own feet. They moved painfully slow, but as the *Carina* and Nautilus's spare airship drew farther away, they kept the storm with them, until Honorine was able to look up and see a patch of open sky, the ocean, and the towering dunes silhouetted against the rising sun. But no Francis.

She shouted for him as they trudged across the rocky ground.

"Francis!" she called. "Francis! Are you out there?" Honorine called until her voice went hoarse from shouting and coughing up sand.

"Are you certain he's here?" Lux asked as they wandered first in the direction of the dunes and then toward the water. "If we don't find him soon, we'll have to head back to the *Carina*."

"He's here! We just have to look a little further!"

Suddenly, the wind swept farther back, revealing a tiny figure standing on the flat plain.

"Francis?" Honorine called out with the last shout she could manage. The figure paused, then began waving frantically in her direction.

"It's him!" Honorine croaked. Her hand slipped from Lux's shoulder, and she was jogging across the sand in an instant.

"Honorine!" Francis called, waving a hand. "You're alive!"

"So are you!" she said as she ran the final few yards toward him. They were both caked in sand and dirt from head to toe, but at least Francis had the sense to wear goggles with black reflective lenses that hid his eyes, which made him look a bit like an insect.

Before she could catch her breath or spit all the sand from her mouth, Francis lunged forward and threw his arms tightly around her.

"I didn't know," he said, his voice cracking a bit, as if a sob of relief was caught in his throat. He coughed it away, and then pulled off his goggles and wiped his eyes, trying to make it look like he was just rubbing away sand and grit. "We found everyone who was on the *Nighthawk* when she went down. Everyone except you!"

Honorine realized that Francis had no way of knowing that she'd been rescued from the cold ocean. For just a moment, she felt the weight that would have hung on to her every moment since the *Nighthawk* crashed, if Astraea had not told her that Francis had survived.

"I wish I could have talked to you," she said. "But look! I'm just fine. Have been the whole time. And I found your note!"

"I was hoping you would," he said.

"I had to try to figure out your bees," she said.

"I had to try to find you," Francis said. "And make sure you were all right."

"Well, I had to try to make sure this storm didn't kill you. You shouldn't have come out in the desert alone."

"Neither should you," Francis said. "Oh, you didn't."

His face went very long as he stared over Honorine's shoulder. She looked back to see Lux standing at a slight distance, his yellow eyes locked on Francis.

"You're not going to shoot him this time," Honorine demanded.

"No, I'm not," he replied without taking his eyes off Lux. "Tell him I'm sorry, would you?"

"Tell him yourself," Honorine said, but when she looked back, Lux had retreated a few paces.

"We shouldn't stay out here," Francis said, pointing at the ball of sand and thunder ahead of them. "When that's over, things are going to get much worse.

Nautilus is planning a full attack on the Mapmaker and everyone who sails with him!"

"The Mapmaker is planning an attack on Nautilus and everyone who sails with you!"

They both looked back at the dust storm rolling toward the dunes.

"We have to get back to the *Gaslight*," Honorine said.

"Is that safe?" Francis asked. "What if Nautilus finds out that you're, well...You're a Mordant, aren't you?"

Honorine nodded. "I think he already knows. My mother was a Mordant. My father was—is—Nautilus."

Francis said nothing for a very long moment.

"Why didn't he tell me that?" he asked finally. "Why didn't *you* tell me that?"

"I didn't know," Honorine said. "I didn't know about any of this until that night you came back home and shot Lux in the garden. And since then it's been all kinds of things I thought were impossible or unbelievable. But it turns out that 'impossible' is much less likely than I ever would have imagined."

"Well, we probably can go back to the *Gaslight*," Francis said, but then paused awkwardly. "You and me,

I mean. I don't know if your wolf should come along just yet."

Honorine turned back to see Lux, a bit farther still, watching her but slowly building a distance between them. Francis was right. He couldn't come along now. The next part, she would have to do alone.

"I'm all right," she called to him. "Go back to the *Carina*. Talk to the archer. He'll tell you the plan, and I'll meet you again soon!"

Lux waited a moment, tilting his head slightly. Then he nodded and trotted off toward the *Carina* and the thunderclouds. Honorine watched him go, realizing for just a second that she might never see him again. But there was no time to linger on the thought.

"We should hurry," Honorine said. "The wind seems to be dying down. Without this sandstorm, they'll surely be able to find us."

"Right this way," Francis said. He jogged toward the ocean, taking a wide path around the storm. Near a worn red rock, partially covered in algae, he had stashed a boat, a curious little thing that looked something like a canoe strapped to a collapsed brass windmill.

"What on earth is this?" Honorine asked. She had left a magnificent flying forest for a motorized dingy that hardly looked seaworthy.

"What?" Francis asked, looking slightly offended as he stood before his boat. "I made this. We do a lot of research on traveling with speed. This is the fastest thing anyone in Nautilus's crew has ever built. Now, come on. Help me launch it."

They pushed the boat out as deep as they could manage before climbing in.

"How did you know I'd be here?" Honorine asked as they settled into their seats. Her head barely cleared the high sides.

"I didn't," Francis said. "But I've looked for you everywhere we went since the *Nighthawk* exploded. I sent notes out every time we landed."

Francis fired up the motor, and a great, round fan blade at the back of the boat began to turn. "What have you been doing all this time?" he asked as the boat began to move with speed across the water. "Who was on that ship with you? What are the Mordant doing?"

"They were just trying to find the last free Mordant before Nautilus could capture them," Honorine said.

The boat bounced and hopped as it reached increasingly high speed. But if they ducked their heads below the tall wooden sides, they could speak over the roar of the engine and the howl of the wind.

Francis was uncomfortably silent for a moment.

"Nautilus isn't harming them," he said. "The Mordant on the *Gaslight*. You should know that."

"But he isn't letting them go," Honorine said. "So they're his prisoners. That's not just a rotten thing to do—it's incredibly dangerous. And the Mapmaker is going to find a way to stop Nautilus...for good."

"We can't let them go yet. We need their help to build a defense *against* the Mapmaker," Francis said.

"There's no need for a defense against the Mapmaker if you just let the Mordant go," she countered.

"Is that what he told you?" Francis said. "Because it's a bit more complicated than that. Just wait until you see what we're working on here."

"Where?" Honorine asked, then turned to see the side of the *Gaslight* looming above them. They were still approaching at a tremendous speed, and it looked as if they were going to smash right into the side of the ship.

Francis began to slow the engine, easing it back from full power to a slow idle, eventually pulling up alongside the huge ship and slipping the little boat through a door right at the water's edge. It led into a chamber that immediately lifted the boat, passengers and all, up to a metal dock inside the ship. From there they climbed a staircase until they reached a narrow door with rounded corners.

"Welcome aboard," Francis said as he opened the door and led Honorine out onto a deck that seemed to stretch on forever in both directions. The lights from thousands of gas lamps gave off heat, creating fine steam that drifted in the damp ocean air. The boards of the deck were warm, and a faint odor of burned chemicals seeped up from below. It rose and spread like a fog, pooling along the rail, corroding everything it touched.

"Oh, what is that smell?" Honorine said with a cough. She held her sleeve over her nose and mouth, trying to filter out the noxious odor.

"That's from the Sidus Apparatus," replied Francis.

The machine. The thing even the Mapmaker feared, hidden somewhere inside the massive ship, perhaps right under the very boards beneath her feet.

Francis tugged her sleeve and waved her toward the enormous crystal dome rising out of the deck. It looked like some manner of spectacular greenhouse, but when

Honorine drew closer, she noticed that it seemed to be empty. There was no floor, nothing inside but open space, specks of light, and a great hole opening into the heart of the ship.

Eerie lights flashed up from below, refracted through the dome's crystal panels and sprayed across the deck like breaking waves.

This was what had stolen Leo and Sirona and a hundred others away.

She hadn't expected it to be so beautiful.

"Wait until you see the rest of it," Francis said. He led her to a corroded metal door surrounded by a strange copper cage.

He closed the copper gate behind them and then sealed the rust-pocked outer steel door, leaving them in a knot of darkness until he turned on a string of bare round bulbs. They were in a short corridor that ended in another rusty door, this one covered in a net of copper straps lined with flecks of starglass.

He turned a brass and wooden lever to release the catch, and the door swung toward them, revealing a sparkling room beyond. "This is the bridge, where the ship is steered."

The *Gaslight*'s bridge was a long hall with a floor of dark, polished wood, a ceiling covered in maps and charts of the ocean and sky strung on lines like laundry, and two long walls made almost entirely of clear crystal panels.

"That's the front of the ship, and the ocean, of course," Francis said, pointing out at a view of sprawling decks lined with tiny electric lights and cannons. Down on a landing deck, the airship was lowering toward the main ship.

"That's our backup airship, the *Black Owl*," Francis said. "Not as big as the *Nighthawk* was, but it has more guns."

"Wonderful," Honorine said, although Francis didn't seem to catch her sarcasm.

Just then, the doors on the far end of the bridge swung open, and in walked Professor du Ciel, led by Nautilus Olyphant in midspeech. He wore his same impeccable suit and piles of silver jewelry, and this time he sported a pair of heavy dark goggles with black lenses hanging around his neck.

"We almost had him!" he said as he marched up to the crystal windows overlooking the laboratory below.

"How did the Mapmaker get here faster? Weren't you monitoring their ship correctly?"

"As best we could," Professor du Ciel said. "As of forty-eight hours ago, they should have been at least another day behind us."

"But they *weren't*," Nautilus said with a calm yet infuriated tone. "And now we've lost the archer."

"I beg your pardon, Captain, but would he have been any help if we had caught him?" Professor du Ciel replied as she studied a collection of papers in her gloved hands. "None of the others have helped. They won't give up the Mapmaker."

"Perhaps not, but he would have been able to defend this ship," Nautilus said. "And now we must…" He trailed off, suddenly noticing Honorine and Francis.

"Captain Olyphant," Francis said, stepping up and standing with a sailor's attentive posture.

"Mr. Vidalia," he replied. "Professor du Ciel informs me that you left your post this morning."

"I did," Francis replied. "I admit it. But I had good reason."

"And that was?" Nautilus asked.

"I went to rescue your daughter, sir," Francis said.

Du Ciel nearly spilled her papers to the floor.

"Daughter?" she asked, but Nautilus stopped her with a short wave of his hand while looking directly at Honorine. She didn't know what to expect from him. Only now, standing in front of him again, did Honorine realize that she hadn't thought much about Nautilus himself since they had first met. She hadn't really prepared, and she braced herself for an awkward reunion, or an angry inquisition.

"The Mapmaker knows you're here?" was all he said.

"I don't know," Honorine said. "If the fight is over, he might suspect by now." She gestured toward the *Black Owl* on the landing deck outside the window.

"Did the Mapmaker send you here?" Nautilus asked.

"No," Honorine said.

"Are you certain?"

"*Yes*," she insisted. "It was my decision. I left the *Carina* to try to find you."

The bridge was completely silent while Nautilus took a moment to consider her. Then he gestured toward Professor du Ciel.

"You've met?" he asked Honorine.

"Well, not officially," she said. She held out her hand, which Professor du Ciel shook very lightly and with hesitation.

"Professor du Ciel," Nautilus said, "this is my daughter, Honorine Olyphant."

Honorine's entire body seemed to lock into place for a moment. She had never been given a full, proper name. It attached her somehow to Nautilus in an instant, and she found, to her surprise, that she did not like it one bit.

But she smiled back numbly as the professor said "pleased to meet you," and mumbled a thank-you as Nautilus placed an unnervingly strong hand on her shoulder.

"You may go along with Professor du Ciel," he said, "and take a look at the work she's doing on this ship."

"Are you...sure?" Professor du Ciel replied uncertainly as she shuffled her papers around to get a better grasp.

"I don't know," Nautilus replied. "Am I still *captain* of this ship?"

Professor du Ciel nodded an apology. Nautilus turned back to Honorine.

"Do get a good look at everything we're doing here," he continued. "It's very exciting work."

She nodded dutifully and took a step toward

Professor du Ciel. Everything about the way he spoke, the way he moved, the way du Ciel reacted to him, though, made Honorine suspicious and uncomfortable. There were no wolves or scorpions or forbidden swamps here, but a gnawing fear told her that this place—even more than any of the others she had been to—was the most dangerous of all.

The Hall of Research

Even though she could never forget why she had come, Honorine could not help being completely captivated by the *Gaslight*. In every hall, in every room, down every corridor, and up every ladder and stairway, she found wonders and excitements and things that made her eyes light up with curiosity.

Professor du Ciel led her from the bridge through a door of copper and glass and onto a kind of revolving spiral staircase that twisted down into the lower levels of the ship. Francis followed along, lost for a moment somewhere above her as the mechanized stairs spun into a vast open atrium, big enough to house the entire Vidalia Manor.

"This is the research hall," Francis called down, leaning over the railing as they moved past stacks of balconies, catwalks, stairways, and brass caged elevators. It all made the atrium look a bit like the back of a dollhouse with the wall removed to reveal the colony of compartments within.

The hall was lined with tall iron columns, cast in the pattern of tree trunks reaching up and bending gracefully across an arched ceiling. Iron branches ended in thousands of lights in fixtures shaped like blooming flowers on curling vines of copper pipe. The decor created the strange illusion of being outdoors and indoors all at once. The scent of things burning and cooking filled the air, some of them very unpleasant, others less so. Honorine detected a hint of woodsmoke from one corner and witnessed a strange mist wafting from another.

"What are they working on?" Honorine called back up to Francis, her curiosity a near fever at this point.

"Just about everything," Francis said. "Anything you can think of to study or build, we probably have someone working on it."

They reached the ground level, and Honorine stepped onto a wood floor packed with miniature laboratory spaces, some secluded behind panels or curtains, most open to the rest of the room. At one station, she observed rows and columns of plants sprouting from miniature crystal vases arranged on a spiderweb grid of fine wire lines. At another, liquids of various viscosities poured from one decanter into another through a series of measuring devices. At a third, inside a greenhouse of apparently soundproof glass, several researchers sat amid a forest of musical instruments. They were recording notes and chords on wax cylinders and playing them back in the direction of several ceramic plates and vases, which were cracking and disintegrating one at a time.

"This way," Professor du Ciel said, leading them through a clear avenue running down the middle of the hall.

They passed towers of books. Endless collections of elixirs, powders, and compounds arranged in tiny crystal bottles. Mice, lizards, ponies, parrots, even a tortoise the size of a boulder, working on tasks and puzzles of varying complexity, while more men and women in blue coats filled stacks of logbooks with an endless stream of data. Honorine felt like she was seeing artifacts, creatures, plants, and even people from every corner of the globe. But she didn't see any sign of the Mordant.

She scoured every partitioned laboratory as they passed, but all the people appeared to be people, and all the animals (she confirmed when a spotted pony lifted its tail and dropped a fragrant pile of manure onto the floor) just regular animals.

"*This* is where I work," Francis said, leading Honorine to an alcove at the farthest end of the research hall.

An arched entryway built from carved, whitewashed wood and panes of blue and silver glass soared more than a story tall. Through it was a wide room partitioned into several levels connected by a series of open staircases, and a wall of tempered glass with an exterior balcony staring out over the sparkling black sea. Everywhere hung charts and globes and models of islands and continents, along with twirling instruments and maps covered in lightbulbs.

"This is the most important work on the entire ship," Professor du Ciel said, stopping Honorine just inside the doorway. "All the rest we just passed was added as we went along." She waved toward the research hall, as if the overwhelming number of experiments and studies going on outside was nothing of any great concern. "We are in charge of all the navigational studies, which have been, since its launch, the original purpose of the *Gaslight*."

"Navigation?" Honorine asked. It seemed a bit underwhelming. They had to be working on more than just sailing around and charting the ocean. Still, she saw no Mordant in the room, and Professor du Ciel was keeping very close.

"Yes," she drawled, walking farther into the room, clearly intending for Honorine to follow. She gestured to a contraption about the size of a tabletop, with a map on a long, continuous, adjustable scroll. Unlike most other maps, this one had very little information filled in on the major continents. The cartography described the oceans, including thousands of islands, all marked *previously uncharted* and most of them marked with a tiny silver X.

"Have you been to all of these?" Honorine asked.

"All of the indicated locations, yes," Professor du Ciel said. "And this is just the Atlantic. There are even more in the Pacific."

Honorine felt the professor's eyes on her as she leaned close to examine the map.

"Do any of these look familiar?" Professor du Ciel asked.

Honorine felt as if the question was looking for more information than it first seemed.

"Should they...?" she asked slowly.

"Have you ever been to any of these?" Francis asked more helpfully.

"Oh," Honorine said with a nod of understanding. "No. Not a one."

"Where did you sail, then, with the Mapmaker?" Professor du Ciel asked.

An uncomfortable weight dropped into Honorine's stomach, like a mouthful of cold, congealed cream soup. This question had an obvious answer, but she wasn't sure she should give it. Or if she wanted to.

"Didn't you go anywhere?" Professor du Ciel pressed.

"Yes," Honorine said. "But we didn't go to any islands." She considered her answer for a brief moment and decided that telling them where the *Carina* had been couldn't do any harm at this point.

"We went to the Amazon forest, the Andes, and then back over here, in the desert. The same places as this ship."

She looked up.

Professor du Ciel was very quiet, her face unreadable.

"You never went to Possideo?"

"The Mordant city?" Honorine asked. "I've heard of it, but I've never been there. I don't know where it is."

"Neither do we, yet," Professor du Ciel said, looking determined. "It's located on an island known as the Insual Stellarum—the Island of Stars, rather fittingly—but that has been, well...It's impossible to find."

"So none of these are the right place?" Honorine asked, looking at the silver *X*s scattered across the parchment ocean.

"No," Professor du Ciel said. "Apparently not."

"Well, we've always known that the quickest way—some say the only way—to find this place is with a Mordant guide," Francis said. "But none of the Mordant we've encountered so far has been able to help us in any meaningful way."

"Yes, and we're running out of Mordant," Professor du Ciel added.

"Well, perhaps they don't want to help you," Honorine said. "Maybe it wouldn't be a good idea for you to find this place."

Professor du Ciel looked confounded, as if she couldn't understand what Honorine had just said. "This ship is on a scientific mission, and part of that mission is to find the island and the city of the Mordant. The knowledge that could be found in their libraries—"

"Yes, but maybe it shouldn't be found," Honorine emphasized. "The Mordant hid it away and guarded it for a reason."

Professor du Ciel huffed and stuttered until she managed to spit out a few words in reply. "Just what are you saying?"

Francis stepped in. "Honorine's never been on a ship like this. She just doesn't know how things work around here yet. Actually, she does know a bit about my project, so I'm requesting a moment to ask her a few questions about my work."

Then he leaned over and whispered something to the professor, who snapped to attention, nodding.

"I have tomorrow's charts to approve," she said. "Take a few moments, and then we'll reconvene."

"Let me show you my experiment," Francis said as he led Honorine away from the scrolling map, and toward the port side of the room.

"What was all that?" Honorine asked.

"Protocol," Francis whispered.

"And what did you say to her?"

"I said that you probably had information about the Mordant city, but you just didn't understand it."

Honorine gasped. Her face turned red with the reply she had ready for Francis, but before she could launch it, he was up a set of stairs to a little niche sectioned off from the rest of the room by a low brass railing.

"Get up here so we can talk," Francis said. "And then yell at me later, please."

Beyond the railing was a half-moon-shaped space, the walls lined with cases of tools and instruments, and dotted with occasional portholes. Fixed to the outer wall was a wide glass plate filled with a brass and copper honeycomb that was mostly empty.

"You're running out of bees," Honorine said.

"Well, most of them went down with the *Nighthawk*. And a thunderstorm got a lot more, you might recall," Francis said. "It takes time to make more. And right now I'm doing a lot of research." He moved to a wide table topped with black marble and began removing stacks of dusty books. "Looking for accounts of the island, descriptions from previous explorers, clues to how others have had success finding it in the past."

"Francis, do you know what's on that island?" she asked. "Has Nautilus told you?"

"The city of the Mordant," Francis said. "There are rumors among the crew here about libraries full of all the knowledge in the world—"

"Libraries?" Honorine interrupted. "Salton and Bloom are in this for the libraries?"

"*All* the knowledge in the *world*," Francis said again. "Maps to lost treasures, the locations of diamond mines, volumes on alchemy—"

"So treasure?" Honorine asked. "They think they'll find gold and riches if they find this island?"

"Some of them, sure. The scientific types have their own reasons. But all anyone really knows is that Possideo is where Nautilus wants to go, and Nautilus is the captain."

"So they don't care why this place is so very well hidden or what might happen if you do find it?"

"Most of the crew is busy with other projects," Francis said, nodding toward the research hall outside. "They give Nautilus the information he wants, and he funds their research. They don't ask a lot of questions. Besides, it's a challenge, finding a place that can't be found."

"But if Nautilus does find it, he might very well kill everyone on this ship and a good part of the rest of the world," Honorine said urgently. "Even if he doesn't find it, if he continues to go after the Mapmaker, he's going to get himself killed at the very least. And where are all the Mordant? I haven't seen *one* since we've been on this ship."

Francis cleared his throat.

"They're here," he said, his eyes locked on the table. "You might not have noticed them."

Honorine wondered for a moment how she could possibly not notice a Mordant. She had only met a few, but they had all been unmistakable.

Francis pointed across the room to another platform surrounded by brass railings. On a tall, narrow table sat a translucent orb, emitting a faint golden glow.

She was across the room in an instant, navigating tables and enormous globes to reach the platform, with Francis following quickly behind. The orb was roughly a foot in diameter, made of amber-colored stone, and hollow. Within it sat a small figure, a young woman in old-fashioned sailor's clothing.

"Who are you?" Honorine asked.

"Pyxis," said Francis.

"Can't she hear me?"

"She can, but she can't answer you from inside."

Pyxis stood up, putting her miniature hand against the amber glass.

"How do you get them out?" Honorine asked, ready to crack the sphere open right on the spot. She was reaching for it when Francis took her hand and waved her away.

"I don't know," he whispered. "And even if I did, you can't just let her out here."

"But that's what I came to do," Honorine said. "Nautilus has to let them all go or the Mapmaker is going to kill him and probably everyone else on board!"

"Not if we can catch him," Francis said.

"I don't think you can," Honorine said. "He's not like the others."

"Well, he's stronger, maybe, but at the end of the day, he's a Mordant. If we know his constellation, we can catch him."

Honorine shook her head again.

"No, that's not the answer. Nautilus can't keep pursuing the Mapmaker, he can't keep the other Mordant here, and he can't keep looking for Possideo."

"Well, you're going to have quite a time trying to convince him of that," Francis said.

"I have to try," Honorine said. "That island doesn't just have a library on it, Francis. The reason the Mordant built their city on that spot was to guard a gateway to an underworld full of monsters."

Francis smirked. "Monsters? What kind of monsters?"

"Who's the worst Mordant you have, the most dangerous? The one who everyone is afraid of?"

"Well, there's Draco," Francis said. "He's a real, actual dragon. Almost got the whole ship on fire when we caught him."

"Well, imagine a hundred times worse than him, that you can't catch, running all over the world."

Francis looked skeptical. "Even if that's true, the Mordant can control them, obviously, if they're guarding them."

"Yes, but you have the Mordant in prison! So if Nautilus does manage to get to that island and accidentally lets the monsters out, he's going to have to let the Mordant go anyway."

Francis was stumped, his eyes scanning over the books in front of him as he struggled to come up with a reply.

"Forget about that island, and forget about capturing the Mapmaker," Honorine said. "Help me find a way to get the Mordant off this ship before Nautilus gets everyone here killed."

"But what about our work?" Francis said, growing frustrated. "You've seen what we're doing here. Having the Mordant on the ship has inspired everyone. We're making developments and breakthroughs almost every day, learning everything we can about the world. Now, I've read a lot of my father's work on this subject. He figured out who the Mapmaker is, even though he never located his constellation. The Mapmaker is the muse of Knowledge. He was the one who showed people how to contact the Mordant the very first time."

"Well, what if I happen to know that your father doesn't want Nautilus to find the island, either?"

Francis frowned. "How would you know that?"

"Because I met him," Honorine said. "He's on the *Carina*. He's been there this whole time—helping the Mapmaker."

The Captain's Plan

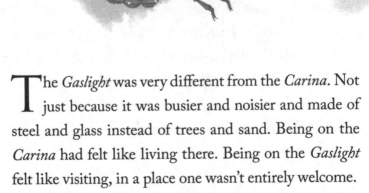

The *Gaslight* was very different from the *Carina*. Not just because it was busier and noisier and made of steel and glass instead of trees and sand. Being on the *Carina* had felt like living there. Being on the *Gaslight* felt like visiting, in a place one wasn't entirely welcome.

This feeling crept over Honorine on the very first day, when, shortly after seeing Professor du Ciel's and Francis's work in the research hall, she was called away and shown to a suite full of marble and polished brass and glossy panels of dark wood. Farther inside was a solarium filled with overgrown palms and ferns, where she found a little table set with china and silver and dishes of food, and Nautilus, busily writing notes in a ledger of some kind while a cup of tea cooled in front of him.

"Ah, welcome," said Nautilus, setting down his pen on the open ledger page. "Please, do sit down."

Only then did she realize that she was to dine with Nautilus, and that it would be just the pair of them. Despite everything she knew about him and his ship, and even the very reason she had come to find him, Honorine felt a twinge of excitement at the prospect of sitting down to have a meal with her father for the very first time.

Honorine took the only other seat at the table, across from Nautilus. With all the frantic and overwhelming activity of the morning, she didn't realize she was hungry until she saw the table piled with plates of potatoes and sausages and rolls and fillets of chicken dusted with herbs. Not exactly traditional breakfast fare, she then realized how long it had been since she'd eaten something other than whimsically flavored fruit.

"My apologies if this is not what you were expecting at nine o'clock in the morning," Nautilus said as he speared a few sausages from a silver dish and slid them onto his plate. "We keep unorthodox hours here— a requirement of our work, after all. Dinner is usually served at sunrise, and breakfast before sunset. Go ahead and help yourself, if you find anything to your liking. Despite all appearances, we don't bother with airs and graces around here."

Honorine gladly accepted the offer. When she had guzzled a full glass of juice and stuffed at least three sausages and a warm roll into her mouth, Nautilus folded his hands over his sparsely filled plate and looked across the table at her.

"I suppose you have some questions for me," he said.

"Well…" Honorine replied. "Did you know I was living with the Vidalias all these years?"

Nautilus looked a bit surprised at this.

"Oh," he said, busying himself with a helping of potatoes and roasted chicken. "I did not, actually. I had no idea of your whereabouts until the night of our arrival at the Vidalia Estate, nearly nine weeks ago."

Honorine's fork dropped to the table.

"Nine weeks!" she said. "I've been gone that long?"

"Yes, I suppose you have," Nautilus said. "Nine

more weeks away from me. But here you are now, back where you belong, with your family."

He gestured at the room around them and the suite beyond the open glass doors.

"This was supposed to be our home. I built this for your mother, and later for you as well. I've never spent the night in this suite. But now perhaps it will finally get some use. Is there anything else you wanted to know?"

"Why didn't you come looking for me?" Honorine asked. Nautilus frowned at his plate and then looked up at her, as if it had taken some serious contemplation to come up with an answer.

"Well, I just told you. I didn't know where you were," he said. "Unfortunately."

Perhaps not, but she had been living in the house of his former partner and fellow explorer. He had not once corresponded with Lady Vidalia, in any way, for the last twelve years? Honorine did not like his answer, but she sensed that further questions on the subject would only result in equally unsatisfactory answers. She turned her attention to a bowl of honey-glazed carrots and another of warm, crusty rolls.

"So," Nautilus said, "what can you tell me about the Mordant on the *Carina*?"

Honorine swallowed a lump of roll before it was quite chewed enough, feeling the rough edges slipping all the way down her throat.

"I thought you already knew everything about them," she said.

"Well, no matter how educated, one can always learn more," Nautilus said with a smile. "Now, who's on the ship? Astraea, Lux, and, of course, the Mapmaker, we know for sure. We suspect he has Scorpio as well, and, after our last few encounters, Eridanus and most likely Sagittarius are there."

Honorine set down her fork and sat back a bit from the table.

"If that's all you want to know," she said, "then yes. They're all there." Nautilus must already know this, she reasoned, and he couldn't reach them on the *Carina* anyway.

Nautilus nodded and then made a note in his ledger.

"And their next destination," he continued without looking up from the page. "Do you have any information on where they might be headed?"

"No," Honorine said flatly.

"Nothing at all?" Nautilus asked. "You didn't hear anything about their next course of action?"

Honorine did not reply. Nautilus waited for a long moment, pen poised over the paper, before looking up.

"Come, now, Honorine. I thought you came here to help me."

"I came here to try to save you," Honorine replied quietly.

Nautilus set down his pen and sat back in his chair.

"Save me? Well, that's quite noble. But just what do you think I need saving from?"

"The Mapmaker," she said incredulously. Nautilus nodded but did not reply. "He wants you to let the Mordant go. He wants you to stop keeping them as prisoners."

"I'm sure he does," Nautilus said. "Even if I set them all free today, though, that wouldn't be enough, would it?"

Honorine sat farther back in her chair. "No," she said. "He doesn't just want the Mordant free. He wants... well, he wants you dead, and your ship destroyed."

Nautilus reached across the table to grab a tall silver teapot, then filled a new cup, creating a ball of steam that curled around him as he spoke.

"Honorine, I'm not a complete fool," he said. "I've been sailing these seas for a dozen years now with the Mapmaker himself waiting for his chance to hunt me down, and I'm still here. You must learn to trust your father, at least a little, especially if you expect me to trust you in return. Now, I would like you to give me any information you have about the Mapmaker. Help me catch him."

Honorine remained silent.

"Don't you want to see your mother again?" Nautilus asked.

"Of course," Honorine said quietly. "But how will catching the Mapmaker do that?"

"Oh, come, now, Honorine," Nautilus said as if lightly scolding her. "Surely by now you've seen what the Mapmaker can do."

"He can show you how to get anything you want," Honorine said.

"Exactly," said Nautilus. "He can show me how to, for instance, find an island where your mother waits right at this very moment, unable to leave and come home to us."

"What do you mean?" Honorine asked. "Because of the gates? Because she can't leave them or the Bellua might escape?"

Nautilus stared at her very keenly.

"You are a clever girl, aren't you?" he said. "Yes. She cannot leave now, because she has taken on the responsibility of guarding the Gates of Hades. But it doesn't have to be her. We can get her back, Honorine, if we can catch the Mapmaker. He can show us where she is, and more important, he can show us exactly what we must do to bring her home."

Honorine put down her fork, unsure of what exactly to say. He was right. The Mapmaker could show them how to get Andromeda back. He had already shown Honorine one vision of how it could be done—the one that somehow involved throwing the Mapmaker into Hades to be swallowed up by the Bellua. But just as she had pushed back against the Mapmaker when he insisted that he had to sink Nautilus's ship to free the Mordant, she pushed back against the thought that the only way to get her mother back was to destroy the Mapmaker.

"That's what all this is for," Nautilus continued, waving a hand dismissively at the ship around them. "All this work going on around us doesn't mean a thing to me if we can't find Andromeda."

"But you don't need all the other Mordant, then," Honorine said. "You could let them go."

"That is out of the question," Nautilus said. "The work we are doing on this ship—the advancements my crew are making every day in medicine, communication, navigation, agriculture are immeasurable. It would be irresponsible to abandon our research now. We're making far more efficient use of the Mordant talents than anyone has in all of recorded history. Not only that, but the Mordant who have been on this ship now know far too much about what we're doing here. We can't have the Mapmaker learning our secrets, or we lose a major advantage over him."

Anger flared in Honorine's cheeks, but she took a breath and tried to push it aside. She wondered if it was supposed to be this difficult, talking with one's parents. Surely it was easier for other children.

"But you could learn all that without keeping them as prisoners," she said.

"Perhaps. But there is one other thing you have to consider." Nautilus folded his hands and leaned onto his elbows. "The Mapmaker truly is dangerous. Without a defense, there's nothing to stop him from causing destruction to anyone who displeases him anywhere in the world."

"He wouldn't do that," Honorine said quietly, not entirely sure of her own claim.

"Oh, he already has," Nautilus replied. "Why, in this day and age, should we be helpless against him and his incredible power?"

Honorine had no answer.

"You help me catch the Mapmaker, you help the world. *And* you get your mother back," said Nautilus. "Seems like a good deal all the way around. Now, are we in agreement?"

Honorine's head screamed *no!* but she nodded obediently. In her experience, obedient children—or at least those who appeared to be—were given freedoms and allowed to wander unsupervised. Disobedient ones were put under strict watch.

"But I don't know if I can help you," Honorine protested. "The only Mordant I've met are on the *Carina*, and from what I've seen, they're protected from your machine. So even if you knew the Mapmaker's constellation, you wouldn't be able to . . . get him."

"Ah," said Nautilus with a growing smile. "You're correct, almost. We've made some improvements since last we met. Our Sidus Apparatus is much more

 • 291

powerful than it was when we met in the jungle. Tonight, we shall try it on Sagittarius."

Honorine's heart went cold.

The archer had pledged to defend the *Gaslight* from the Mapmaker, which he likely couldn't do if he was trapped in an amber prison. Honorine felt the worry like ice against her cheeks, but Nautilus didn't seem to notice her pale expression.

"I have a few things to tend to before this evening's work begins," he said. "You probably want to get a bit of rest. The whole suite is yours, of course."

He made his way to the door of the solarium, then turned back.

"If you do want to be out on the rest of the ship, I ask that you be escorted. For your own safety, of course. We start work one hour before sundown."

Then he left. The moment the suite door closed behind him, Honorine leaped from her chair and paced the room.

She had until sundown to find a way to stop Nautilus from using his machine on the archer. If she failed, none of the people on the ship would live to see another sunrise.

CHAPTER
• 20 •

Sabotage on the *Gaslight*

The *Gaslight* was very quiet in the afternoon. Honorine spent a few hours retooling her Mordant watch with things she found in the well-appointed suite, adding more indicators from the constellations she could remember from Lord Vidalia's books. Then, when the ship seemed to grow quiet around her, she slipped out and started exploring.

She wanted to find the laboratory she had seen in the Mapmaker's vision and the machine that captured the Mordant. The only thing keeping the Mapmaker from sinking the *Gaslight* was her agreement with the archer. But once Nautilus captured him, it would be swift and brutal revenge for the entire *Gaslight* crew. She had to find the machine before sundown and make sure it was not working when Nautilus tried to capture the archer.

Honorine found the ship nearly deserted and most of the doors unattended and unlocked. A spare few deckhands wandered about, but most of the scientific crew was not yet awake, and Honorine was reminded of the empty halls and parlors of the Vidalia Estate after supper had been cleared and the house went still.

It seemed so much further away than nine weeks. Every single part of her life had changed since then, except for maybe Francis.

The bridge was manned by a pair of blue coats busily engaged in conversation at the far end of the room. Honorine easily slipped from the hatch at the top of the stairs to the open doorway beside it on the wall. Her bare feet made no sound at all as she padded along the hallway, moving in the direction of the laboratory.

The first door she encountered opened onto a narrow balcony of pipes and grates, surrounded by a helpful fog of steam. The balcony ended in stairways on both sides, one leading down into the hold and one leading up into the crystal dome capping the whole of the laboratory.

Honorine grasped the railing and leaned out, searching for a view of the room below. She got brief glimpses, but the steam quickly saturated her clothes and dripped from her hair. Better go down, she thought, and took a step toward a staircase, when the entire, delicate pipe balcony began to rattle and shake. Gruff voices on the stairs rose up with the steam. Someone was up and about in the laboratory.

Honorine turned and ran the other way, past a wide pipe vent funneling the steam outside, until she had climbed up into the crystal dome itself.

The light was blinding, shining straight in from the heavy red sun burning low in the sky above the ocean. It was already nearing sundown. She might have waited too long to leave the suite. She climbed a bit higher, the stairway contorting into a narrow ladder that continued up into the dome, toward a network of slender pipes and pendulous glass globes suspended dozens of feet off the ground. Far below, a handful of crew members tended and cleaned the machine, providing a good amount of noise to cover up the sound of

Honorine shimmying about on the catwalks and ladders above.

She started up the length of the adjustable ladder, studying the intricate twists of the pipes leading to each globe. They all ended in a valve, presumably there to shut the gas off while the globes were being fixed or replaced. With a few turns of the gears at the top of the ladder to shift its position, Honorine maneuvered toward the nearest globe, the one closest to the copper rim of the dome. It was precarious, but if she rested her chest and stomach against the rungs of the ladder, she could get her hands on the valve, which she turned until it appeared to be closed. Then she swung the ladder toward the next globe and repeated the procedure.

By the time she had done this for several dozen of the hundreds of globes scattered through the dome, the sun had dipped lower outside, and the work below was beginning to pick up. Hoping she had done enough to at least postpone the night's hunt, she reeled the ladder back in and started to climb down.

More crew members began to gather below. She had to be extremely cautious, creeping along the wall, moving softly across the metal balconies, until she had snuck back out into the hallway.

She intended to slip back down to the suite, but just as she reached the door to the bridge, Nautilus stepped through it and nearly walked right into her.

"Oh!" she said. "There you are."

"What are you doing all the way up here?" Nautilus asked.

"I...was hungry," she said. "Just looking for the galley."

Nautilus frowned. "Well, we can't have you wandering around." He looked about, as if searching for a place to store her. "I'm on my way down to see Professor du Ciel. Come along. We'll have to have something sent up for you."

He led her back through the bridge, down the spiral staircase, and into the research hall, which was still mostly empty and silent.

"Good afternoon, Captain Olyphant," said Professor du Ciel as she emerged from a curtained alcove, dressed in her work clothes, but clearly having just woken from a hard slumber.

"Professor du Ciel," Nautilus replied. They retreated to a corner of the room to study a gigantic chart.

Francis was already up in his little study. He waved Honorine over when Nautilus's back was turned.

"What are you going to do?" he asked. "You talked to Nautilus? What did he say?"

Honorine shook her head. "He was no help at all. We'll have to do this on our own."

"Do what on our own?" Francis asked, looking alarmed.

"First, I need to find the Mordant," Honorine said, ignoring his concern. "Where does he keep the rest of them?"

"Secured," Francis replied. "It was a massive undertaking just to get Nautilus to let us keep Pyxis out here so Professor du Ciel could work whenever she liked."

"We have to try," Honorine said. "And I need your help."

Francis looked very uncertain. "You're going to try to let them go, aren't you?" he asked.

"Of course," Honorine said. "We get them off this ship, and then maybe I can persuade the Mapmaker not to kill anyone."

"But what if we just help Nautilus find that island first?" Francis asked. "Then I'm sure we could get him to let them go."

Honorine had no more patience for explaining

herself. She had expected more from Francis. She had thought he of all people would understand her.

"Did you ever think about what these machines are doing?" she asked suddenly. "What happens when you take a Mordant out of the world? Did you ever think about whether Nautilus should be doing this?"

"No, not at first," Francis admitted quietly. "Until after I brought you to the *Nighthawk*. When I realized what you...are...I was afraid to bring you back to this ship. I was afraid of what Nautilus would do if he found you."

Honorine frowned at him. "You were afraid he would lock me up, just like the rest of them," she said, crossing her arms.

"Well..." Francis said. "It's really not that bad."

Honorine narrowed her eyes. "That's exactly the kind of thing someone says when they've done something terrible and they want to confess."

"Maybe," Francis said. "But the confession part is supposed to be a good thing, isn't it? What if you realize you did a bad thing, but you were doing it for the right reasons?"

"It's a start," Honorine said. "But there's another

step. You have to make up for the thing you did, too. Not just admit it."

"*I know!*" Francis grumbled. "I know, you're right. It's just—"

"What, scary?" Honorine asked. "Francis, we're going to do this together. I need your help."

"What do you want me to do?" he asked reluctantly.

"Wait until they're distracted, and then go find the Mordant," Honorine said.

"Why would they be distracted?" Francis asked, his eyes going wide as he realized that whatever Honorine was planning had already been set in motion. Before she could answer, Nautilus interrupted.

Du Ciel and Nautilus were busy marking possible island locations on a gigantic map, and then arguing about the probability of any of them being strong-enough candidates to take the entire ship in that direction. Every one of the locations was in vast open water, with nothing around their ship for hundreds of miles but deep black ocean.

"Francis!" Nautilus called from across the study. "Honorine! We are about to begin this evening's experiments. Time to retire to the laboratory." Honorine wanted to tell Francis what was about to happen but decided—though she felt a bit terrible about it—that it would be better if he didn't know. Then he wouldn't be tempted to warn Nautilus. She kept quiet and followed the procession through the research hall.

The dome above was a cap of darkness, and the polished wood, hammered copper, and smooth brass of the machine all around them reflected the light of many incandescent bulbs, turning the entire laboratory into a glowing golden bowl.

The room was far more crowded in the evening, with pairs of blue-coated crew members manning a dozen stations, each a cacophony of dials and levers and banks of gauges monitoring every system of the massive machine.

"Stand over here, please, and put these on," Francis requested, handing Honorine a pair of goggles with smoky black lenses and a black leather strap. Francis was already wearing his. "It gets very bright in here once things get moving."

Honorine was reminded suddenly of watching fireworks on Lady Vidalia's front lawn many years ago, perhaps for Francis's birthday. They'd exploded in the sky with such deep, resonating blasts that the sound had echoed inside Honorine's chest. Now she could feel something like that in the hum of electricity, the vibrations moving through the room like ripples on water.

The electric bulbs illuminating the floor rattled slightly. The pipes whistled and emitted intermittent wisps of steam.

"This machine, the Sidus Apparatus, is my masterpiece," Nautilus said, with a sweep of his arms, as he stepped up in front of Honorine and Francis. His own black-lensed goggles were rimmed in pearl and had silver scrollwork on the sides. They rested on his forehead as he pulled on a pair of black deerskin gloves. "It took a decade to build, years more to perfect, and now we are only weeks—or perhaps days—away from our final goal."

He lifted the goggles to lower them over his eyes, pausing to look directly at Honorine.

"And you will be here to see it," he said. But before she could inquire as to what this final goal was, he had secured his goggles and was striding away, shouting important-sounding orders.

Crew members began turning gears and flipping levers. The whine and whistle of heat and gas moving through pipes escalated as little gauges wriggled and spun all around the room. High overheard, lights began to spark and pop inside the globes, burning in blues and greens, golden yellow and smoldering violet. It was intense and beautiful, the colors reflecting off the crystal panels of the dome above, scattering out in flashes that shot across the room and bounced off every polished surface.

Honorine watched, captivated, as the lights bloomed across the net of pipes, until the gas hit the ones she had tampered with that morning. When the first globe attempted to ignite, it did not do so in a controlled burst of flame as the others had. Instead, the entire globe filled instantly with flame, exploding into a spray of glass shards and sending a spout of blue fire across the ceiling.

"Whoa!" said Francis with a grin as the blue light filled his smoky goggle lenses. But he was less delighted by the second explosion, and downright concerned by the time several dozen globes had exploded into jets of flame, surging together to create a multicolored fire-ball. It rushed upward, bursting through the crystal dome, which exploded into a cloud of violet smoke and shards of iron and copper.

Honorine dropped to the floor in a heap, shielding her head from the falling glass, as Nautilus's crew flailed about, shutting down the machine as quickly as they could manage. She stayed in a huddle until the room was filled only with the sounds of boots pounding across the floor and salty language being lobbed through the air.

Honorine peeked under her arm, hoping to see no one engulfed in flame or impaled with a thousand shards of crystal. She breathed a sigh of relief when everyone seemed to be unharmed. The machine was greatly damaged, seeping oil like blood from gashes in metal and broken pipes. The crystal dome was shattered on one side like an eggshell, the pipes bent and useless, the gauges all still and dead.

"Are you all right?" Francis asked as he, too, slowly looked out from under his arms.

"Fine," Honorine said before actually checking. "You?" She looked him over, finding the hem of his coat singed, but the rest of him untouched.

Nautilus was marching toward them, pulling his goggles off, his face set in a scowl.

Honorine stood up and moved back in one automatic motion, like a startled horse beginning to spook.

"Francis!" Nautilus shouted. "Something is terribly wrong! Get her out of here at once!"

He did not even look at Honorine as he stormed past into a cloud of sulfur steam and errant sparks.

"Well, let's go, then," Francis said, holding out his hand to help Honorine down from the platform. He looked shaken, his mouth curled up in a painful expression, his hand gripping Honorine's uncomfortably tight.

Together, they made their way back to the suite. Inside, with the doors closed, it seemed that they were on another ship entirely, insulated from the noise of the crew members and the damaged ship.

"What could have happened?" Francis said, finally taking off his goggles and flopping down onto a dusty sofa. He stared vacantly across the room.

"Haven't you ever seen something like that before?" Honorine asked, trying to sound just concerned enough that Francis would not suspect her. But he had no reason to, and he did not even glance over at her.

"No!" he said. "A problem with a globe, maybe. One or even two breaking during a single evening, sure. But I've never seen the thing explode like that!"

Then he turned toward Honorine, his face slowly crushing into a frown as he started to put the events of the evening into a useful order.

"What did you mean when you said they would be distracted?" he asked. "Did you do something—"

The doors to the suite burst open, and Nautilus strode across the brushed silk carpet, directly toward Honorine. Her first instinct was to flinch, but when he reached her, Nautilus dropped to one knee and put both hands on her shoulders.

"Are you quite sure you're all right?" he asked. He turned her around in a full circle, brushed back her hair from her forehead, looked over her bare palms and wrists. "No cuts, no burns?"

"No, nothing at all," she replied, holding up her hands to show she was unharmed. "No damage whatsoever. I promise."

Nautilus stood up and put a hand to his forehead, rubbing his eyes in an exasperated gesture.

"Good. Good," he said, drawing a long breath in through his narrow nose. Then, when he had composed himself, he looked her straight in the eye. "That was my fault. I shouldn't have brought you down there right away. I should have tested, run some simulations, been absolutely certain of the effect you would have on the ship—and the machine."

Honorine would have been happy to let him go

on taking the blame, but his words suddenly stopped making sense.

"What effect?" she asked.

"Well, every time we bring a constellation on board, it changes things," he said. "Every Mordant exerts an influence over the world around them. It's like they each have their own unique kind of gravity. When we add one to the collection, it creates changes in other, unexpected ways."

He stopped there. Honorine nodded and waited for the rest.

"And...?" she finally asked.

"Well, you're one of them, at least partially," Nautilus replied. "I knew it would have an effect. I confess I did hope you would strengthen the apparatus's reach, whatever your particular power may be."

Suddenly, something shifted deep in Honorine's heart. She wondered if she was not, in fact, just another Mordant in Nautilus's collection, one without an amber sphere to hold her.

She took a moment to compose her thoughts. Since arriving on the *Gaslight*, she had felt overwhelmed with amazement at the ship, anger at Nautilus for what he was doing to the Mordant, and fear that the Mapmaker would turn up before she could find a way to keep Francis and Nautilus safe. When she saw the glass explode and the look in the crew's eyes as their work erupted into flames, she had felt a pang of regret. But now, as she stood before Nautilus, she began to feel something new. Something she had never experienced before.

All the time she had been with the Mapmaker, she had been making sure that he wouldn't come after Nautilus's ship. She had made bargains and agreements and done things that terrified her to her bones, all to keep Nautilus and Francis safe. Lux and Astraea had promised her mother they would do whatever they could to guard her from harm. Lord Vidalia had gone into hiding for twelve years, worked side by side with a dangerous creature, to keep his child and his friend's child safe.

And Francis, when he learned who she was all those weeks ago in the forest, had first tried to protect her, then tried to reach out to her, and finally snuck out in the middle of a sandstorm to bring her to the place he thought she would be safe.

Nautilus, on the other hand, had spent his time on his machines and his quests to find Andromeda and to capture the Mapmaker. The more that Honorine worked the idea over in her head, the more she was convinced that he was really and truly not interested in her as anything more than a tool, another component of his machine, to use for his own selfish goals.

Never had he mentioned coming to look for her. Never told her that he had stayed away for her own good. Never asked her a single question that wasn't about the Mapmaker or the other Mordant or what she could do to help him. And now there she was, standing on his ship, and he was using her to give him some kind of advantage over his adversary.

Honorine continued to feel a strange kind of knot in her chest. It wasn't anger, really, or sadness. It was disappointment. Growing up believing she was an orphan, she always dreamed of meeting her parents. But now, having met one, she was stuck with the reality that her father was brilliant but quite cold. And she did not like him very much.

There was only one thought that rose through her disappointment and gave her a glimmer of hope. Nautilus did not suspect in any tiny, fractional way that Honorine had intentionally tampered with his machine.

Which was exactly what she needed him to think, because she was definitely going to do it again.

The Rogue Mordant

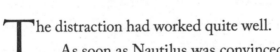

The distraction had worked quite well.

As soon as Nautilus was convinced she wasn't hurt, he instructed Honorine to stay in the suite, which she definitely did not do. The Mordant were somewhere on that ship, and she was going to find them.

Francis insisted he did not know where they were kept.

"I never see them except in the hall when they're brought in for research," he explained again as they ducked out of the main hallway and into a service corridor.

"That's all right," Honorine said, holding up her arm

with the Mordant watch still strapped to her wrist. "You just help me navigate the ship. I'll do the hard part."

They stayed out of the main halls and cabins, even though it was loud and dark in the bowels of the *Gaslight*. Noises rattled in the walls, bare steel grinding and groaning as the engines fired, pushing the ship through the dark water toward the northern seas. The Mordant watch only worked on a few of the dozens of Mordant in the world. But, thankfully for Honorine, it did work on Sirona, who was somewhere on this ship. They wandered around for quite a while, ducking behind pipes and down dark halls when they heard footsteps, hitting dead ends in storage closets and unused pantries.

Francis grew anxious as the hours spooled off the night, and they were still scurrying about like rats in places they weren't supposed to be.

"Nautilus is going to notice we went missing," he warned as they passed an open doorway and saw a clock reading very late in the night, or possibly very early in the morning.

"Well, if we get this right, that isn't the only thing he'll notice," Honorine replied, and then gasped with delight as the little stones on her watch finally began to glow.

She followed the dimming and brightening of

Sirona's tiny spots of light on her watch as they wound their way through a maze of passages and utility rooms full of tools or spare machinery, down hallways clad in rusted metal with pools of briny water on the floor.

"Are you sure you know where you're going?" Francis said. "I've never been down here before."

"This is the right way," Honorine said as the stones finally began to grow brighter and brighter on her arm. After a few more turns and corners, they came to a place Francis did recognize.

"We're near the crew quarters," he said. "They wouldn't be down here. I've never seen them." Another turn more, and the trail stopped at a wooden door.

"This is it," Honorine said.

"This is right next door to Nautilus's cabin," Francis replied, looking up and down the corridor with a confused expression. "No one uses this. And it's locked anyway."

When he said the word *locked*, it echoed in Honorine's mind as if he had just rung a bell. She suddenly remembered something the Mapmaker had said to her.

An ironwood key will unlock any door.

She happened to have an ironwood key still in her pocket.

Despite the heaviness of the wood and the rustiness

of the lock, the ironwood key did, in fact, unlock the cabin door easily.

The door creaked open to reveal a standard cabin built to accommodate four sailors, but in this one, there was only a single cot, raised on a metal loft over a spare wooden desk. The other walls were covered with maps and charts, a trunk, a shelf with neatly arranged books. It was all very orderly, very precise, and very deliberate.

"You're quite sure?" Francis said. It was dark and cold, more like a vault than sleeping quarters. On the wall opposite the desk and the bed was a door made of solid wood, which looked completely out of place on such a ship. This door was rough and stout, the planks made from ragged timbers. It looked more like something that belonged on the *Carina*. Honorine walked across the room and placed her hand on the door.

It was warm.

"*This* is it," she said. Once again, the ironwood key worked perfectly on the rusted iron lock, and the door swung open, revealing a room from another world.

There were no windows here, only dark walls and the scent of damp earth, moss, and slowly rotting leaves. Here was a great desk covered in notes and maps splashed with ink, books with ribbons marking dozens of pages, globes with routes painted in shimmering golden ink, and a hammock in the corner piled with ragged blankets and a flattened pillow.

The room was bathed in the light of a hundred golden globes hanging overhead. Some were very round, others pear-shaped, and they each were wrapped in a small net and hung from thin cords at various lengths to keep them from knocking together as they swayed with the ship. Honorine and Francis could see small, moving shapes inside them.

Honorine dragged a chair in from the next room and climbed up to reach the nearest globe. Inside was a bird, black like the crow, but slimmer and lighter, with a long beak, long neck, and long legs. It was a crane. Other movements in the globes nearby caught her eye: a rabbit, a small man with a bow, and then, at the end of the row, an old friend.

"Sirona!" Honorine said, standing up on her tiptoes to get a closer look into the globe. Sirona stood and pressed her hands to the inside of the amber shell.

"Honorine!" she replied, though the sound didn't make it to Honorine's ears.

"How do we get her out?" she asked. Francis shrugged and shook his head.

"I told you, I don't know," he said.

She turned the globe carefully in her hands. It was smooth and solid, without a seam or hinge or lock. This was something the ironwood key couldn't open.

"Well, something on this ship must do it," Honorine said, and began spouting every idea she could think of. "Copper? Iron? Heat? Starglass—wait! Those stone bullets in your pistol—would they work?"

"You want me to shoot at…that?" Francis asked incredulously.

"That would work, wouldn't it?" Honorine asked.

"It might, but I don't have my pistol, and I don't know if we want to fire off a bunch of rounds in here. And someone will hear us."

He was right, though Honorine didn't want to hear it. Nautilus would come looking for them before long. She studied the hanging globes. There were perhaps a hundred of them, and it was very unlikely that she could get all the Mordant free before Nautilus caught her.

Her mind raced through possible plans, trying to find a solution. She could come back later, but there might not be time for that. They had to act now.

"We'll have to test our hypothesis," she said finally, searching through the globes while Francis looked on quizzically. "Aha!" she said finally, grasping a particularly large one in both hands and yanking it down from the ceiling with all her might.

"*That* one?" Francis asked. "Why are you—"

"We have to get going," Honorine said, handing the globe to Francis as the sound of boots rattled down the hallway. She looked around the room at the rest of them, all watching her from inside their little prisons.

"We'll be back for you very soon," she said.

They snuck back into the hall, dodging the crewmen as they stomped back and forth to their cabins.

"Honorine, what are we doing?" Francis whispered as they slipped down hidden hallways and back up stairs. "What's the plan?"

"The plan has changed a little bit," Honorine said. "Well…a lot. It's a completely new plan. We can't free all the Mordant, so I think there's only one thing we can do."

"What's that?" Francis asked.

"We have to find Possideo," Honorine said.

"We're already doing that," Francis said. "This whole ship is working on it."

"No, I mean *we*," Honorine said, pointing from herself to Francis. "You and me. Right now. We find that island, and the city, and Andromeda. Then Nautilus will stop looking for and hunting the Mapmaker, and then, maybe, we can get this sorted and get everyone out alive."

Francis looked shocked. He clutched the amber orb to his chest, holding it like a little child might clutch a toy bear for comfort.

"I know it's going to be dangerous," Honorine said. "I know it sounds absolutely mad. But Nautilus is going to get that machine fixed, no matter how hard I try to stop him. And when he does, he'll capture the archer, and there will be nothing stopping the Mapmaker from sinking this ship. But there's one more thing."

She took a deep breath and then put a hand on Francis's arm.

"Lord Vidalia is not well," she said. "He needs Sirona's help and care. And soon. If we don't get this matter settled..."

Now Francis looked as if he might burst into tears.

"I'm sorry," Honorine said. "I shouldn't have told you that. Now you'll just be worried."

Francis shook his head and swallowed a sob. "No," he said. "Now I understand. We're going to find that island, and that's why..." He looked down into the orb in his hands.

"Yes!" Honorine said. "So let's get going."

Francis, thankfully, knew the fastest way back to the outer deck. He stopped by his cabin to retrieve his pistol, extra stone ammunition, and a pair of his spare boots for Honorine. They were a size too large, but would do in a pinch. Then they were off to begin their tiny mutiny.

When they emerged out on the deck, they were met with a stiff wind and a cold early morning, but the sky was clear. There was no forest hovering above, only the full pale moon, shining spectacularly over a calm black sea.

"Perfect," Honorine said as they tucked into a little alcove along the outer deck, where they might make their getaway without being seen. It was going to be some feat, she thought, once she freed the particular Mordant they had liberated from the cabin. Honorine set the globe on the deck but held it with one hand to keep it from rolling overboard on the smooth wood.

"Now, well, you might want to stand back," Francis said as he pulled out his pistol.

"I'll pull my hand back when you say when," Honorine said. It sounded in her head like a terrible plan, but Francis nodded and leveled his pistol at the globe.

"Now?" Honorine asked.

"No," Francis said.

"Well, when?"

"That's what I'll say when I'm ready, so don't you say it."

"Say what?"

"When!"

And Honorine pulled her hand back. The globe began to roll at once. Francis raced to cock and aim the pistol, then fired it wildly, missing the globe entirely and leaving a giant burned mark on the wooden deck.

The globe rolled toward the outer railing.

Honorine dove after it but slipped and kicked it farther. It rolled under the lowest bar of the railing and began to fall. She watched in horror as it plummeted toward the black water. It might be lost forever with the Mordant trapped inside!

Just before she could find her voice to shout, the pistol fired and found its mark. The globe burst into thousands of tiny particles fine as sand and scattered in the wind. A great ball of flame rolled up, and from it emerged Pegasus, his black-and-copper wings unfurling as he rose up into the dark sky.

"Francis, you did it!" Honorine shouted with glee, flinging her hands around his neck as the Pegasus swooped toward the deck and landed with a spray of sparks. He left hoofprints singed into the deck.

"Well, if Nautilus doesn't know what we did yet, he'll figure it out when he sees this," said Francis as he stepped over the smoldering horseshoe burns.

Pegasus bowed his long neck, his ears pricked forward, and sniffed at Honorine with his delicate nose.

"Hello," she said quietly, and reached up—very gently—to place her hand on his velvety muzzle. It felt like that of a mortal horse, fuzz dotted with sparse whiskers. But then there was that electric hum under her fingertips, especially when he pressed his nose forward into her hand.

"My name is Honorine," she said. "It is a pleasure to meet you."

Pegasus took a step forward, pressing the length of his head against her entire body, his ears brushing her cheek. He stayed for a moment, then stepped back and raised his head proudly, nodding and tossing his mane and a spray of silver-black sparks.

"We need to find Possideo," Honorine said. "As fast as possible."

Pegasus nodded his noble head and stretched out his great wings, as if graciously inviting her aboard.

She reached up and placed a hand on Pegasus's back, which was as high as she could reach, and realized that she had no way of getting astride the huge beast. "You know…I've never actually ridden a horse before."

"Good," said Francis as he gave her a leg up. "Because I don't think this is going to be anything like riding a horse."

He was right.

The moment they were on Pegasus's back, he was off into the darkness, flying with impossible speed at impossible heights. Francis sat close behind Honorine, both of them twining their hands into Pegasus's long, tangled mane. His wingbeats were so powerful and so swift that Honorine could barely breathe through the searing cold wind that whipped around them. She tucked her head, closed her eyes tight, and clung on with all her strength until the flight began to calm.

When she opened her eyes, they were soaring over the rivers of silver mist, back in the Sea of Ether. Honorine glanced back to make sure Francis was still safely aboard. He was staring all around them, not speaking, not even blinking, as if he were afraid to miss a single second of the heartbreakingly beautiful view. He reached out his hand, trailing his fingers through the shimmering silver mist, and then let out a single laugh of amazement.

"Pretty, isn't it?" Honorine said, and then "Hang on!" as Pegasus tucked his wings and descended, leaving a wake of silver star mist behind as they sailed back toward the world below.

There were no branches or trees this time. Honorine's view was completely clear in all directions. They were soaring over open water, headed north, with great bands of shore on either side of the wide, rolling ocean. She could barely breathe at the sight of it all.

Behind her, Francis sputtered and tripped over his own words as he tried to express what he was seeing.

"This isn't possible," he said finally, turning about on the back of the horse to take it all in. "I can see half the world in the same view!" Pegasus tossed his head and banked a bit to the left.

"Are we there already?" Francis asked.

"This is a very fast way to travel," Honorine said, just before Pegasus began to dive even faster.

The drop was even more terrifying than the ascent. Francis flew backward so quickly that he nearly pulled Honorine off, and the pair of them only managed to stay aboard when Pegasus gave a little buck to knock them back into place.

The beautiful landscape spread out before them narrowed into an angry, surging sea. It was still dark where they flew, but the sky above became blotted by heavy clouds and flashed with distant lightning.

Below, the water churned, sending up swells that would have toppled any ship smaller than the *Gaslight*. Then a faint sliver of pale shore appeared between the crests of huge waves.

Pegasus soared up and over the tremendous waves. The tips of his wings brushed the rising water.

"What's that light?" Honorine asked as a streak of bold blue, like a comet or a shooting star, flashed through the clouds above and fell back toward the sea. Pegasus tossed his head and whinnied in alarm.

"What light?" Francis replied. Indeed, the blue streak had vanished, leaving a handful of sparks quickly fading among the flickering lightning.

"It was just there!" Honorine insisted with an uneasy feeling in her gut, and not just from the plummeting descent or the bumpy ride. The blue sparks looked uncomfortably familiar. Like the ones Corvus left in his wake as he flew.

"I see something!" Francis shouted.

"Where?" Honorine asked, scanning the clouds.

 • 323

"Out there," Francis pointed over the waves. "That's an island!"

It was becoming easier to see. There was a violet light glowing under the black sea and around a bright white crescent of land. "We're coming in a bit fast," Francis said.

Honorine agreed, but there was nothing she could do but hang on and close her eyes as the shore came toward them with frightening speed.

Pegasus's legs began to race beneath them, pantomiming a gallop as he sailed low and swift over the ground, until his hooves began to graze it and then slowly take the weight of his body. Within a few strides, they were galloping along the shore, right at the boundary of the sea and the land. With hooves firmly on the ground, Pegasus slowed to a trot and finally came to a halt with a snort and a whicker.

Honorine untwined her fingers from his mane and tumbled to the ground.

The beach was covered in something rough and sharp, like shards of broken pottery.

"What is this?" she asked as she took a few shaky steps on the unstable land. Francis grabbed her sleeve and pointed at a round white skull lying between them.

Bones. The beach was covered in bones.

The Island of Stars and Bones

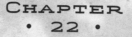

There was not a grain of sand or bit of shell to be seen. The entire beach was made of bones of every shape, skulls with long noses and strange flat teeth, femurs cracked in two with the splintered ends caked with dried marrow. They were every size as well, from great, rounded pelvic bones with odd-shaped openings big enough to stick a foot through, all the way down to little, pebble-sized vertebrae and the tiny fragments from inside fingertips. There were more than a few human skulls in the collection as well.

"It's just bones," Francis said, trying to sound confident, though his voice cracked and quivered.

"But it's a lot of them...." Honorine replied. The loose bones shifted about and made horrible noises as they scraped together. Honorine shivered at the sound.

Pegasus watched the sky a moment longer, then, with his head lowered and his wings raised, he ushered Honorine and Francis away from the water's edge.

"Did you see the crow?" Honorine whispered. Pegasus nodded, his eyes still scanning the sky as they made their way uphill, away from the shore.

"Was it...just the crow?" Honorine asked as she stepped gingerly over the bones. "Or was it the Mapmaker, too?"

"He's here?" Francis said, looking quickly back over his shoulders, then up into the sky.

Pegasus flattened his ears and flapped his wings, hurrying them all toward an ominous forest of scorched pine tree skeletons standing in a crust of snow.

"Yes, let's get out of plain sight," Honorine agreed, though she knew there was no hiding from the Mapmaker. Francis hurried along after her, and together they followed Pegasus into the pines.

Beyond the beach the ground rose uphill quite steeply. Above the tree line, the snow faded away, revealing a mountain of jagged black stone reaching up toward a single narrow peak. The entire island smelled of smoke, the air choked with a mist of salt and charcoal.

"Something very bad happened here," Francis said.

"Isn't there supposed to be a city?" Honorine said as she took her first step into the snow.

"Perhaps this is all that's left," Francis said.

Honorine shook her head. It had to be here, the city they were looking for, and within it, Andromeda. Ahead, she saw two pillars of white stone spattered with black ash. What had once been an arch lay in a pile of rock between them. Beyond the pillars was a paved road snaking up the mountain.

"That's the way to Possideo," she declared. Pegasus nodded in agreement.

Francis craned his neck back to look up at the steep grade of the mountainside.

"Up there?" he asked. "How far?"

"Well, we won't know until we start walking," Honorine said as she stepped over the crumbled arch and onto the flat paving stones of the old road.

Francis walked beside her, and Pegasus followed a few steps behind as they headed off into the silent, dead forest. The climb was steep, and the road was in poor condition, missing many paving stones, which made the ground mushy in places and icy in others. Pegasus kept his head low, sniffing the ground and listening intently. As they moved farther uphill, the air became warmer, and the snow and ice melted away. Faint clouds of smoke began to gather among the dead trees.

"Where is that smoke coming from?" Honorine wondered aloud. "Is the forest still on fire up here?"

"I don't see any flames," said Francis as they came upon a thin line of smoke rising swiftly through a narrow split in the ground. "This is coming from underground."

The ground rumbled very faintly, as if thunder had cracked deep under the earth. Pegasus spooked, fluttering into the air briefly, like a pheasant flushed from the underbrush.

"The Bellua," Honorine whispered. The ancient and horrible beasts that even the Mapmaker feared. Pegasus settled back to the ground, folding both his wings and his ears down tightly, and nudging

Honorine with his muzzle, encouraging her to move just a bit faster.

"And what are they again?" Francis asked.

"The only thing that can kill a Mordant," Honorine said.

"Ah yes," Francis said, nodding toward the crack in the ground as they carefully picked their way around it. "So don't go down *there*. Got it."

Farther up the mountain, the smoke grew thicker, rising in sheets toward the sky, like a waterfall in reverse.

"Something moved over there," Francis said, stopping suddenly. "Something white."

"It was probably just smoke," Honorine replied, too busy trying to keep track of the road to look up. Higher uphill, they finally moved away from the sheets of smoke and onto a ragged slope of exposed stone, hard and jagged as broken glass.

Here, the road came to an end. The flat paving stones disappeared under a field of pointed black stones.

"Obsidian," Francis observed, picking up a chip of sharp rock. "And this is all hardened lava over here. We're standing on a volcano. Wait! There it is!"

Francis pointed over the landscape of black rock to a white flash that was gone before Honorine could get it in her view.

"I saw a blur," she said. "What was it?"

"An animal," Francis replied. "Some kind of white animal. Like that wolf."

Honorine froze.

"*A* wolf?" she asked. "Or was it Lux?"

Then she finally saw it, first as a flash of white in the other direction. She looked harder, and the blur focused into a white animal bounding over the black stone, head held low, a trail of faint white sparks following it like a comet.

"Lux?" she called as the creature streaked away over the curve of the mountainside.

"Was that him?" Francis asked.

"Why would he run away?" Honorine asked as she started out in the direction of the vanishing white streak. Over a ridge of obsidian, they found a vast field of black scattered with stark white stones, but no white wolf.

"What is all this?" Francis asked as they stopped to examine the pale stones. "It looks like marble."

"A headstone? Is this a cemetery?" Honorine scanned the vast field. Most of the lighter stones were great square hunks and slabs, but among them were a few round disks with notched edges or carvings of curling leaves. Francis squatted down to examine a round white shape jutting out of the ground.

"Doesn't look like a tombstone," he said. "Wait, this is part of a column!" He patted one of the great, round disks.

"That's a roof!" Honorine exclaimed, pointing to a steep ramp of reddish tiles.

"Well, I think we've found the city," he said, tapping his foot on the ground. "Buried. Must have been an eruption. Lava came down and covered the whole place, or most of it, at least."

"The whole city was destroyed," she said, trying not to let Francis see just how angry and disappointed she was. "What are we supposed to do?"

"What we came here to do," Francis said. "Find Andromeda."

He looked just as scared as Honorine felt, but neither of them dared mention the thought aloud—that there might not be anything to find here.

"And there's that creature again," Francis said, pointing toward the very peak of the mountain.

There it was, a white beast with four legs and a shimmering white coat. But it was not Lux. It was a dog. A tall, elegant white dog with long fur and a curling tail.

"There's another one," she said as a second, identical hound stepped beside the first, glowing against the black landscape all around them. They looked like phantoms. Honorine took a step up the mountain.

"Wait, are we going after them?" Francis asked. "We're sure they're friendly?"

"I have no idea," Honorine said. "But I have nothing better to do than investigate a little further."

Over a lump of treacherously sharp rock, they found a wide, charred marble staircase leading up to the peak of the mountain and the remains of what must have been a spectacular palace. Great, round sections of fluted marble columns lay scattered about. Among the wreckage lay uneven patches of a terrace inlaid with a spiraling mosaic of gold and silver and rich blue gemstones.

In the very center of the wrecked terrace stood a massive, ancient tree, its trunk twisted and pocked with gaping black knots, its branches gnarled and covered with galls. All around the tree, steam rose up through cracks in the ground.

"This is it," Francis said. "This is all there is."

"Wait, I've seen a tree like that before," Honorine said. "That's an ironwood tree. There was one on the *Carina*."

"And what happened to the dogs?" Francis asked, only to be answered by a low, mournful howl.

The dogs appeared over the broken marble steps, trotting to the base of the tree. They were tall and sleek and made of ivory-white light, with long Roman noses and curling tails that made them look as if they were in midflight even as they were standing still. Just behind them came a woman, walking up the hillside and under the boughs of the ironwood tree.

She looked as if she had been made of the night itself, with huge eyes that glittered like stars. Her hair was a magnificent spray of icy white ringlets that rose all around her, the ends waving as if weightless and leaving tiny silver embers drifting down around her. She wore silk in the deepest violet set with tiny spots of light, fixed to her like gems.

"Andromeda," Honorine whispered.

"That's her?" Francis whispered back as Andromeda approached them.

She stared down at them, the little chips of light
falling over her shoulders and drifting to the ground as
slowly as dandelion down.

"You shouldn't have come here."

The Surprisingly Dangerous Key

Andromeda cast off so much vibrant white and purple light, it was difficult to look directly at her. But faced with a second long-lost parent who didn't seem at all pleased to see her, Honorine found looking at the dark ground preferable. It helped hide the warm tears welling up in her eyes.

"We didn't know where else to go," Francis said as Honorine lifted her head with a sniff. "Nautilus is trying to find you, and the Mapmaker is trying to kill him."

"All this time, and they still haven't worked it out?" Andromeda said with a shake of her head. Then she smiled very slightly. "I remember you, Francis. You look just like your mother. And, of course . . ." Andromeda reached out her hand and placed a finger under Honorine's chin, raising her face until she was looking the girl in the eyes.

The color in Andromeda's eyes shifted, growing bolder and then softer, just the way the Mapmaker's did. But Andromeda's eyes were gray, just like Honorine's.

"You are still too young to be here," she said. "I had dear allies who had promised to look after you. Perhaps they are allies no longer?"

"No," Honorine said. "I mean, yes, they did look after me, as much as they could. But now we have to return the favor. They need us."

A growl rumbled up from somewhere deep beneath the mountain. Honorine froze, her eyes wide.

"Is that . . ." she whispered as she looked past Andromeda toward the smoking vents surrounding the ironwood tree. "The Bellua?"

Andromeda shook her head.

"No," she said. "They are farther down below. The mountain shakes and shudders. That's its nature."

The mountain rumbled again, but this time the ground lurched up, shaking loose large boulders of obsidian. The sound of stones rolling down the rocky slopes echoed up from below. Pegasus leaped into the air, but this time, he didn't settle back down. He flew higher, circling the mountain.

"Are you sure that's nothing to be worried about?" Francis asked.

"Oh, it very well could be," Andromeda mused. "It's just not the Bellua."

"What else could it be?" Honorine asked as a single streak of blue sailed by high over the mountaintop. A very familiar blue.

"Corvus!" Francis whispered.

"It's the Mapmaker! He's here!" Honorine shouted. The entire mountain heaved as if it were resting on a carpet that had just been tugged away, knocking Honorine and Francis to the ground.

Andromeda took each one by the hand and lifted them to their feet in one swooping motion, moving them down the marble steps, away from the peak of the mountain.

They had just reached the last splintered marble step when the ground heaved again, even more violently, shaking great sheets of mountainside free and sending them crashing down toward the ocean. This time, the shaking didn't stop. Andromeda kept them moving out onto the field of black stone and broken marble as the peak of the mountain above them split in two, one side shearing clean off and sliding past them. Andromeda pulled Honorine and Francis closer and shielded them from the scattering shards until the trembling stopped and the mountain went quiet again.

"Honorine?" Francis said through a cloud of dust and smoke.

"Francis? Are you all right?" she replied. She felt his hand reaching out and took it, holding tightly as they waved away the chalky clouds around them.

"You know," Francis said. "Ever since we landed on that beach, I've been thinking, 'At least things can't get much worse.' And then they do."

"Then don't look up there," Honorine said as she inched her way onto a fallen boulder to see what had become of the mountaintop.

All that remained was the old ironwood tree resting on the precipice of a newly formed cliff of irides-cent black stone and a narrow, rocky ledge. Facing out of the cliff, and tangled into the exposed roots of the ironwood tree, stood a gate made of iron bars and polished black bones of every kind of creature imaginable, and some unimaginable as well. Every bar and bone of the gates stood silhouetted by an unsettling violet light.

"No, I don't like that, either," Francis agreed. "And yet, I feel certain it is about to get worse. Again."

And then, of course, a shadow moved through the violet light. Honorine and Francis both took a sideways step toward each other.

"This is why you shouldn't have come," Andromeda said. "And why you should go now."

"But we just found you," Honorine protested.

"Yes, how unfortunate," said a voice booming down from the crumbled remains of the top of the mountain. All heads turned to see the Mapmaker striding over the ruined peak, past the violet light of the gates.

He was furious. Honorine could feel it rolling off him like a mist. Even from a distance, she could see his eyes, no longer blue, but dark, reflecting the light like smoky mirrors, revealing not his mood, but instead just how ancient a creature he truly was.

"Andromeda, my dear, we have a bit of a situation," he said. "Actually, *you* have a bit of a situation. Your long-lost love has decided to, once again, interfere in affairs that are none of his concern."

"So you come here? You threaten me? You ruin the last protection we have against destruction by the Bellua?" she replied, crossing her arms and glaring. She nodded toward Honorine and Francis. "You could have killed them."

The Mapmaker shrugged. "The boy, maybe."

"You didn't need to come here," Honorine said. "We were getting this all sorted out."

The Mapmaker's eyes snapped to her, burning with intense blue-white light.

"Oh, you were?" he asked. "Is that what this is? Because if I remember correctly, we had an arrangement."

"And we still do," Honorine replied.

"Oh no, no," said the Mapmaker. "The only thing you were supposed to do was to remain loyal to me. But you ran away with Nautilus. *Again*."

"No, I ran away with *Francis* again," Honorine corrected.

"As if that's any better."

The ground heaved as if the mountain had taken a tremendous breath. Francis and Honorine hung on to each other to keep from toppling over.

The Mapmaker hardly twitched. "That wasn't me."

A horrendous, howling bellow rolled up from deep underground, echoing through the hollow mountain and erupting from the steaming fissures running across the stony ground.

"This is a dangerous game," Andromeda said. "You'll risk upsetting the peace."

"The peace is already gone!" the Mapmaker replied. "I've had enough. I've waited for centuries to be able to rest. It's time to settle this. Every one of you had your chance, and the situation has only grown worse with every passing moment. So now we finish this my way."

"What are you going to do?" Honorine asked.

"Oh, I've already done it," the Mapmaker said. "That's the beauty of it. Nautilus has been chasing me for years. He's been capturing the Mordant and holding them on his ship, as if he has any right to do such a thing, claiming he just wants to find this island. And now, would you look at that!"

The Mapmaker clapped his hands as he stared out past Andromeda, Francis, and Honorine, toward the ocean behind them. They turned to see a bright, glimmering light moving swiftly toward them from the eastern horizon.

It was the *Gaslight.*

"You brought Nautilus here?" Honorine asked.

"Actually, Astraea did," the Mapmaker said. "At my request. I'm done waiting. I'm done warning. I'm done hiding and running and making bargains. If this is what Nautilus wants, then let him have it. Let him see just what happens when he gets what he thinks he wants."

"This is all a foolish waste of time," Andromeda said. "As long as I'm here, the gates remain closed, and the Bellua remain trapped. Nautilus cannot make me leave this island."

The Mapmaker's eyes sparkled with wicked glee.

"Oh, but, my dear, I think he can."

"Then we have to stop him!" Honorine shouted.

"Oh, *now* we have to stop him?" asked the Mapmaker. "What about when you were on his ship? Did you stop him then, when you had the opportunity? Did you free the imprisoned Mordant? No. When you left his ship, did you come to me? No. You are still trying to protect him from me."

"I'm trying to protect the both of you!" Honorine said. "I came here to find a way to stop you both from hurting each other or anyone else."

"How noble," said the Mapmaker. "But I don't believe it." He took a single, lunging step forward, sending a tremor through the ground that knocked Francis to his knees. The Mapmaker reached toward Honorine but was stopped by a blaze of white fire that raced from Andromeda's hand and rolled across the ground between them.

"Don't you dare harm her," Andromeda said, her figure smoldering brightly.

"Just what do you think I am?" asked the Map-maker. "I'm not going to hurt her. I'm going to show her what she needs to see."

Honorine's heart thudded in her chest. Her skin prickled as a cold breeze blew across the mountain. The sound of the *Gaslight* pulling toward the island grew louder every second. The gates at the top of the mountain rattled.

"What is he doing?" Francis said as he stared out toward the water. Honorine turned to see the *Gaslight* steaming toward them. Bright light shone through the shattered shell of the greenhouse dome.

Andromeda began to glow as well, first faintly and then with a searing white light that turned her into a silhouette, then simply a great knot of burning heat.

"He's using the machine!" Francis continued. "On Andromeda!"

"But he can't!" Honorine said. "It's not strong enough for this! She's safe here!"

The Mapmaker shook his head. "What did I tell you about that word, Honorine?" he chided. "Nothing is safe. Not in this world or any other."

"How can he use that machine here?" Honorine said. "This place is protected!"

"No place is protected anymore," the Mapmaker said, standing back and throwing his hands out to his sides. "Not this island. Not the archer's desert stronghold. Not even the *Carina*. Not since you spent time on his ship."

A swirling ball of sparks began to orbit around Andromeda. She sent out another flare of white fire, but it was contained within the shell of sparks.

"Oh, one more thing, before you go," the Mapmaker said, reaching into Honorine's pocket and drawing out the key in one swift motion, like a heron snapping a fish from a pond. "Your daughter thought it wise to make an ironwood key. And then to bring it back to Possideo."

Andromeda's eyes widened, then her mouth, as if she were about to shout something, but she was a moment too late. In a flash, she was gone, imploding into a tail of embers and burning dust.

Out on the water, the glow of the *Gaslight*'s dome turned from multicolored to bright gold.

"He did it," Francis said in a quiet, terrified tone. "He caught Andromeda."

"That's right, he did," said the Mapmaker. "With Honorine's help."

"But I broke that machine," Honorine said. "I didn't help him rebuild it. This has nothing to do with me!"

"It has *everything* to do with you," the Mapmaker said. His voice dripped from his lips like poison. "Nautilus and Lord Vidalia combined never came close to building anything like that steamship until after you were born. But then they each held you when you were just a mewling infant, and even that was enough to inspire Nautilus to build his most devious contraption. And look at Francis! He grew up beside you and his genius exceeds that of even Nautilus."

Honorine stepped in front of Francis.

"He didn't do anything wrong, either," she said, staring the Mapmaker in the eye.

"Oh, really?" he replied, leaning forward. "He didn't spend years on that ship, building that machine, right alongside his mentor? And what happens when Francis is a grown man—which will be in a flash of time—and decides he wants to avenge his father?"

Honorine felt the blood drain from her face.

"What have you done to Lord Vidalia?" she demanded.

"Nothing," the Mapmaker insisted. "But he's very elderly now. He's lost valuable years that he will never get to spend with his son. What if I let Francis go tonight? In a few years' time, I'll have to endure his attacks as well? You don't understand where this will all lead. You don't understand what's to come. Terrible things. Generations of terrible things, and the Mordant have to watch it all. So much more than temples and coliseums and steam engines and gaslight. So much more destruction. Nautilus may be the first, but he won't be the last. Better to stop it all now."

The ground began to swell. Honorine took a step back and reached out for Francis's hand.

"What's happening?" he asked as cracks began to form and then split, revealing red light and noxious steam from deep underground.

"Well, all that shaking and rumbling has probably

woken a few of our old friends down there," the Mapmaker noted. "They'll be coming up to check on the situation surprisingly quickly. And thankfully, you brought this."

He held up the key.

Honorine gulped.

The Mapmaker smiled. "Didn't I tell you?" he said, shaking his head as he took the last few steps up the mountainside, toward the rattling black gates.

"Ironwood keys can open *any* lock."

"Don't!" Honorine shouted as the Mapmaker reached for the black bones. "Why would you do that?"

"Nautilus must let the Mordant go," he replied as he brushed aside a loose vertebrae, uncovering a stout iron lock on the old bone gates. "And he doesn't seem to want to. So we'll just press his hand a bit."

The ironwood key slipped into the lock.

"He has his beloved back, and his daughter, right here, to complete the family! All Nautilus has to do to save you both is let the Mordant go," the Mapmaker said as he turned the wooden key in the iron lock. "If that's *really* all he wants."

"Francis, we have to get off this island," Honorine said

as the ground continued to splinter and tremble around them.

"You probably won't be able to save Francis now," the Mapmaker said, strolling along a ridge of black stone that continued to rise from the smoldering ground. "Yourself, perhaps. This will be a chance to find out just how mortal you are. But the boy, well, in a few minutes, this entire island will be a cauldron of death from his perspective. Unless Nautilus has a machine that can capture a Bellua."

"Over here!" Francis said, leading her toward a pile of rubble forming a more manageable slope. "We can climb down here. Maybe." As he reached a toe out to test the footing, a blast of boiling hot steam erupted from under the rubble, sending a spray of red-hot embers and chunks of razor-sharp stone blasting into the sky.

"Okay, not that way," Francis said, pulling his singed, damp boot back from the widening crater on the mountainside. Honorine led him back from the edge of the crumbling cliff, closer and closer to the black bone gates.

"Are you just going to leave us here?" Honorine called up, searching for the Mapmaker. All she could see above them was black stone and traces of night sky through a sheet of smoke and steam.

"No, of course not," called back the voice of the Mapmaker. "I'll be with you the whole time! We can see just how brilliant your Nautilus Olyphant really is together."

Honorine growled in frustration. There was no use in being scared, she thought, but she could hardly help it. The mountain was falling apart, the ground was splitting in pieces, and she was trapped. But then, through the smoke and the blurry red light, she saw something move on the pile of black rubble below them. Something large and dark and outlined in piercing green sparks. It was monstrous-looking, but not a Bellua.

It was Scorpio.

It wasn't just the Mapmaker who had come to the island. The others were probably here, too, and the *Carina*, somewhere.

Above them, the Mapmaker turned the key in the lock.

The ground trembled.

The smoke billowed.

And the black bone Gates of Hades silently

unlocked and started to swing open before shaking apart and falling into a pile of smoldering black dust.

"Francis, I think—" she began to say, but she was interrupted by a vicious growl rolling up behind the bone gates from somewhere not just deep under the mountain—it was a howl from another world.

Chapter

· 24 ·

The Stars of Stolen Fire

The volcano was a problem. The Gates of Hades standing open, letting any monster from the underworld escape into the night, was also a problem. The incredibly high and precarious position of what was left of the ledge on the crumbling side of the cliff was a third problem.

But there were also a scorpion and a winged horse still somewhere in the vicinity.

"I'm not one to complain," said Francis, "but if you

have any ideas at all about how to get out of this situation, I am ready to hear them."

"Let's just start this way and see how far we get," Honorine suggested finally, inching her way to the cusp of the ledge. The rock was unstable and the drop quite steep, but there were enough tiny footholds along the broken stone to at least get them lower down on the mountain.

A pair of black wings rushed past, but it was not Pegasus.

"Astraea!" Honorine shouted, waving into the sky with one hand as she clung to the rock with the other.

Astraea circled back, using her wings to hover very near Honorine and Francis.

"We need Pegasus!" Honorine shouted across a swath of searing steam. "He brought us here—he's still up there somewhere."

"Hang on," Astraea said. "I'll send him to you. Keep climbing down! Don't stop!"

"No worries there," Francis said as the mountainside buckled.

They reached a little plateau of broken stone and took just a moment to catch their breath, which was exactly when the pile of sharp gravel under them began to shake and slide down the mountain.

Sitting on a sheet of tumbling stones was already uncomfortable before they sailed through more than one vent of hot steam, which stung just enough to be excruciating without leaving lasting burns on their exposed skin. Honorine tumbled and bounced, gathering bruises and scrapes along the way, trying to keep an eye on Francis, which was nearly impossible in the dark and the fog. Eventually, they sailed into melting, slushy snow, which was a relief—until they realized they were sliding even faster down the increasingly steep side of the mountain, which disappeared only a little way ahead.

Astraea swooped by a moment later.

"There's a cliff!" she called out. "Very steep! When you go over the edge—"

"What?" Honorine protested.

"We'll catch you!" Astraea finished.

It sounded impossible, yet as there were no other plans, Honorine simply shouted back, "All right, I suppose!" and braced for the fall.

And fall they did, Honorine right onto the back of Pegasus, and Francis right past him.

"Francis!" Honorine shouted as they plummeted after him.

Between Pegasus's teeth and Astraea's lucky grab, they caught him just before he would have crashed onto a slab of black granite. With Francis hanging between them like a bit of damp laundry, the Mordant glided swiftly down to the beach.

Pegasus held him up by the sleeve of his shirt until he regained his footing.

"We need to get back to the *Gaslight*," Honorine said. "Nautilus has Andromeda. He's done something to his machine. He got her, even though she was still on the island."

Astraea crossed her arms and nodded.

"Then this makes a bit more sense," she said, tipping her head toward the chaos on top of the mountain.

"And what about that?" Francis asked groggily as he pointed back at the side of the mountain that had once been the Gates of Hades.

A fissure had opened in the side of the mountain, spilling out bright, bloodred light. Slender, many-jointed legs rose from beneath the ground, planting themselves into the mountainside. There were far too many legs for just one beast, yet before they stopped unfolding, they began to lift a writhing body with pincers and wings and glittering eyes on short black stalks. Honorine had never seen anything more horrible in her life. It looked like some kind of flying scorpion, with legs and wings that were far outsized for its body.

"That would be the Nightmare," Astraea said.

The newly hatched Nightmare howled, or screeched, or made whatever kind of call a hideous beast from beneath the earth makes. It was somewhere between a tiger's growl and a banshee's wail, and it chilled Honorine immediately, as if she had just been dropped into the icy sea.

"There's still time to stop this, but we mustn't wait a moment longer," Astraea said. "Get back to the ship. Find Andromeda. Send the others to help. I'll do what I can to keep the Nightmare from getting off this island, but I won't be able to keep it here for long."

Honorine nodded and twisted her hands tightly into Pegasus's mane.

"We'll find her," Honorine said as Francis climbed onto Pegasus behind her. "I can get her back."

"I know you can," Astraea said, and then leaped into the air.

Pegasus took off in the opposite direction. In a single stride, they were aloft, soaring back toward the *Gaslight* and its cargo of prisoners. And cannons.

"Oh, that could be a problem," Francis said as they flew low over the black water, toward the giant steamship. Honorine could see men gathering at the railing, aiming cannons at the Nightmare as it began to crawl over the mountainside.

"I don't think those cannons will help," Honorine said.

"No, but they'll definitely knock this horse out of the sky," Francis replied as a hunk of fiery green rock sailed past his head.

Pegasus raced toward the ship, dodging the whistling cannonballs as he aimed for the main deck, lit by thousands of crystal lamps. A fragment of ammunition caught him in the flank, and his back end briefly sputtered out. Honorine felt herself beginning to fall for a moment before Pegasus regrouped and she felt solid horse under her once more. Francis nearly tumbled into the sea as well, only catching the hem of Honorine's tunic before he was bounced back aboard by a rough kick from Pegasus's re-formed legs.

They touched down, leaving long, smoldering gashes across the wooden deck. Honorine hopped down before Pegasus had come to a complete stop.

"Andromeda!" she whispered aloud, searching up and down the deck until her eyes landed on the greenhouse dome. She had to still be in the laboratory.

Down into the ship she ran, skipping over steps and leaping over railings, with Francis rushing to keep up. When they burst through the laboratory doors, Honorine found exactly what she was looking for, in an unexpected way.

Andromeda was there, but not in a globe. Not captured or held prisoner, but standing in front of Nautilus, her shimmering light casting long shadows on the far walls. She looked up as Honorine and Francis tumbled into the laboratory. She did not look pleased.

"There you are!" Nautilus said as if he had been searching for them for a very long time.

"You have to get back to the island," Honorine said between gulps of breath. She pointed frantically in the general direction of the erupting mountain.

"Honorine, you look upset," said Nautilus.

"Yes, I certainly am!" she replied. "The mountain is erupting! The Bellua are escaping! There's nothing holding them back because *you* took my mother away from there!"

"Then that's it," Andromeda said, turning to Nautilus. "Your experiment is over. Set the rest of the Mordant free so we can stop this from escalating."

To Honorine's shock, Nautilus resisted.

"But none of the Bellua have even escaped yet," he said, shaking his head.

"The Nightmare has," Honorine replied.

"Well, that's only one," Nautilus said. "Surely Astraea and Sagittarius and the others can handle one Bellua on their own."

Andromeda crossed her arms and began to burn with low, intense light.

"You want the handful of Mordant who have managed to escape your persecution to now fight and protect you? To clean up the disasters that you created?"

"They don't need to defend me," Nautilus said. "I have this ship. They only need to hold back the Bellua."

Andromeda's light swelled. She took a step toward Nautilus, who immediately retreated.

"Well, it's their duty, isn't it?" Nautilus continued. "Isn't that part of the job?"

Andromeda's light grew so bright that Honorine's eyes had difficulty adjusting. The Mordant queen continued to advance toward Nautilus, the light now pooling and falling from her dress. She pointed her hand toward the far wall, and a trail of white fire raced across the floor in a thin line. It climbed the far wall, forming a rough circle that continued to burn hotter and brighter until a great slab of iron fell away, leaving a gaping hole.

"You can't expect me to abandon all the work we've done here," Nautilus said as Andromeda sent the fire deeper into the ship. "You haven't even seen what we've built here! At least take a look—"

"I've seen enough," Andromeda said as another layer of wall crumbled, revealing the cabin full of imprisoned Mordant. "This ends now."

Nautilus opened his mouth to reply, but he was interrupted by a hideous crash from outside the ship.

"What was that?" Francis asked. "That Nightmare thing?"

Lightning flashed overhead, followed by a wild crack of thunder.

"No," Honorine said with a hesitant smile. "That's Eridanus."

The ship rose suddenly and pitched sharply, knocking everyone aboard except Andromeda off balance for a moment.

"Enough," she said. "There's no more time to waste here."

The next moment, Professor du Ciel appeared on the bridge overhead, knocking sharply on the window. She was drenched from head to toe.

"Captain!" she said through the amplifiers inside the bridge. "There's a rogue storm approaching, very fast. The volcanic activity is increasing exponentially, and also, well, there's a...monster on the side of the mountain, not one of the Mordant. It's...I think you need to see this."

The entire crew hurried up to the bridge. Out across the deck, a wild storm had begun circling the island, curiously staying out at sea, creating a barrier of lightning and thick black clouds. On the island, a creature that looked a bit like a squid covered in barbed hooks crawled across the beach while another beast, much more solid and stout, pounded its way around the hillside, using huge tusks to fling enormous boulders into the air, which landed with sprays of hot ash and splashes of lava.

"And what are *those*?" Francis asked.

"The Leviathan and the Rhectae," Andromeda said in a very unamused tone. "This is not going well."

Far up above them, the Nightmare crawled toward the peak of the mountain, its wings catching the growing breeze.

"Why isn't it flying?" Francis asked.

"It's going after the tree first," Andromeda explained.

"You mean that old ironwood?" Honorine said.

"It's the last of the Silva trees on the island," said Andromeda. "The last defense against the Bellua escaping. The sap of a Silva tree will harden the volcano's lava and rebuild the old gates. We need it to lock the Bellua back in."

"And if that beast tears it down?" Professor du Ciel asked.

"Then it will be a battle," Andromeda said. "One I don't think we can win."

A tiny silver streak raced across the sky toward the Nightmare.

"Astraea!" Honorine said.

"She won't be able to hold him off for long on her own," Andromeda said.

"The storm is closing in," Francis said as the wall of clouds met and washed over the ship, pouring a torrent of rain down over the *Gaslight*.

"Eridanus is hiding the ship," said Andromeda.

The clouds blocked the ship from view of the shore, but also blocked the view of the Nightmare. Lightning flashed and rain splattered across the deck as winds whipped in every direction. The sailors out on the deck ran to secure the ship, to protect the exposed equipment from the sudden rain, and also to save their own lives.

A blue light flashed brightly over the ship, but it was not lightning. Corvus swept low, landing on the deck. The Mapmaker slid from the back of the crow and stood facing the bridge and the greenhouse dome beyond.

"That will not be good," Honorine said. The Mapmaker raised his hands, and the ship rose and heaved under a tremendous wave, tipping treacherously back before plunging down into a spray of salt water. He raised his hands again, and the deck began to splinter, a sharp crack appearing straight across the width of the ship from starboard to port.

"He's going to sink the ship!" Nautilus shouted.

"He just wants the Mordant free!" said Honorine. "Let them go!"

Andromeda turned and leaned down beside her. "It's time to be courageous," she said. "I have to go back down there and get them out."

She pointed back toward the laboratory and the imprisoned Mordant.

"Right," Honorine said. "Let's go!"

Andromeda shook her head.

"You stay with Francis. Keep him safe."

"No," Honorine said, shaking her head. "I have to go with you! I promised I'd help them!"

Andromeda smiled. "And you did," she said. "You found me. Now, be brave. I'll be back in but a moment."

Andromeda left the bridge, Nautilus protesting and ranting behind her, Professor du Ciel on his heels.

Out on the deck, the Mapmaker continued to send waves over the ship, one after another, shaking railings and fixtures loose from their fittings, widening the fissure in the wooden deck.

"He's not going to stop," Honorine said. "He's really going to sink the ship. We have to do something."

"Well, there's one thing...." Francis said as he watched the Mapmaker snapping the boat in half one deck plank at a time. "There's always the machine."

"No!" Honorine said with a gasp. Even though she knew he was right, and that if they didn't act quickly, the Mapmaker would simply tear the ship to pieces, Honorine still wished there was another way. If they used the machine against him, then he would be right. Honorine would have betrayed him.

"Except that we don't know his constellation," Francis continued. He seemed almost mesmerized by the sight of the Mapmaker's rampage on the other side of the glass.

Honorine breathed half a sigh of relief and then stopped cold.

She did know his constellation.

The moment she thought of it, the image filled her mind—the last constellation in the room under the swamp, behind the only locked door on the *Carina*.

Honorine looked out at the Mapmaker, remembering the vision he'd shown her, himself in the globe, his stars extinguishing one at a time in the dark sky. It had probably been a test to see if she would use that knowledge against him.

"What if we do?" she whispered.

"You know his constellation?" Francis asked in disbelief.

"I might," Honorine said. "But do we have to capture him? Can we just…hang on to him for a moment and give Astraea and the rest of them the chance to fight back?"

"We can try," Francis said.

Honorine opened a logbook, grabbed a charcoal pencil, and jotted down the pattern of stars as she remembered them, still hoping in a small way that she was wrong.

"I saw this on the *Carina*," she explained, suddenly remembering something that Lord Vidalia had said to her on the ship. "And your father mentioned the Stolen Fire."

"Prometheus?" Francis asked after a moment of contemplation. "But he doesn't have a constellation."

"Or maybe he does, and he's been very good at hiding it," Honorine said, handing him the drawing. "Of course, this might not be correct."

"We can give it a try," Francis said. "It will give us something to do besides wait to be drowned or eaten by monsters."

As they hurried back down toward the laboratory, figures began to emerge from below. A magnificent black swan, its wings edged in silver, its eyes blazing red. A ram with curling golden horns, a blue-black hare with points of light speckled through its coat, a hunter with a bow and a silver sword, a great lizard with scales of black and gold. A chariot drawn by a team of horses with silver coats. A magnificent dove, its feathers made of swirling white and blue lights shot with streaks of gold.

Francis and Honorine ducked and swerved as the Mordant escaped past them, out into the night air.

"Prometheus," Francis said with a shake of his head, "who stole the secret of fire from the gods and gave it to man. Of course! The Mapmaker is the muse of Knowledge. He was the one who first taught people how to communicate with the stars."

In the laboratory, they found more Mordant pouring through the hole that Andromeda had burned into the wall. Professor du Ciel stood near the controls, watching helplessly as figure after figure raced past them. She was too confused and overwhelmed to object when Francis ordered her to stand aside.

"The machine isn't ready," she said as she considered Honorine's hasty rendering. "We don't have globes in place for these stars."

"Well, start anyway," Honorine said. She headed to the wall and began climbing the rusting metal staircases toward the dome above.

"What are you doing?" Francis called as he tried to follow her.

"Stay there!" Honorine called back. "Tell me which ones!"

She pointed to the globes high above. Most of them had been replaced, but some still hung in shards from the singed ends of the copper pipes. The dome above had not been fully repaired, either, and cold wind whipped in, bringing sparks and jets of sulfurous smoke.

"There are thirteen stars in Prometheus!" Francis called up to her. "And from down here, it looks like most of the ones we need to use are broken."

"Wonderful," Honorine said as she made her way out onto the adjustable ladder. With the help of Francis's wild gestures and frantic shouting, she swung around to each of the thirteen globes that were required to light the constellation of Prometheus. Most of them were shattered, and there was no time to wait for replacements to be carried up. She had to substitute intact globes from other locations, detaching and reattaching them, but eventually, amid the gusts of wind that shook the ladder, enormous waves that almost threw her to the ground, and falling sparks that singed the back of her neck, Honorine thought she had the globes in place.

"All right! Give it a try!" she called down.

Francis scowled. "Not while you're still up there!"

"I'm not coming all the way down! I'll need to come back up if it doesn't work. Just hurry!"

Something groaned in the water deep beneath the ship, making the walls shudder and the glass globes ring.

Francis and Professor du Ciel began turning the dials and adjusting the levels. The copper pipes rattled faintly as the globes filled with gas. Soft pops echoed around the dome as flames erupted gently into the globes.

Honorine watched intently as each one flickered to life in different shades of fire. One, two, three, all the way up to five looked good, and they continued to light.

Then she saw it.

Across the open dome, one of the globes right in the middle of the constellation was too loose. She had replaced the broken globe with one that was a size too large. She hadn't tightened it enough. As soon as the gas ignited, it would come completely off, and fall.

She began to swing the ladder out, into the most open space in the laboratory.

"Wait! What are you doing?" Professor du Ciel shouted.

"It's about to light!" Francis called. "Get out of the way!"

Globes around her burst to life as Honorine reached the loose one and grasped the sides of the glass with both hands. Leaning all her weight on the ladder, she tightened the connection as fast as she could manage.

She could hear the gas flowing down the pipe and filling the globe, hear the tick of the ignition as it attempted to light the flame. After only two faint clicks, the Sidus Apparatus came to life, and a pulse of energy burst out through the connected globes and across the dome.

Honorine was instantly thrown off the ladder and into the vast open space between the dome and the hard, glass-strewn floor.

The Lost Constellation

H onorine felt the solid metal of the ladder slip
away and expected to fall to the floor. Instead,
she dropped just enough to feel her stomach lurch into
her throat, and then there was a tremendous flash and
the sound of air rushing past her, though she felt no
wind. And then...not much else.

She was not on the ground, but she was not falling,
either. She was looking out over the laboratory, filled with
the reflections of the light from the globes. Far below
stood Francis and Professor du Ciel, looking terrified.

Then something else moved in the room. The Mapmaker sailed past her and became a whole, solid form collected out of the air from bits of electricity and cinders. He was standing on a kind of flat disk of pale light.

He looked completely confounded, both at finding himself standing inside the ship and at seeing Honorine there, hovering somewhere above him.

"Ah," he said after a long moment to contemplate his situation. "So this is Nautilus's magnificent machine. And you clever people have finally figured out how to use it against me."

"I'm not going to do it," Honorine said. "What you showed me, in that vision. I won't destroy you. And I won't let anyone else do it, either."

"Yet you'd use this machine to imprison me?" he asked.

"Or to keep you safe," Honorine said. "Just for a little while. When this is over, I'll set you free again. I promise."

The Mapmaker's eyes grew wide, and he looked as if he was about to say something, when Honorine noticed the key still in his hand. She reached out, trying to get her fingers around it, when Professor du Ciel made an adjustment on the machine. Suddenly, he was surrounded by intense golden light drawing closer and tighter until, with a flash, the Mapmaker was encased in a small amber orb, just as the rest of them had been.

And then she was falling.

Not to the floor, but into a cloud of sparks and blinding light. A moment later, Honorine felt solid ground under her feet and slowly looked up to find herself sitting on the metal grate of the laboratory floor.

Francis and Professor du Ciel stared at her in shock.

"What just happened?" she asked. She had the ironwood key in her hand.

"You...well, you..." Francis said, trying to find a way to explain. "You remember when I hit the wolf with that starglass bullet?"

Honorine's eyes lit up. "I did the sparks thing?" She waved her hands in the air to imitate the explosion. "What color sparks were they?" She felt suddenly shocked with energy. Her heart was pounding. She could feel it in her ears.

"Gold, I suppose," Francis said. "It was so fast I don't really remember."

"You got a bit tangled in the machine," Professor du Ciel explained. "It didn't know what was the

Mapmaker and what was you for a moment. But we straightened it out."

Honorine peered into the amber orb resting in a scorched silver metal bowl, rocking slightly from side to side and giving off a faint wisp of smoke. Instead of a little figure, she saw only a tumbling knot of dark smoke swirling inside. "Are you sure you got him?"

"I think I see a figure inside," Francis said.

"There wouldn't be a physical orb unless we had caught something," Professor du Ciel added.

"Don't worry," Honorine said, wrapping the Mapmaker's amber prison in her sash and slinging it over her shoulder. "You're staying with me for now. And Francis," she said, looking up at him. "Andromeda and the Mordant are handling the mountain. So I think we should go find your father."

Francis's eyes popped.

"The *Carina* must be here somewhere. And that was the last place I saw Lord Vidalia."

That was enough to persuade Francis.

They headed out into the storm, looking for Pegasus. Who they found was Corvus, rain and sea spray flashing off his feathers. He cawed loudly at them as they approached.

"Now, don't be upset with me," Honorine said as she showed Corvus the globe containing the Mapmaker. "We need to get him out of here, and we need to find Lord Vidalia. Can you to take us back to the *Carina*?"

Corvus obliged but made no effort to be pleasant about it. He waited just long enough for Honorine and Francis to climb aboard before launching into the air and up through the storm clouds.

The lightning was blinding and the thunder deafening until they emerged above the clouds into a clear, cold night, and a scene of complete chaos.

The peak of the mountain, rising up above the clouds, was ripping apart. Everything was a smoldering mess of jagged gashes and smoke, topped with the ruins of buildings and the stone palace and the withered, old ironwood tree.

The beasts below had completely broken through the shell and swarmed over the crumbling mountain. They were huge, dark, impossible shapes. Their legs were too long and too many, their eyes shone black and red and sometimes blank, horrible white. Their teeth were too long, their jaws too wide. Everything about them was destruction and evil and death.

The Mordant circled in the sky and stood guard on the land, fighting them back, keeping the Bellua from leaving the island.

"That doesn't look good," Francis said, staring down at the glimpses of apocalypse between the beats of Corvus's wings.

Corvus swept up to the *Carina*, sailing through the branches to land in the redwood forest near the base of the mast tree.

Honorine hopped down at once, landing on the sandy deck. Francis followed more slowly, looking about in awe as Lord Vidalia struggled to make his way up from his study to see what the commotion was all about.

"Honorine!" he said, struggling over the roots with his crooked, old cane. "What are you doing here?"

"Well, things went a bit sideways down there," she said. "I need a place to keep Francis safe...and I have this."

She pulled the sash over her head, opened the silk, and held up the Mapmaker in his globe.

"He needs to be here until this is all settled," she said. "If Nautilus finds him trapped..."

Honorine had a flash of the Mapmaker's prediction, but instead of herself throwing the Mapmaker to the Bellua, it was Nautilus, tossing his rival down into the pits of Hades, to be rid of him forever.

Lord Vidalia nodded. "He'll be safe up here," he said.

"And him, too?" Honorine asked, pushing Francis forward.

The reunited Vidalias stared quietly at each other for a moment.

"Francis, this is your father," she said. "Lord Vidalia, this is your Francis."

Lord Vidalia, unable to find the words, waved his son closer. Francis reached out tentatively, putting one arm over his father's frail shoulder, before grabbing him in a long, joyful hug.

"You're alive," Francis said as he took a step to the side, keeping Lord Vidalia's arm over his shoulder to help support the elderly man.

"Indeed," he said. "And you look well."

"Where are Lux and the archer?" Honorine asked.

"They thought they would be of more help down on the ground," Lord Vidalia explained. "And I rather agreed."

Honorine ran to the railing of the ship and looked

down at the island ringed with storm clouds and speckled with fire. It was quite a sight with the Mordant climbing and soaring and swimming about. There didn't seem to be a lot of them, but the Bellua were huge and wild, and it was clear that the Mordant could not hold them back forever.

Then, through the flashing green lights and billowing smoke, came the silhouette of the Nightmare in flight, accompanied by a handful of Mordant, all herding it back toward the island. Honorine spotted a swan, an eagle, and a chariot pulled by four winged horses. There were others as well, on the ground and in the water, obscured by the dense smoke but visible by their trails of colorful sparks. Andromeda and Pegasus landed on the beach.

Almost at the peak of the mountain, the archer was battling through plumes of steam and around scuttling monsters, with Lux galloping along beside him, making their way toward the summit and the still-standing ironwood tree.

"They need my help," Honorine said, to the immediate protests of Lord Vidalia and Francis. But she was already swinging herself up onto Corvus's back and whispering for him to fly. She didn't wait to say good-bye to Francis or Lord Vidalia, or give them a chance to try to talk her out of leaving. She had promised herself and many others that they would all get out of this alive. And now it was time to be true to her word, not sit back and hope that everyone else fulfilled that promise for her.

Corvus was obliging and swooped back down toward the island at a ferocious speed, headed straight for the peak of the mountain, where the archer stood with a raised bow.

Honorine expected him to fire at the Nightmare when it sailed past, but instead he fired a single silver shot straight toward the ancient ironwood tree, just as Corvus reached his claws out to land.

At that exact moment, the Rhectae rooted a tremendous heap of rock from the hillside, and the entire mountain heaved. Everyone was thrown to the ground as a jagged crack wrenched the remains of the terrace in half. Honorine slipped from the crow's back and hit the stony ground. She struggled to her feet immediately, only to find herself on the far side of a gulf of smoke and steam and licking fire.

She was alone on the scrap of terrace along with the ancient tree—and the shining silver arrow, which had missed its mark and sunk into a pocked chunk of hardened lava stone.

"The arrow!" called the archer from the other side of the divide as the ground shivered and heaved again. Honorine planted her legs and managed to stay upright until the shaking stopped. "Do you see the arrow?"

"Yes!" Honorine called back. "It's stuck in a rock!"

"Get to it!" Lux shouted. "Use it to cut into the ironwood tree!"

Overhead, the Nightmare was circling back, surrounded by a swarm of Mordant. It ducked and soared just under the hull of the *Carina*, its whipping tail striking the ship. The *Carina* listed sharply to starboard, sending a cascade of white sand over the side, shimmering as it fell. And in the middle was a single glowing golden orb.

The Mapmaker. Falling toward the open chasm, just as he had predicted.

"Hurry!" Lux shouted.

Honorine ran for the arrow and plucked it out of the rock. Just as she approached the ironwood tree and lifted the arrow to plunge it into the twisted bark, a rush of black raced past her.

Corvus!

She watched the giant crow swoop across the sky and grab the golden orb in his beak just before it plunged into the fiery mountain. Then, in a single wingbeat, he was off into the clouds, and Honorine felt her hand stop hard as the tip of the arrow sank into the dry bark of the ironwood tree.

A single drop of glowing blue sap oozed from the sharp gash in the rusty orange bark. The drop swelled and trembled, and then fell with a splash onto the terrace stones below.

All around the darkened island, the once dead trees began to bloom leaves of shimmering light in every color. The illuminated leaves burst open in a wave moving quickly up the hillside, skipping among the taller trees, pouring down onto the shorter ones beneath, and finally building to a rush that swept up to the crown of the island, where the ancient ironwood tree erupted with hundreds of thousands of needles made entirely of blue light.

The light coursed through the branches and down into the trunk of the tree, where a thick, glowing sap began to ooze and flow, spilling onto the stones. The liquid rushed toward Honorine, and she climbed quickly onto a flat obsidian boulder, letting the sap flow around her and down the mountain. It poured through the crevices and trenches, soaking and dripping like glowing blue honey.

Above the island, stars began to brighten and send out trails of golden sparks that pooled together and created a web of flowing gold that draped like a dome over the entire island.

"Our last defense against the Bellua," Lux said, coming up behind Honorine. "The net will close over the mountain and pull them back down. We have to hurry, or we'll be drawn in along with them!"

Honorine looked up at the great golden net, dripping shimmering embers over the island. The Nightmare was caught on the inside, skimming through the air and searching for a way out. Already, the golden snare was beginning to shrink, to close down over the entire island like a fishing net being drawn up by a trawling boat. The Leviathan squirmed and struggled, pulling itself toward the water, even though the net was closing in rapidly.

Andromeda, finally making her way to the summit of the mountain, leaped across the divide and landed on the terrace beside the tree. She sent out trails of fire that pushed back the Bellua still on land, away from Honorine.

"Run," Andromeda commanded. "Get as far down the hill as you can while the net is still large."

"But what about you?" Honorine asked. "Aren't you coming with us?"

"I wait until the end. I am the last to leave."

The golden net was drawing ever closer in the sky. The Nightmare thrashed against it. He made a great clatter of noise and explosions of sparks, but the net held strong and began to close even faster.

Honorine looked to the sky, where anything with wings or the power to fly began to gather over the peak of the volcano, racing toward the net while they could still fit through the gaps in the golden threads.

Several of the Mordant hung back, snaring the Nightmare with hooks and lines made of shimmering light, binding it like an insect wrapped in spider silk, and dragging the beast back toward the ground. Farther down the mountain, another group drove back the Rhectae, pushing it toward a gaping chasm of red light.

Andromeda stood proudly and boldly, her dogs at her sides.

The net was drawing closer. The light from the golden threads burned as hot as the noon sun, and sparks began to fall onto the hard stone ground, and into the illuminated forest below.

"Honorine, you must go," Andromeda said quietly but firmly. "I will see you on the other side."

Andromeda turned to look at Honorine, and for a moment, there was no exploding mountain, or monsters, or Mapmaker screaming for their destruction. There was just Honorine and her mother.

"We must go now," Lux said, nudging Honorine's hand with his nose.

The net was already half its initial size. Some of the larger Mordant had escaped through the shrinking gaps to the outside. The Bellua fought and strained against it.

"Honorine?" Lux insisted, not shouting or commanding, but asking.

"I know," she said with a nod, and turned with him to begin their descent off the mountain.

They stumbled down the mountainside as quickly as they could manage, hopping over stones, sliding on melting ice, dodging falling sparks as they raced toward the rapidly closing net.

"Duck!" Lux cried, and Honorine looked up to see the net before them, like a spider's web drawing closed.

Honorine was right behind him, but the hole had closed almost by half, and she had to pull her legs up nearly to her chest to get through. Lux took a mighty leap, tucking himself into a slender arc of white light, and still he singed the tip of his tail off.

The golden net shrank more quickly, pulling the Bellua back down into the earth, growing brighter and brighter as the threads drew together, until it was a golden shell writhing with angry beasts. Then the shell itself shrank and dove into the very stone of the mountain, fading until it disappeared completely.

The blue sap of the ironwood tree instantly began to cool over the volcano's red-hot molten lava, sealing the caverns below once again under a layer of impenetrable, solidified light. Then the whole shimmering forest began to fade out, one tree at a time, until all was finally calm, dark, and silent.

CHAPTER
• 26 •

The Shipwreck

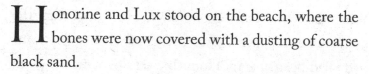

Honorine and Lux stood on the beach, where the bones were now covered with a dusting of coarse black sand.

Down at the farthest end of the beach, before it curved out of sight around the slope of the mountain, sat the wreck of the *Gaslight*. Her hull rested at a sharp angle, the bow cracked nearly down to the sand, the greenhouse dome shattered. Gray steam trickled from one bent smokestack, and rattled sailors were slowly assembling outside. The figures were too small and far away to identify.

"Look what you've done, Honorine," Lux said, and for a moment, she thought he'd meant the shipwreck. "Over there."

She turned to look down the beach in the other direction.

From the ground, the air, and even the sea, the Mordant were gathering. The archer, the ram, the lynx, the swan, the eagle, and so many others. The collected light of their shimmering bodies lit up the dark island as if it were morning.

"They are free," Lux said.

"Except for her," Honorine said, looking up at the mountain. They had barely made it out before the golden net collapsed. There was little chance Andromeda had been able to. Honorine sat down on the sand, feeling a bit dizzy and a bit nauseated as the excitement began to wear off. For a moment, between the crushed shell of the *Gaslight* strewn on the beach and the cold, still mountain above, Honorine feared she had just lost both of her parents in one night. Again.

Then a shimmering cloud of silver and gold crossed Honorine's view and drifted around the slope of the mountain, sinking slowly and gracefully toward the beach.

It was a patch of forest.

"That's the *Carina*," Honorine said, rising to her feet as the ship touched down on the black sand. "And Francis!"

He was waving from the railing. Lord Vidalia stepped up beside him, stooped but waving joyfully as well. And then there was a third figure.

Andromeda.

"She made it," Honorine whispered.

"It seems I still know how to sail," Lord Vidalia said, shuffling down to the beach with his son's assistance. "And we found someone we thought you'd like returned to you."

Andromeda followed, walking slowly to accommodate Lord Vidalia's careful pace.

"You're free!" Honorine said. "And so are the rest of the Mordant!"

"Yes," she replied. "And there's just one more bit of business to attend to now."

The rest of the Mordant, Francis, and Lord Vidalia all waited on the beach as Andromeda and Honorine walked toward the *Gaslight*. The sailors and scientists gathered around the broken hull stepped back as they approached.

"Is anyone hurt?" Andromeda asked, and the crowd went completely silent. "Sirona and Serpens will help anyone who needs medical attention."

There were a few nods and even fewer murmurs of thanks, barely loud enough to hear over the roll of waves onto the shore.

Inside the *Gaslight* was not quite as bad as Honorine had expected. It was a mess of broken furniture and sputtering electrical wires, but they were able to find the laboratory, which was flooded up to Honorine's knees and dark except for a single flame burning gently from a crack in a copper gas line.

Nautilus stood in the middle of the room among the wreckage of his masterpiece, the great machine that had made him more powerful than even the Mapmaker for a short while.

"I'm glad to see you made it through," Andromeda said, stopping just a few steps inside the laboratory.

"You two, as well," he said. "And I believe I owe you an apology. I know you may not believe it, but I built this ship for you. So we could all be together again."

Andromeda's jaw clenched, and her light brightened.

Tiny drops of white fire dripped from her gown and floated across the water. "And you succeeded. Here we all are, together."

They were quiet for a long moment, and in the silence, Honorine understood that there was more Andromeda should have said. They were together again *for the moment*. But the moment would not last.

"What are you going to do now?" Andromeda asked. Nautilus waded a few steps toward them.

"I suppose I don't know," he said. "Start over again."

"Why don't you stay here?" Honorine asked quietly, but her voice echoed in the hollow bowl of a room.

Nautilus was silent for a moment.

"I don't think the rest of the Mordant would appreciate that very much," he said. "I still have one airship. It's probably best to leave now."

Honorine crossed her arms angrily until Andromeda put a hand on her shoulder.

"He's right," she said. "No one is going to be able to stay on this island, after all."

"And why not?" Honorine replied.

"It's too dangerous," Andromeda said.

"But there used to be a city here, and libraries, and people came from all over the world to study here. You could build that again," Honorine said, imagining the city of Possideo full of Mordant and people alike. It was the kind of place Francis would want to live. And Lord and Lady Vidalia. And Lux, and even Astraea. Somewhere they could be together.

"Not on top of the gates," Andromeda said. "It will be many years before the forests have regrown and the gates are at their strongest again."

Honorine felt a nervous panic rising in her gut. It was all going away, and she'd barely even put it together.

"What if we don't need the forest?" she said, looking around the room at the plates of iron and rivets and the half-submerged wreckage of the Sidus Apparatus control panel. "What if we can build a new gate? Even stronger."

"No one could build such a thing," Andromeda said. But Nautilus slowly nodded.

"She could," he said, pointing at his daughter. Honorine, despite being furious with him for the damage he had caused, smiled.

"Take the ship," Nautilus said, gesturing at the broken hull around them. "There should be everything you need here. Then you won't have to wait for your forest. You can start rebuilding Possideo at once."

"It will be a tremendous amount of work," said Andromeda.

"I have a crew," Nautilus said. "I'm sure many of them would stay."

"And what about the Mapmaker?" Andromeda asked.

"I don't know," Nautilus said. "What even became of him?"

"He...escaped, with Corvus," Honorine said.

"Well, then I would keep an eye out for him," Nautilus said. "I'm sure he'll be back here before long."

Andromeda's fire scorched to blinding white. She gestured toward Nautilus, sending a line of fire that raced across the water and encircled him, with flames dancing up to his chest.

"What about *you* and the Mapmaker?" she asked. "If I'm to let you leave here, it must be with a solemn promise to leave him be. Your feud with him is ended. There can be only a truce now between you."

"All right," Nautilus said.

Andromeda's flames roared around him.

"I swear!" he added. "I give you my word. I will not engage with the Mapmaker anymore."

"I accept your oath," she said. "And you accept the consequences if you break it."

Nautilus nodded. Andromeda gave him one last look and then turned to go, leaving Nautilus caught in a circle of white fire until she had left the laboratory.

Honorine followed, looking back over her shoulder every few steps until the flicker of white light went dark behind her.

In the end, nearly half of the *Gaslight* crew decided to stay, even Bloom and Professor du Ciel. Salton went on ahead with Nautilus. He had never been very interested in the scientific research part of their expedition anyway.

It took just one more day to prepare the *Black Owl* with the cannons removed and enough food and supplies to last quite a long journey.

Honorine was on the *Carina*, docked along the black sand beach, when Nautilus left. He hadn't set foot on the island except to say a brief good-bye before he had finished readying the airship for his journey.

"I'll be back someday," he told her. "If you need me before then, you can send a message."

"How?" Honorine asked.

"You'll find a way."

Honorine didn't know quite what to say. She didn't want any harm to come to him, but she didn't feel the same way toward him as she did toward Lux or Francis or Andromeda, or even—though she would never admit it to anyone but herself—the Mapmaker. They were her family, and Nautilus, somehow, was not.

"Well," Honorine said, "it was very good to meet you."

"And you, too," Nautilus said with a short nod.

The next night, he and the other half of his crew set sail on the evening tide. The *Black Owl* launched from the deck of the *Gaslight*, soaring gracefully up into the sky until it became just another shimmering star on the horizon.

The Seedling Forest

The *Gaslight* looked quite different without her elegant crystal dome. She was undergoing many renovations, but the missing greenhouse was the most glaring. A new one would soon be installed with a redesigned version of the Sidus Apparatus that communicated with the Mordant, rather than imprisoning them. That had been Francis's idea, a sort of floating extension of Possideo where Mordant and human beings could travel together, gathering knowledge.

Honorine's plan for a new, mechanically reinforced gate had come together quite quickly once she had the time, the materials, and the crew.

The lava eruption had sealed the mountain shut, but the entrance to the underworld still existed just beneath the surface, and a thin crust of stone would not be enough to keep it closed now that the ancient ironwood tree had been destroyed. Fortunately, there was a single tree left on the *Carina*, and it'd been able to provide seeds. Unfortunately, even Mordant Silva trees took time to grow, and the Bellua were not likely to be patient or cooperative.

Iron, it seemed, was a good tool against the Bellua, and as Honorine pointed out, the *Gaslight* happened to be built of the stuff.

The Mordant residents of Possideo, along with the former *Gaslight* crew, spent a month dismantling the iron framework of the greenhouse dome and bringing it up to the top of the mountain. It took another month to clear the old buildings and begin to repair roofs and walls and roadways. They built steppes from black obsidian and white marble around the peak of the mountain, and they filled them with rich earth from the remains of the dead forest below. The Mordant guarded the mountain closely every moment, watching for signs of unrest under the ground.

The forest looked much different now. Instead of a lurking canopy of charred pine skeletons, the ground was covered in a field of tiny seedlings, their leaves bright against the black surface of the mountain.

Within six months, the fastest-growing trees were already as tall as Honorine, though still as thin and wispy as twigs. They even began to grow tiny lantern buds. Honorine and Francis were walking through a stand of silver maples when the lanterns finally grew in and began to bloom. It was a welcome occasion, because the sun never rose over the island. It was always night there.

And, Honorine noticed, the island was often in a different place from night to night. Sometimes there were other landmasses in the distance, sometimes a coastline, but often there was nothing at all but rolling black sea and a sky full of millions of stars.

Lord Vidalia chose to build a cottage near the beach because Lady Vidalia had always loved the ocean. When it was ready, he sent word—and a Mordant escort—to bring her back, if she wished to come. His health seemed to improve greatly once Sirona was free to provide remedies again. But he made the most improvement when he received word that Lady Vidalia was on her way to join him.

Though he was free to roam anywhere in the world now, Lux, too, chose to stay on the island near Honorine. She took long walks with him through the forest, quietly exploring the trees and the changing landscape. They passed through gardens, stretches of wild forest, and over a cold, rushing stream, which they would cross again as a waterfall pouring into a clear pool, where they would stop to say good evening to Eridanus.

"Storm tomorrow?" Honorine asked.

"Just a little one," Eridanus replied.

"We could use some rain," Lux agreed.

They continued on up the winding road, paved in crushed black lava stone, toward the town. The outer edges were still the roughest, with most of the buildings cleared from the lava but not yet restored. Up another few hundred yards were buildings with doors and windows refitted and roads cleared for traveling.

Above the buildings were the new laboratories, sprawling collections of glass domes rising like bubbles around the crown of the mountain. Fixed into the stone around the domes, per Lord Vidalia's suggestion, were starglass omen stones to detect the Bellua. Honorine was also working on a monitoring system that would measure any movement of the ground and track the changes in heat from the lava still pooling below.

"If they ever wander too close to the surface, we'll know," Lord Vidalia said. So far, the stones had remained dark unless a Mordant came near. Honorine had not made them glow yet, though she had made a habit of checking, even keeping a tiny pebble in her pocket, waiting for it to one day begin to burn with light.

Above the laboratories was a single narrow path leading up to a courtyard and a little house made of white stone, surrounded by terraces that looked out over the sea. Honorine stopped in the courtyard to pick a cinnamon-flavored apple, before heading into the house with Lux at her side.

"Ah, there you are," said Andromeda from out on the eastern patio.

"Eridanus is sending rain," Honorine said, pausing to give her mother a brief hug. They had this house at Honorine's insistence. Andromeda clearly found it strange, but she obliged her daughter. And Honorine, though she couldn't exactly express it, was more grateful for the little stone cottage on the edge of the mountain peak than she had ever been for anything in her life. She could see it from almost anywhere on the island, the little chip of white right up at the top. Her home.

Honorine proceeded through the house and the courtyard beyond to a hidden, winding set of narrow steps that led to the last little terrace at the very summit of the mountain.

"There it is, as always," Lux said as he paused at the last step.

It was just a little round patch of rocky black earth. But right in the center grew a thin, spindly sprout that would one day be a tree. The ironwood sapling seemed to grow much slower than the rest of the trees on the island. That was fine with Honorine. She had plenty of time now to wait for it, on the top of the mountain, under the stars.

Occasionally one would shoot past, and she wondered if it was a meteor or perhaps Pegasus...or the Mapmaker. She didn't know what had become of him. He might already be free, or he might still be in his amber prison. But he would not remain confined forever. One day, the Mapmaker would return. And she would be ready.

From her perch at the top of the mountain, she could see the ocean all around, and the scattered laboratories like sprouting mushrooms all over the slopes. The remaining *Gaslight* crew originally intended to help in building. But being on the island, and especially around Honorine, had made them astonishingly productive. Many of them had postponed plans to build houses as they found they were spending so much time working in the laboratories. Professor du Ciel was one of the most dedicated, spending all her time developing navigational equipment unlike anything Honorine— or any other living soul—had ever seen.

Honorine looked down the hill at Professor du Ciel's laboratory, a little glass dome glowing with the lights of her inventions. Down a trail marked with white stones was Francis's laboratory, closer to the beach.

He was working on engines, something that had been his favorite area of study on the *Gaslight*. Now that they were rebuilding it, he was planning to install a new system that would power the ship with heated seawater.

"There's so much work going on down there," Honorine said as she sat on a little ledge of obsidian, letting her bare feet dangle over the black slope below.

"And there will be more," Lux said as he sat down beside her. "You know that it isn't just a talent you have when you work with machines."

He looked out over the island, dotted with lights and fine plumes of steam.

"You truly are a Mordant," Lux said. "One day you will be the muse of Invention. You will recognize it in those who don't even see it in themselves, and others will seek you out, despite time or geography, to understand the need that calls them."

Honorine looked down at her feet.

"It sounds like a terrible amount of responsibility," she said.

"There's still time," Lux said. "You are not a child anymore, but you are not yet ready to take on what this life will ask of you. But you will be. I promise."

"And..." She had never asked this before, but now, in the quiet night, she thought she was ready to hear the answer. "I will have a constellation of my own?"

"Of course!" said Lux. His coat shimmered with light. "Someday."

"How do I know which stars are mine?"

"When you're ready, you'll see them," Lux said.

She looked up into the sky, so thick with stars that

they changed the very color of the night. The ones that belonged to her were already there, shining down. Just as Francis, Lux, Lord Vidalia, Andromeda, and even Astraea had always been out there, even before she knew them.

One day, just as she had found her family, Honorine would find her stars.

The CARINA

Acknowledgments

There are so many people to thank for their love, support, and encouragement over the many years it took to make this story happen:

All my fellow writers who took the time to read bits and pieces, and sometimes whole drafts, while this unruly manuscript slowly became a book. My eternal gratitude to you.

All the distant branches of my giant family tree. We're lucky to be connected to such amazing people. And especially my parents, Mom, Dad, and Dad again.

My teachers who made a wild little kid into a writer—Miss Gallo (Mrs. Perugini), Mrs. Buzzard, Mr. Strom, Mrs. Johnson, Mr. Dougherty, Mrs. Teegarten, Mrs. Frank, and of course, Mr. Parker. Thank you for introducing me to so many stories and for helping me create my own.

My agent, Natalie Lakosil, and my editor, Deirdre

Jones, for their belief in this story and all the hours they spent making it a real book. It has been a wonderful experience.

And lastly, all my thanks and love to my two favorite people in the world: my son, the brightest star in my life, and my Ben, the fuzzy old scoundrel who measures things in sharks.

Ben Lewandowski

Lindsey Becker writes stories about ghosts, monsters, and daring children who love adventure and magic. *The Star Thief* is her debut novel, and she invites you to visit her online at literarylilycate.blogspot.com or @lcatebecker. She lives in Wisconsin.